DIE FOR ME

Also by Diane Hester

Run To Me
Hit And Run

DIE FOR ME

DIANE
HESTER

Slender Thread
Publishing

This book is a work of fiction. All names, places, characters
and events are products of the author's imagination. Any resemblance to
actual people, living or dead, events or locales is purely coincidental.

Cover art by SelfPubBookCovers.com/INeedABookCover

ISBN-13: 978-0-9953713-1-6

For Michael

CHAPTER 1

She'd known the risks when she left the house. This deep into a New England winter – three weeks shy of spring in fact, though it hardly felt like it – the weather was grossly unpredictable. Still, jogging had always been her escape, and right now she needed it more than ever.

Lauren pulled up her track suit hood against the first stinging needles of icy rain. Just about time to turn back anyway. Trouble was, the road she was on – a winding course through one of the Cape's old housing estates – hadn't looped around as she'd expected and there were no side streets leading to where she'd left the car. She knew it was off to the left somewhere, so when a path opened up in the woods on that side she veered to take it.

Twisting branches of scrub oak and pine closed overhead, clawing at the menacing sky. Though the roads had been clear, beneath the trees a blanket of snow still covered the ground, clearly scored by multiple tracks. It gave her a trail to follow at least, for which she was grateful. In her fondness for running in unfamiliar places she sometimes found herself getting lost.

The path commenced a gradual descent till the woods

bottomed out on a snow-covered field. A row of houses backed up onto the opposite side, the trail she followed leading across and between two yards. And there, just visible beyond the gap, stood her car, parked on the side of the road.

She stepped out from the cover of trees and started across. With the snow deep in places she slowed to a walk, cursing the dampness that seeped through her socks. She trudged, head bowed, till she came to a spot where the snow was churned as though children or a dog had been digging.

At a glimpse of what lay beneath, she stopped. Ice. Not the ice of a shallow puddle, but the crust atop a deep dark void.

A shiver went through her that had nothing to do with the cold. The field wasn't a field at all. She'd blundered onto a frozen pond.

She looked behind her, then ahead. She was already halfway across and others had passed this way before her; by the look of it, only that morning. Her car was in sight, and if she turned and went back, it would take her a good half hour of walking in the freezing rain to reach it.

She continued on. Her fears receded with every step. No ominous cracking sounds, no deep-throated rumble, not the slightest tremor in the soles of her shoes. The ice was solid. Perfectly safe.

Until the instant it shattered beneath her, opening a maw that swallowed her whole into water only two degrees above freezing.

Lauren shot to the surface, gasping. Cold branded every inch of her flesh, slashed at her scalp, knifed her face. She floundered for the nearest edge.

Sliding her gloved hands over the ice, she groped for a bump, the smallest notch. A surface smooth and seamless as glass offered nothing on which to take hold. She managed to haul her shoulders out, but the weight of water-logged winter clothing dragged her back in. She clung to the edge.

Two to five minutes.

The thought burst unbidden into her head. Where had she heard it? Was it true? Two to five minutes. The time she had before hypothermia sapped her strength to the point she couldn't pull herself from the water.

In sudden panic she threw out her arms, kicked with her legs. If she couldn't pull herself out she'd swim out! But already the cold was taking its toll, making her movements stiff and ungainly. She rose for an instant then slid back again.

Stay calm. Don't panic. Surely a fit twenty-eight year old was at the upper end of that five-minute range.

"Help! Help me. Somebody. Please!"

No answer. Not even a barking dog.

Somehow her legs had drifted ahead of her under the ice. She fought to lever them back behind her.

The ledge she clung to broke free in her hands.

She scrambled for purchase, gained it by nothing but the tips of her fingers. Fingers rapidly losing sensation.

The drag on her legs kept pulling her under. Realization struck like a blow. Not a pond, but a stream. This water was *moving*. If she lost her grip...

"Help! Somebody. Anybody. Help!"

Movement flickered at the corner of her eye. An elderly man was lumbering toward her from one of the yards. *Oh, thank God!*

Another chunk of ice broke away. She clawed her way back, the weight of her arms now all that was keeping her from going under.

The man was still ten paces away, moving so slowly.

What was he doing? What was wrong with him, couldn't he see—

Her hopes dissolved. He walked with a limp, his left arm bent and clamped to his side. How could he pull her out with one arm? How could he pull her out at all when the ice kept...

"Stop," she wheezed. "Go back. Get help."

The man kept coming.

At the edge of the stream he picked up a branch and pushed it ahead of him onto the ice. Sliding his feet on the treacherous surface, he started toward her.

"No. Stop. It isn't safe." Her words emerged in breathless gasps. He'd never hear them.

He continued his slow relentless approach. Five yards from shore and the ice was still holding. She could see his eyes now. Faded with age yet wide with concern. Almost as frightened as she felt herself.

The branch inched toward her. Two yards away. One yard away. Less than a foot.

The ice shuddered against her neck.

"No!" she screamed, panic giving her the volume she needed. "It's cracking. Don't come any closer."

He shuffled to a halt, the salvation of the branch just out of her reach. Leaning forward, he stretched out his arm. The branch skittered the last few inches.

If not for seeing the wood jab her hands she'd never have known; her flesh was stone. She tried first one, then the other, but neither would move. Too late? Was her five minutes already up?

No, her gloves had frozen to the ice!

She pulled out her hands. Fingers fixed into useless claws, she hooked them over a joint in the branch.

The man started backing away, his weight enough to anchor each step as he hydroplaned her onto the surface.

Face down, her nose fairly scraping the ice, Lauren watched it slide beneath her, fearing that at any moment those frigid jaws would open again and snatch her back.

Movement stopped.

She turned her head.

There he stood at the fringe of vision, her unlikely hero. Why had he stopped? What was filling his gaze with such panic? Something he could hear that she couldn't? Something he could feel? *Oh, no please...*

The jaws cracked wide and he was gone.

"NO!"

She flailed at the ice, her frenzied strokes propelling her forward. Gliding on her belly, spreading her weight, she aimed for the downstream side of the hole. She scraped off the snow, and peered through the ice.

A hand clawed the underside of its surface!

"Oh God, help! Help me please! Somebody! Help!"

She lurched to her feet, stood splay-legged over the spot. She kicked with her heel, again and again. But the surface was now defiantly solid.

The hand vanished, replaced by a head – strands of grey hair softly waving, drifted serenely along with the current. She staggered after him. Screaming her loudest. Screaming. Screaming.

The ghostly tendrils slowly submerged, vanishing into the frozen depths.

She dropped to her knees, brought her nose to the surface once more. And shrieked when he reappeared below her. His eyes huge, bulging with fear. Their faces only inches apart.

Lauren pounded the ice with her fists, blood from her

knuckles spraying the endless carpet of white. She forced more screams from her ravaged throat, watched as his movements gradually slowed.

Dazed, helpless, she peered in his eyes. And beheld the moment, the very instant, life ceased to shine in his gaze.

CHAPTER 2

A crowd had gathered.

Seated at the table, Lauren stared blankly out the kitchen window at the row of people lining the stream. They'd been kept from venturing onto the ice by the police tape now strung between trees. Where were they all a half hour ago when she'd been screaming to rupture her throat? Nothing attracted spectators faster than the sight of police and emergency vehicles.

A uniformed worker – a fireman, she thought – tethered by a safety rope at his waist, knelt on the ice, cutting a hole in the frozen surface. Shavings flew from the whirling blade, its chainsaw-like buzz filling the air. Somehow the noise seemed an affront. Like shouting at a funeral, laughing at an open grave.

The paramedic stepped in front of her again, blocking the scene. He took the empty mug from her hands and replaced it with another. Only half full. Just as well. Any more and she'd spill it the way she was shaking.

"The officer just wants another quick word with you, then we'll get you off to the hospital."

Lauren stared down into the coffee and pulled the blanket

closer around her.

"I know it's uncomfortable, but your shivering's actually a good sign. It means your temperature didn't get too low." He slid his fingers inside her wrist and consulted his watch. "Hypothermia doesn't get serious till your core temp drops below ninety-five. I'd say you were just on the edge. Any worse and you'd be showing signs of confusion, lethargy, trouble breathing. The heat and fluids should be enough, but we'll get you checked out just to be sure."

She knew what he was doing. Chatting to distract her, keep her engaged. And not for any medical reasons.

He parted the collar of the shirt she was wearing and pressed a stethoscope to her skin. "I gather these clothes aren't yours since they're dry. Did she give them to you?" He jerked his head toward the stocky figure standing in the yard, her back to the window.

Lauren frowned. She vaguely remembered staggering to the nearest house and pounding on its door. The woman who answered, not much older than Lauren herself, had given her clothes, called 911, then sat her here at the kitchen table and started pouring hot coffee into her. Only after the ambulance arrived had the woman gone outside to talk with the police.

The medic lifted one of her hands and flexed her swollen bloodied fingers. Lauren winced but didn't pull away.

"You sure did a number on yourself, didn't you?" His voice was soft. "Your hands were probably numb by that stage. Lucky you didn't break a finger."

Lucky. Right. More lucky than some.

The silence stretched.

"Look, I heard what you told the cop before. By the sounds of it, there really wasn't anything—"

He cut off when she met his gaze, leaving his attempt to

console her unfinished. Sensing she was still too shocked to process? Or unable to override his own doubts?

She drained the cup and handed it back to him. He got up, gave her shoulder a squeeze and stepped to the counter to get her another.

She was left with a view of the crowd once more. Most were talking in quiet groups. Strangers lured by the prospect of drama, sharing what few facts they had, speculating on what might have happened.

The buzz of the saw abruptly cut off. The woman in the yard took a step forward; all heads turned toward the uniformed worker. Wielding a gaff, he hooked the slab of ice he had freed and pulled it out.

Lauren braced as he reached in the water. A sound like a wounded animal escaped her on catching a glimpse of the hand that emerged, white and stiff as the ice around it.

She jumped when she felt someone looming over her.

"I'd just like to go through this one more time." Oblivious to the effect he'd had, the officer commenced reading her statement.

She kept her gaze fixed straight ahead, nodding confirmation whenever he paused. Bad enough she'd had to speak the words initially; hearing them recited back at her felt like he was passing judgment.

"Thank you, Miss Donnelly, that's all for now." He closed his notebook and looked aside. "What hospital you taking her to?"

The medic's reply was a toneless drone. Down at the stream, the police were hastily erecting a screen to block spectator view of proceedings. Not fast enough to prevent her seeing the body being slid from the hole in the ice.

"We'll be in touch if we need anything else," the officer

finished.

She took his arm as he turned to go. "What was his name?"

Startled by the contact, perhaps finally noting by the tremor in her voice the state she was in, he followed her gaze. "Miss Donnelly, perhaps—"

"Please," she said.

He exchanged a look with the medic then regarded her again, not unkindly. "Roger Phelps."

She released his arm. "Thank you." At least now she would know who to mourn.

CHAPTER 3

Mel walked ahead of her into the house and marched straight for the kitchen. "I came by before I picked you up and put something in your oven. Smells like it's ready."

Lauren closed the door behind her and stood gazing about her foyer, the thought that had baffled her all the way home still swirling in her mind: *A man died today because of me. How can everything look the same?*

In addition to the kitchen, the lights were on in the living room, dining room, and the hallway at the top of the stairs. She'd seen the house aglow in the darkness before Mel had even turned up the driveway. "Do you have shares in the electric company or something? What's with all the lights?"

"I thought bright-and-cheery would be nicer to come home to. I got a fire going for you as well."

"I had an accident, Mel, I'm not afraid of the dark." She shrugged her jacket off her shoulders and let it slide down her arms. Unable to hang it with her bandaged fingers, she left it draped over a chair.

She crossed to the kitchen and stood in the door, surveying the room as though it were a stranger's. So much white. Walls, ceiling, cupboards, tiles. Whatever had possessed her? The only real color was a vase of red tulips in the middle of the table that hadn't been there when she'd left that morning.

Her gaze wouldn't leave it. Red against white.

Blood on snow.

She stifled a shiver. "What's that smell?"

"Hello, I just told you, I made you something." Mel produced a dish from the oven and set it on the table with a flourish.

At some distant level of awareness Lauren felt a welling of gratitude. Where would she be without Mel Haynes, her number one worker, best friend since college, and the closest thing to a sister she had? "That's not your famous mac and cheese, is it?"

"I thought you could use some comfort food."

Mel stepped around the table and enveloped her in a motherly hug; something she was somehow able to do despite being a foot shorter. "How are you holding up?"

"Okay." Lauren stood stiffly in her embrace, the woman's long, wavy, red hair pressed to her cheek. It wasn't that she didn't want to respond; it just seemed that a part of her had shut down. And for the moment she was happy to leave it that way.

"Are you sure? I can spend the night if you want. Peter won't mind."

"No." She stepped back. "I'm not going to ruin your anniversary. I'm fine, really. I want you to go."

"Well, our reservation isn't till seven so I have a few minutes. Enough time for you to tell me what happened." Mel slid onto the nearest chair.

"I told you what happened on the way home."

"Yeah, but, don't you want to…"

"Talk about it? No."

Lauren took the seat across from her where a place had been set. She kept her features as neutral as possible as her friend studied her in dubious silence.

I hope you don't blame yourself for what happened.

Of course not, why should I, it was an accident.

Mel finally nodded and picked up the plate. "Well how about I tell you who your new workers are then?"

"My new…?" Lauren bowed her head. "Oh God, I completely forgot. The interviews were this afternoon."

"Relax, I took care of it." Mel spooned casserole onto the plate. "When they called from the hospital I figured you'd be in no condition so I did them for you. I hope you don't mind."

"Mind? You're an angel. I trust your judgment as much as my own. So who did you go with?"

"Claudia Weekes and Josh Stedman."

"Josh Stedman." Lauren frowned. "I remember being impressed by his application but I can't remember why."

"Probably because he owned his own nursery once upon a time." Mel set the mounded plate back in front of her. "You'll be impressed by more than that when you meet him."

"Yeah? Good looking?"

"Let's just say the old girls in the orchid club will be getting their pace-makers checked more often."

Lauren felt another rush of warmth at the woman's valiant attempts to cheer her. Though it felt surreal talking about such ordinary things, in a strange way it was also comforting. "Anything to bring in more customers I guess. Did he say what happened to his business?"

"I didn't ask. The same thing that's happened to half the businesses in the country I assumed."

"Well, maybe he'll have some brilliant ideas on how I can

salvage this one."

Mel grew serious. "Lauren, you know that if there was any way I could buy in, I would."

"Of course I do."

"It's just that right now, with Peter out of work…"

"Look, I told you, forget it. You can't, that's it, I understand. I'll find another solution I'm sure." Lauren did her best to sound convincing, but wasn't sure she pulled it off. Mel going into partnership with her had been her best hope for saving the business. Not only would it have gotten her out of her current financial hole, there was no-one she trusted or respected more.

With that option gone, her only choice now was to take out a loan. And the way the nursery had performed the last two summers there was a very big question as to whether she'd get it.

"When do you see the bank manager?" Mel said, as though reading her thoughts.

"I haven't made an appointment yet. I'll do it tomorrow."

"Well, don't worry, you'll get the loan. And I'm sure that new line is going to work out. I don't know anyone else on the Cape who stocks Nowell & Johnson. It's sure to lift sales back to what they were."

"Absolutely."

With their hollow assurances fading around them they sat staring down at Lauren's plate.

"So are you going to eat that, or what?"

"In a minute. It's still a bit hot."

Mel checked her watch. "Well, I better be going. That is, if you're sure—"

"Yes, I'm sure. I'll be fine."

They got up and headed for the front door.

"So who was the part-time worker you hired? Claudia…?"

"Weekes. Nineteen years old and saving for college. I know how you like to help struggling students." Mel shrugged. "She has a tattoo and an eyebrow ring but I figured that wouldn't bother you."

"As long as they both get along with Simon I don't care how many tattoos they have."

Lauren submitted to another hug, promised to call if she needed to talk, no matter the hour, and waved her best friend out the door.

Back in the kitchen, confronted with her plate of mac and cheese, she felt the slightest welling of nausea. Still, she hadn't eaten all afternoon and Mel had gone to the trouble of fixing it. She picked it up clumsily between bandaged hands, scraped half of it back in the baking dish, and carried the rest into the living room.

On the couch, clutching the spoon in her fist like a child, she forced a mouthful past her lips. Despite Mel's hopes, the sight of the fire didn't cheer her. More than her body had been numbed this day, and though feeling had returned everywhere else, inside she still felt totally deadened.

She took another mouthful then set down the spoon. Chewing the cardboard-flavored paste, she fumbled the remote from the coffee table and clicked on the TV.

The scene of her accident flashed on the screen as a news reporter delivered the details. "In a tragic twist the sixty-four-year-old then fell through the ice himself and became trapped. Rescue workers later freed him but he was pronounced dead at the scene."

A paramedic spoke to the microphone thrust in his face. "As a stroke survivor, Mr. Phelps would have succumbed to the cold far more readily than a healthy person. He wouldn't have had the strength to swim, let alone fight the current."

Lauren dry-swallowed her mouthful of food and pushed her plate onto the coffee table.

"Sadly, the twists in this story don't end there." The reporter was briefly back on the screen before yet another cut, this time to a familiar face – the woman on who's door Lauren had knocked seeking help – looking tearful and clearly distraught.

"Can you tell us what happened?" said a voice off-camera.

"I heard someone screaming. Before I could go out and see what it was, she was banging at the door. Dripping wet, crying. Ranting about the stream out back."

"Miss Donnelly?"

"Yes. I figured she fell in and somehow managed to pull herself out. I never realized...I had no idea..." Her voice choked off.

Lauren felt the food congeal in her stomach.

"So you brought Miss Donnelly into your home," the reporter prompted. "Gave her dry clothes, helped her get warm..."

"I called 911. Then I realized my father wasn't in the house. He'd gone for a walk. He does every morning. He should have been back, but he wasn't home yet."

My father. Lauren covered her mouth. Pressure was building at the back of her throat.

"I went outside, but I couldn't find him. My neighbors, they helped me; we looked all over. It wasn't till the firemen...till they cut through the ice, that they told me... Oh God..." The woman broke down.

Lauren jumped up and ran for the bathroom.

CHAPTER 4

Her favorite mug. The one with the whimsical picture of a moose standing at the edge of a moon-lit lake. The one Marc had bought her in Boothbay Harbor the summer they'd vacationed in Maine. The pieces lay strewn across the office floor. The doctor had told her to keep her bandages on for three days. At this rate she'd have no dishes left.

Lauren swept and mopped up the spill, her third of the morning, and threw the broken remains in the bin. At her desk, she sat staring at her mutinous hands. She flexed the fingers, feeling the swollen joints strain at the bindings. In a way she almost welcomed the pain. It helped her focus on the here and now.

She opened the ledger and forced her thoughts to the task at hand, the reason she'd come down to work so early – how much would she need to borrow to keep her ailing business afloat? She scanned the columns, determined to find some hidden equation, some elusive sum she had overlooked the hundred other times she'd done the figuring. The numbers danced before her eyes, refusing to make sense.

A blue jay landed on the leafless branch outside the window. Across the yard, the potting shed and annuals greenhouse stood ready for her workers' arrival. The gates were unlocked, the heaters going, and there was plenty of water in the urn for coffee. Monday. The start of pre-season work. The day she'd looked forward to all winter.

Yet she felt strangely removed from it all.

Josh Stedman climbed from his car, closed the door and surveyed his surroundings. The parking lot lay at the top of a rise, the nursery's buildings spread out behind it, bagged trees and shrubs arranged into orderly rows below. His was the only car in the lot, no sign of anyone else around. But then he was a few minutes early.

Bracing himself, he walked toward the entrance – a drive-through archway separating the nursery's shop from a well preserved shingle-clad barn. On one side was a heated koi pond, its fountain burbling a cheerful greeting, on the other a collection of garden statuary in traditional, modern and fanciful designs.

Beyond the archway, waste-high benches stood in a circular yard, bare but for a dusting of snow. He could imagine them at the height of the season crowded with flats, a colorful and welcoming sight for customers. With the archway's wisteria blooming overhead…

He nodded approval. Someone knew how to create an impact. Still, the entrance he'd designed for his own place had been every bit as impressive. He ventured further into the yard.

The driveway curved around the back of the shop before disappearing through a stand of blue spruce. At the top of the hill he could just make out the roof of a house to which the drive presumably led. Closer to hand three large greenhouses stood in a row, receding toward the rear of the lot.

"Hello?" he called. "Anyone here?"

When no-one appeared, he turned and wandered toward the barn. At the top of the ramp, he peered through its windows and let out a low appreciative whistle. A bobcat, a forklift, a ride-on mower, a twenty horsepower roto-tiller, and an assortment of barrows, carts and wagons.

He'd have died for this much equipment at his place. Not that his work had suffered for the lack; he'd made good use of the pieces he'd had. In fact the pain of selling them one by one – a crazed surgeon hacking off bits of living tissue in hopes of reviving a dying patient – had been one of the hardest things about going bust.

The landscaping side of the nursery business had always been his primary love. Nothing gave him greater satisfaction than transforming a neglected piece of land into a satisfying integration of plantings and contours, line and color. Yet the thought he might, in his new position, be called upon to use those skills for the ultimate profit of someone else, the very person…

He swallowed the bitter taste in his mouth and turned from the window.

A path beckoned down the side of one greenhouse. At the end he found the utility area with bins of the usual potting materials, piles and pallets of landscaping needs. Everything from compost to flagstone pavers. Yet no-one in sight.

A flicker of light through the greenhouse wall – heaters providing the critical warmth for the annuals they'd be potting today – told him he was at least expected. Maybe *she* was waiting inside.

Humid, loam-scented air enveloped him as he stepped through the door. He drew the fragrance deep in his lungs. Earth. Renewal. A sense of purpose, pride in ownership. It had been too long.

Like an ice cave, the structure stretched before him, its glass walls diffusing the thin morning light to a dazzling almost rapturous glow. Flats of seedlings lined the near benches. Impatiens and pansies by the look, most only an inch or two high. One industrious specimen however had not only outgrown its brothers but produced a single trembling bud.

Josh pinched it off, crushed it in his fist, and dropped it to the floor.

He stood recalling all he had seen on his tour of the grounds. The spoils of a cutthroat thriving enterprise. This mocking glimpse of the world he had lost.

Yes, he'd once had all this and more.

Till the day Lauren Donnelly stole it away from him.

CHAPTER 5

Lauren set her cell phone back on the desk. Even as she'd talked with her bank manager, arranging the appointment early next week to discuss her application for a loan, her mind had been elsewhere. Twice her words had trailed off to silence. Only his voice, his puzzled inflection, had brought her back to the point.

Now, with nothing left to engage her, she felt her thoughts drifting off again, her mind's eye fixing on a field of white. Splatters of red. A cloudy surface on which she knelt. A murky image, ghostly pale, rising slowly from shadowy depths…

She shut her eyes, covered her face. Anything to stop that image from surfacing, as it had in her dreams throughout the night.

With her eyes still closed she drew a deep breath, then slowly exhaled. Naturally she was still a bit shaken, both physically and mentally, by what had happened. But she had to pull herself together. Too much was riding on the decisions she'd be making in the next few days.

If her business went under, she wasn't the only one who would suffer. With Peter out of work, Mel needed her income desperately. And though Simon wouldn't struggle as much financially, what he'd lose in purpose and self-respect would be every bit as devastating for him. She couldn't afford to go to pieces.

The mental pep talk seemed to work. The image threatening to engulf her receded. She lowered her hands. Opened her eyes.

And shot to her feet at the sight of Roger Phelps' face, wide-eyed and staring, pressed to her window.

At the sound of a car coming up the drive, Josh walked back out through the archway and into the parking lot. A Mazda sedan pulled up beside his Sierra and a familiar energetic figure emerged, long red hair tossed by the breeze. Melanie Haynes, the woman who'd hired him.

"I was just having a look around," he said in greeting.

Her welcoming smile turned to a frown. "You're here on your own? Lauren's not with you?"

"Haven't seen anyone. The heaters are going in the greenhouse though, so someone must be here." He looked about them. "Beautiful spot. You've laid it out nicely."

"Not me. Lauren. Well, her parents actually. They started the business before she was born; when they died she took it over. Lauren still lives in the house out the back."

Josh hid a smirk. So the enterprising Miss Donnelly had simply inherited her success. The fact fit neatly with the impression he'd already formed of the woman. Her home, her business, all he could see had been given to her, her every desire just dropped in her lap.

"And if you think the place looks beautiful now, wait till you see it in summertime." Mel joined him in taking in the view – the iced-over pond that wrapped around the side of the property, the snow-frosted corn field that stretched before them down to the road, the cranberry bog framed by woodland on the other side, and the sliver of ocean along the horizon.

"Even at the tail-end of winter it's pretty." Her troubled gaze swung back to the entrance. "But I'm surprised Lauren didn't come out to meet you. I know she'd want to give you a tour of the place."

"She might be in the office. I thought I saw movement when I looked through the window just now but I couldn't be sure."

Relief suddenly flooded her features. "Ah, there she is."

Josh turned around. Standing in the archway was a tall slender woman dressed in jeans and an Aran pullover, her tawny hair swept up in a twist. Younger than he'd been expecting, about his own age. With two bandaged hands cradled to her chest she seemed strangely hesitant, almost apprehensive. Hard to believe she ran the place.

So this was his new boss. Her appearance was almost disappointing. No horns, no pitchfork. Just your run-of-the-mill cutthroat bitch.

Even as he fought to hide his reaction, another car pulled into the lot and swung to a stop in front of the woman. The passenger door flung open wide; a small man got out and ran toward her, throwing his arms around her neck. Clearly a reunion of old friends. Yet the clumsy over-zealous gesture made Josh look twice to confirm this actually was an adult.

"That's Simon," Mel said. "Come on, I'll introduce you."

Lauren lingered in Simon's embrace surprised by the comfort she derived from it, a solace it seemed only he could provide. Love unreserved. No secrets, no judgments, nothing withheld. In her current state, a gift unequalled by all the platitudes and logic in the world.

"We're back!" he shouted too close to her ear.

"Yes, we're all back. Hurray for us." She hugged him tighter. "It's so good to see you."

She stepped back and gazed at his open face, his adoring smile. This beloved child in the body of a man. His joy for life, the pleasure he took from the simplest things had always been contagious. She hoped it would infect her now.

Behind him, his father climbed from the car and started toward them. She was glad to see that Ezra had gotten over his bout of bronchitis; his grey hair was a little thinner perhaps, his frame a bit lighter, but otherwise he looked to be his usual hearty self.

From the other direction Mel approached with the man she'd been talking to, presumably Josh, their new full-timer.

The group converged. Simon gave Mel an enthusiastic hug as Lauren greeted Ezra. Then Mel commenced the introductions.

Lauren thrust out her hand in greeting.

And looked up when Josh made no move to take it.

CHAPTER 6

"Oh! You're hurt!" Simon gasped.

Lauren quickly drew back her hand and pulled her sweater sleeve over the bandages. For an instant she'd stood unable to move as the group stared in silence at the evidence of her recent mishap.

Simon's anxious words broke the spell.

"It's okay, honey, I just had an accident. I'll be fine in a day or two."

He still looked dismayed, which tore at her heart. She forgot sometimes how badly Simon reacted when someone was injured, especially someone he cared about. "Come on, now, smile. This is a special day, remember?"

She watched in relief as a grin slowly transformed his features, then turned to the man whose hand she'd been reaching to shake. At least she knew why he hadn't reciprocated. "Sorry, I keep forgetting. It's good to meet you, Josh. Welcome aboard."

He thanked her and returned her greeting. A bit reserved, but pleasant enough.

"Well, I guess I better give you the dime tour."

"Josh already had a quick look around," Mel said. "He

couldn't find you so he went exploring."

"Really?" Lauren turned to him. "How long have you been here?"

"Twenty minutes, give or take."

She shook her head. "I'm sorry, I didn't hear you pull up. I was in the office, you should've come in."

"The shop door was locked. I knocked a few times but nobody answered."

Lauren's frown deepened. Her office was just up the hall from the shop. How could she not have heard someone knock? Unless it was one of those troubling moments her mind drifted off on flashes of yesterday.

At a thought, she looked up and studied his face. If he'd been wandering around looking for people... Yes, of course, the man at the window. With his dark hair and intense blue eyes he looked nothing like Roger Phelps. But the fact she'd been thinking about Phelps at the time...and with the glass all misty...

"Simon, why don't you take Josh down to the greenhouse and show him what we'll be doing today."

Mel's words reached her from far away. When she looked around, Simon and Josh were going through the archway and Mel was staring at her with concern. "Are you okay?"

Lauren straightened. She must've been staring longer than she thought. "Yes, I'm fine."

Ezra stepped closer. "Yes, I saw what happened on the news. You poor child, it must have been terrible. I certainly hope you don't—"

"I should go with them." She gestured after Simon and Josh.

Mel held her back. "Why don't you hang in your office today? You won't be able to do any potting with your hands like that. Just take it easy. I'll look after things in the greenhouse."

Lauren gazed at her bandaged hands. She hadn't considered how useless she'd be in her present state. Just what she needed – an entire day alone with her thoughts.

Mel let go of her arm. "You never called last night so I assume you were all right."

"Yes. Fine."

"Simon doesn't know," Ezra told them. "He didn't see the news and I wasn't sure how to explain it to him. You saw how he got just from seeing your injuries."

"Don't worry, we won't mention it to him." Lauren smiled. "How has he been?"

"You know my boy – couldn't wait for work to start again. Drove me crazy counting the days. It's wonderful what you and your parents have done for him all these years, Miss Lauren. He'd be lost without this place."

She drew herself up. Yes, dear Simon lived for his job. A job she would have to make damn sure he kept.

CHAPTER 7

The day crawled by. Determined to do her share of the work, Lauren spent all her time in the shop. Despite her efforts, and brief spells of chatting with the others at breaks, she struggled to focus. Time and again the image of Roger Phelps's face beneath the ice muscled its way into her awareness. By late afternoon she had lost the battle and could think of little else.

"So what's the verdict?"

She looked up from staring at the local paper to find Mel in the chair in front of her desk. How long had she been sitting there? "About what?"

"Josh, of course. Your new employee? The one I hired only yesterday?" Mel gazed off in the direction of the greenhouse. "I know he was a little quiet today but I think that's just him – the strong silent type. He'll work out. He'll have to be better than George, at least."

"I'm sure he will." She frowned at a thought. "You're not worried about him, are you?"

"Well, you know, it's a big responsibility hiring workers, especially full-timers. You get it wrong and things could be hell around here for a while."

Lauren leaned toward her. "I wanted you for a partner,

remember? That means I trust your judgment on this and everything else to do with running the place."

"Thanks." Mel smiled and sipped her coffee. "So what did you do all day while the peasants toiled?"

"Sorted some stock. Placed a few orders. Sterilized the fridge. Tidied the store room."

"And that's your idea of taking it easy."

Lauren gazed down at the paper again. She hadn't wanted to talk about it but perhaps she needed to. Just this once. "Mel, there's something I don't understand."

"Yeah, what's that?"

"Have you ever been skating – on *solid* ice I'm talking about now – and heard the ice crack?"

Something flickered in the woman's soft gaze. Reluctance? Concern? "Sure, lots of times. Sounds like thunder. Scares you to death, but it's nothing to worry about."

"Because the ice is thick. It's just buckling as it expands under pressure. But what about thin ice?"

That flicker again. "What about it?"

"You ever stepped on the edge of a pond that wasn't completely frozen? The ice doesn't sound like thunder then."

"Well no, it's sort of higher in pitch."

"Exactly. The sound it makes is totally different, there's no mistaking it."

"I suppose. And?"

"I never heard it."

Mel stared back.

"Yesterday when I crossed that stream… I never heard anything. Not a sound. If I had, I'd have known enough to turn back. I never would have gone blundering on, endangering myself and…and—"

"So maybe you were distracted by something, some other

sound. It rained yesterday, were you wearing a hat?"

Lauren took a deep breath to settle herself. "I had my hood up."

"Well, there you go; that explains it."

"No, it doesn't." She shook her head. "Mel, that ice should not have been thin. Think about it. Okay, it's March, but this has been our coldest winter in ages and it's still damn cold out. We haven't had a thaw since the middle of January. Every other stream on the Cape is frozen. Plus there were those tracks I saw."

"Tracks?"

"Footprints – looking remarkably fresh – leading across the exact same stretch I walked on. How could the ice be solid one minute and—

Mel reached out and touched her hand. "Maybe you should talk to someone about this. A grief counselor, or a trauma expert."

"I told you, I'm fine." She pulled her hand away.

"Yeah, I can see that."

Before her friend could press the point, Lauren went on. "I do need a favor though. Would you mind looking after things here on Friday? I have to duck out in the morning for a while."

"Sure. What's up?"

She turned the paper and slid it across to her.

Mel scanned the page. "Phelps's funeral?" She looked up, concerned. "Are you sure you want to go to that?"

Lauren stared at her bandaged hands. "You know how I told you I banged on someone's door afterwards trying to get help?"

"And some woman called the ambulance. Yeah?"

"She was his daughter."

Mel slumped back in her chair and winced. "Oh Jeez."

"At the very least I have to go and pay my respects. But I also want… I mean I'd like…if she'll even talk to me—"

"Whoa, whoa, hang on a minute. Look, I know you want to do the right thing but I'm not sure this is such a good idea. I mean…considering how shaken up you still are, do you really want to put yourself through that?"

"Mel, she helped me. I was in her house and I never said anything. How could I ever leave it like that?"

Mel heaved a sigh. "You are one obstinate customer, you know that. Well, if you're going, I'm going with you."

Lauren managed the ghost of a smile. As much as she loved her, Mel could be a bit interfering at times. "Thanks, but no. I need you to look after things here."

Josh reversed his car from its spot and started for the drive at the end of the parking lot. As he passed the archway he saw the two women coming out and waved goodbye. Only Mel waved back.

He let out a huff. Clearly Miss Donnelly wasn't your warm and personal employer. Not only did she leave the hiring to others, she'd barely given him a civil greeting and shown not a pretense of interest in him.

When he'd run his business he'd made a point of working side-by-side with his people, getting to know them, never asking them to do anything he wouldn't chip in and do himself.

He shot a last look in the rear-view mirror before turning out onto the driveway. It might have been her hands he supposed, being bandaged and all – some minor accident Mel had mentioned but declined to go into. But something told him the lovely Miss Donnelly, despite her charms, was the sort who considered herself too 'above' her employees to ever get down and dirty with them. Which meant she probably wouldn't be around much to supervise his work.

And actually that would suit him just fine.

CHAPTER 8

The last of the late-comers had gone inside. She couldn't put it off any longer. Time to either follow them in or turn her car around and go home.

Lauren picked up the plastic bag from the seat beside her and gingerly stuffed it in her handbag. She'd removed her bandages only that morning and her fingers were still clumsy and sore. With a deep breath she climbed from her car and started for the funeral home's back door.

Icy wind tore at her clothes and hair as she hurried across the parking lot. Hopefully the service had already started and she could slip inside without being noticed. There was always the chance someone would recognize her from her brief appearance on the news the other night, but she very much doubted it. She'd hardly recognized herself in the footage of a woman being escorted to an ambulance with a blanket draped about her head.

The wind's roar dropped away abruptly as the building's door closed behind her. She stood in the stillness of a shadowed corridor gazing towards the lobby at its end. Even if no-one recognized her she would still draw attention. Standing apart on her own at a funeral? Someone would surely come up and talk to her, ask her how she knew the deceased.

And when she answered, what then? What would they do? Show her a seat or throw her out? Open their hearts or demand to know how she could even dare to show her face there? The woman whose presumed carelessness had cost them the life of their loved-one.

She stood for a moment, eyes closed, jaw clenched. It didn't matter what they said or did, she had to do this.

She started forward, her steps soundless on the plush floral carpet. She'd never set foot in Eastmore House but the soft lighting and stately decor were so reminiscent of where her father's funeral had been, she felt she was there. *We unite in grief on the passing of Kenneth Raymond Donnelly...*

She entered the lobby and crossed to the only occupied viewing room.   Through its archway she could see a coffin, a table of flowers and framed photographs, a pastor speaking from a lectern, and the backs of the mourners seated before him. And there in the front row – head bowed, shoulders hunched – sat Ada Phelps, the man's only daughter, the woman she had come to see.

And the person least likely to want to see her.

Lauren stood just outside the door as a series of friends and relatives rose, stepped to the lectern, and shared some anecdote about the deceased. With each reminiscence Ada's shoulders grew more hunched as though the memory added weight to her loss. With each new insight, Roger Phelps became more a real person in Lauren's mind, the ramifications of his passing all the more painful.

An attendant approached, gesturing for her to go inside and sit with the others. She shook her head and he walked off again.

When she looked back, people had started to rise from their seats. As they came up the aisle, making for the table of refreshments in the lobby, her courage faltered. She turned and headed for the lady's room.

Inside, she stood at the marble sink staring in the mirror. She wouldn't cry. Crying seemed somehow self-indulgent. *She* had survived. What did she have to cry about?

A moment after stepping into one of the stalls she heard voices approaching. A group of women, three by the sounds of it, came in to use the amenities and catch up on gossip. Weddings and funerals – the only time some families got together. Their conversation held no interest for her until…

"Poor Ada. How will she survive now without Roger's disability payments?"

"She'll just have to go out and get a job like the rest of us."

"A job, are you kidding? Doing what? She's got no training, no qualifications."

"Oh well, who knows, maybe she'll get married."

A burst of group laughter. "Julie, you're terrible."

"Hey, let's fix her up with Lydia's ex. He's still available, isn't he?"

"I don't know who I'd feel more sorry for!" Their giggles receded as they went out the door.

Lauren left the stall. At the sink, she dabbed her face with cold water then stared into her red-rimmed eyes. What would the conversation have been among her relatives at her father's funeral?

You can't tell me she didn't know.

If she'd bothered to visit them once in a while she'd have seen what was happening.

She yanked a paper towel from the dispenser, blotted her face and walked from the room.

Back in the lobby, she worked her way through the crowd

of mourners now gathered around the refreshment table. Unwanted snippets of conversation continued to reach her. "Still, you gotta feel for the kid…all those years she gave up to stay home and look after him…what's she got left…what'll she do…just don't expect us to take her in…"

Unable to spot the woman herself, Lauren continued back toward the viewing room. But at the sight of Ada standing alone gazing down at her father's casket, the urge to turn and run from the building nearly overcame her. She managed to force herself halfway up the aisle before her feet turned to stone.

Sensing the presence of someone behind her, Ada turned. The smile she had forced to her lips slowly faded as recognition seeped through her grief.

Lauren opened her mouth to speak.

Nothing emerged.

From the lobby door came a man's voice. "Ada, can I get someone to bring you a coffee?"

"Thank you, Uncle Ted." The woman's gaze flicked back to Lauren. "And could they please bring one for Miss Donnelly too."

CHAPTER 9

"I thought so hard about what I would say before I came here. All I could think of was I'm sorry and that just seems so inadequate. I hope you can take some comfort in the fact your father was a hero, that he died saving someone else's life."

Lauren sat with her handbag on her lap. The woman before her seemed to have almost gone out of her way to minimize her few attractive qualities. Her mousy hair was cut in a skull cap, her doughy features unadorned by make-up, her blocky figure made all the more lumpish by a shapeless long-out-of-fashion dress. Yet just at that moment, as she gazed toward the coffin, there was something serene, almost angelic about her smile.

"Knowing that would've made him happy," Ada said. "After his stroke he couldn't do a lot of the things he used to. I think he decided he wasn't much good for anything anymore."

"Well he was to me. If it wasn't for him I wouldn't be here."

The funeral director came down the aisle and handed them each a cup and saucer.

Ada watched him walk away, her gaze fixing on the

others in the lobby. "They think they know, but none of them has any idea."

"Excuse me?"

"The rest of my family. They'd never say it to my face but I know what they think. Poor Ada. How awful that I had to look after Dad all these years. How terrible that I never got married. What hope will I ever have of it now?"

Lauren waited, reluctant to confirm the woman's suspicions yet sharing her scorn. With her bland looks and retiring manner she was perhaps too easy a target. But that was no excuse for unkindness, especially toward someone as selfless, devoted and forgiving as Ada.

"What none of them has ever understood is that I didn't mind; my dad wasn't all that hard to look after. He couldn't talk or use his right arm, but he could walk on his own; it wasn't like I had to carry him. He went for a walk every morning in fact. Though sometimes I think he just did it to get out of my hair for a while, to give me a break. That's how he was, always thinking of others."

Ada sipped her coffee and stared into space. "He just needed help getting dressed. And washing and shaving, combing his hair, using the toilet. And of course he couldn't drive anymore so I had to take him everywhere." Her gaze flew to Lauren. "But how hard is that to do for someone you love? After all the things he did for me?"

Sensing the woman's need to talk, and that she wasn't often given the chance, Lauren just nodded.

"It was the little things that really frustrated him. Like feeding himself. He had trouble swallowing, you know. Gosh, he made a mess! But the thing is, he always did his best. He never wanted to be a burden to me."

"I'm sure he didn't."

"Do you get to spend much time with your Dad?"

Lauren blinked. The question caught her completely off guard, plucking a nerve she feared would remain forever sensitized. "No." She swallowed. "Sadly, he died a few years ago."

"Oh, I'm sorry. I bet you still miss him."

"Every day."

"And your Mom?"

"She died soon after my father."

Ada nodded. "You hear about that. It's like one can't live without the other. My Mom died when I was little. Do you have any brothers or sisters?"

"No. I always wanted some, but mom couldn't have any more after me."

"Really? Same here." Ada tipped her head. "Our parents both gone, no brothers or sisters... I guess you and I have a bit in common."

The director caught her eye from the aisle. "We're ready to leave for the cemetery whenever you are."

"Oh, yes, please, tell them to come in. We're finished here."

The two women rose and stepped to one side as ushers approached, turned the casket and began wheeling it up the aisle. Ada watched it all the way to the door. When it finally disappeared from view, she turned back to Lauren wiping her eyes. "Will you be coming to the cemetery? You'd be welcome."

"Thank you but, no, I feel that's private, just for the family."

They walked toward the lobby and stopped when they reached it.

"I nearly forgot." Lauren reached into her handbag. "I

wanted to return the clothes you gave me." She held them out. "Thank you so much for all you did. It wasn't only your father who saved me – if you hadn't helped me I'd have frozen to death."

Ada smiled accepting the bag. "You didn't need to give these back. In fact you didn't have to come here at all today. But I'm glad you did." She looked down, shyly. "I really liked talking to you, Lauren. Do you think maybe sometime..." She waved off the thought. "Sorry. Never mind."

"No, it's okay. Sometime what?"

"I just wondered if..." Ada looked up to gauge her reaction. "Maybe we could see each other again. The one thing I didn't get to do much with Dad was meet new people."

Lauren stood stunned. She'd been worried this woman would throw her out and here she wanted to be her friend? There'd seemed a note of near desperation in her words. Was she shunned by others besides her family?

"But I'm sure you're busy. You probably have friends and a family and work and—"

"Yes, I'd love to see you again."

Ada blinked back. "You would? Really?"

"Why don't we have lunch together next week? If you give me your number I'll call to arrange it."

"That would be wonderful."

Lauren entered the number into her phone.

Ada took her hand as they said their goodbyes. "You know something? My dad would have liked you."

Lauren swallowed, feeling the tightness pinch at her throat. She'd been holding it together until that moment. Now she desperately needed to go. "I'm sure I would've liked him as well."

CHAPTER 10

Lauren hurried across the lobby. *My dad would have liked you.* Ada's words, spoken in kindness, had inexplicably breached the barrier holding her brittle emotions in check.

She turned down the hall to the building's back entrance and spotted two figures inside the door – one, a woman holding a microphone, the other, a man with a video camera. A news crew? Here? Did these people have no respect? Head down, she barreled toward them.

"Hey, that's her." The man aimed his camera and started filming.

"Miss Donnelly, a word, if you would." The woman shoved the mike in her face. "Are you here for Roger Phelps's funeral? Have you spoken with his daughter? Does she blame you for her father's death? Has she forgiven you?"

Lauren saw the rain sheeting down outside and never slowed as she burst through the door.

Halfway across the parking lot she was soaked to the skin. She rifled through her bag as she ran, bruised fingers screaming. She found her keys, pulled them out, and promptly fumbled them. They bounced off her foot and disappeared beneath her car.

She dropped to the ground and groped in the gloom but couldn't feel them. Icy water seeped through her pants, lumps of gravel dug at her skin. It was all too much. There on her knees, in the driving rain, her sobs escaped.

With her eyes streaming and bleary with tears, she couldn't identify the person who suddenly took her arm. Whoever it was, pulled her to her feet, opened her door and pushed her in behind the wheel.

Her door slammed shut. A shadow passed in front of the windshield. The reporter? One of the bereaved? She fought to pull herself together.

Beside her, the passenger door swung open and the car rocked as someone got in. Her mouth dropped open.

"Josh. My God, what are you doing here?"

"Frankly, I've been asking myself the same question." He dropped her keys in the cup container and swept wet hair back from his face.

"You…but… I don't understand."

"Mel sent me. At least I think she did. Her instructions were a bit on the cryptic side so it was hard to tell."

Lauren slumped. Hearing Mel's name gave her an inkling what this was about. "What did she say?"

"She asked me to run out and pick up something for afternoon coffee, but said she wanted it from Elroy's bakery and nowhere else." He pointed toward the shops across the road. "She said, after I came out I was to drive over here and wait in this parking lot for half an hour before returning to the nursery. She said I was to keep an eye out for you and to give you a hand if it looked like you needed it."

Lauren's embarrassment flared in her cheeks. Mel's misguided concern often led her to do something over the top. But the woman had really outdone herself this time.

"I thought maybe you'd gone to a garage sale and needed help loading something heavy into your car," Josh went on. "Obviously I got that wrong." He peered through the rain at the back of the funeral home. "What is this place anyway?"

"Josh, I'm sorry. Mel should never have—"

"So what's going on?" He turned to look at her.

Lauren blinked back. Under different circumstances those intense blue eyes, the strong male presence, his close proximity in a darkened car, might have led her thoughts astray. But there'd seemed the slightest edge to his tone. Not the concern she might've expected, more a note of…disapproval?

"I thought this would be something to do with my job," he said. "Or is it just some strange initiation you put all your new workers through?"

Her frown deepened. She definitely hadn't imagined the tone, though she couldn't quite see what she'd done to cause it.

All at once her composure returned. She drew herself up. "Look, again, I'm sorry. Mel shouldn't have asked you to come here and it's certainly nothing to do with your job."

He waited for her to explain further.

She sat immobile, staring back. She'd told him all she intended to.

His jaw twitched. Clearly he was itching to say something else but thinking better of it. His first smart move since getting in the car.

"Well, I'll leave you to it then." He reached for the door.

"Stedman."

He turned.

"Seeing as you've been so inconvenienced, why don't you have the rest of the day off."

That twitch again.

He nodded, opened the door and got out. "See you Monday."

CHAPTER 11

In her rain-soaked jacket, bag in hand, Lauren stood in her office doorway.

"Oh hey, you're back." Seated at the desk, Mel resumed writing. "That shipment of osteospernum came in. I got them to unload the flats to the greenhouse. We'll get started on them straight after lunch." When Lauren said nothing, the woman looked up. "You okay?"

"Why did you send Josh to the funeral home?"

Mel carefully set down her pen. "I gather you saw him."

"We had a nice little chat in my car. He was a bit confused about why he was there however. I tried to explain to him the obsessive behavior of my lunatic friend but I don't think he quite understood."

Mel shrugged. "I was worried about you."

"So why'd you send him? Why did you have me look like a fool in front of someone I hardly know?"

"So you *were* in a state when you left the funeral."

Lauren pursed her lips and waited. She was still trying to work out why Josh's remarks had bothered her so much. Was it simply a matter of looking weak in front of an employee? Not being in charge? Or was it more the disquieting sense that a man she'd known less than a day seemed to have taken an instant dislike to her?

"Look, I had no choice," Mel protested. "I was going to come myself, but just as I was about to leave, that shipment arrived. I couldn't very well send Simon, could I?"

"Why did you feel you had to send anyone?"

"I just thought, given the situation, you might need a bit of moral support."

Lauren nearly laughed. Her encounter with Josh had been brief but intense, generating in her lingering sensations she didn't care to examine too closely. But of all the things he'd made her feel, 'supported' definitely wasn't one of them.

"So did you?" Mel said.

"Did I what?"

"Need some su—"

"No!" Lauren thumped her handbag down on the desk and dropped into the seat in front of it. No need to tell her well-meaning friend how Josh's presence had affected her. What happened in the car was between her and him.

"There's nothing wrong with admitting it, you know. I realize that's always been difficult for you, but sometimes you just—"

"When has it ever been difficult for me?"

Mel shrugged. "Your break-up with Marc. Your troubles with the business. Your problems with your mom." She lowered her voice. "When your dad died."

Lauren turned and looked out the window.

"I just wanted you to know, one way or the other, that I've got your back."

She blew out a sigh. Despite insisting she'd needed no help, if Mel had shown up herself today, they wouldn't be having this conversation. No, her problem wasn't with her friend, it was with the man she'd sent in her place.

"If there's one thing you never need to tell me, it's that," she answered at last.

"Well, I'm glad to hear it." Mel leaned back. "So how did it go? With the daughter I mean?"

"Better than I expected actually."

For the next five minutes she filled Mel in on what she had learned of Ada's situation – her father's stroke, the years she'd sacrificed looking after him, how her family both pitied and laughed at her.

"Sounds like she should have a real axe to grind."

"And yet she was wonderful; totally forgiving about what happened. Proud her father died a hero and holds no grudge against me at all."

"It's great she could see it that way. You must be relieved."

"Yes." Lauren frowned then pushed to her feet. "Well I better give you a hand with that order. I'll just run up to the house and change."

"Take your time."

She grabbed her handbag from the desk, crossed the room and stopped in the doorway. "By the way, I gave Josh the afternoon off."

"What?" Mel looked up again, suddenly stricken. "What about my chocolate eclair from Elroy's?"

Josh took a deep swallow of his beer and stared at the TV behind the bar. The words he'd spoken that afternoon had left a sour taste in his mouth – it was going to take more than his usual three to wash it away.

He didn't know what the hell had come over him. Even for something as big as this it wasn't like him to hold a grudge.

Sure Lauren Donnelly had cost him his business, his comfortable lifestyle, his relationship with Fran, but wasn't it time he let it all go and tried to move on?

Hell, he *had* moved on. Or thought he had. It was finding himself in the impossible situation of working for the woman who'd caused his demise that had stirred things up again.

She hadn't been down to the greenhouses much since he'd started there, so this had been their first real one-on-one encounter. A great way to start things off.

He didn't like remembering how startled she'd looked at his prickly tone, that flash of concerned confusion in her eyes. And really how could she react any differently? She had no idea from where his animosity had sprung.

She'd gotten over her fear fast enough. He smiled at recalling how she'd rallied to issue a subtle warning with a nice touch of sarcasm thrown in. A comeback that had, despite his reluctance, spawned in him a grudging respect for the woman.

Unbidden, other images flashed in his mind. The way her wet clothes had clung to her body. The strangely appealing bedraggled look of water dripping from her untethered hair.

He pushed the images firmly aside.

Still, it wasn't right. He couldn't go on sniping at her when she didn't know what he was blaming her for. As far as he could see, he had three options: forgive her totally, bury his resentment, or quit the job.

Well, it seemed he wasn't quite ready for the first. And he sure as hell couldn't afford the last, not if he hoped to start up another business of his own one day. He needed this job in order to save, to add to the sum he'd managed to salvage and sock away in a term investment. Assuming he even had a job to go back to after today!

So of the three options he'd given himself, that left pretending there wasn't a problem. Something he'd never been much good at.

He lifted his drink, downed the dregs and froze when a familiar face appeared on the screen above the bar – someone who looked a lot like Lauren running down a shadowy corridor, a woman with a microphone chasing after her.

The voice-over said, "The memorial service for Yarmouth man, Roger Phelps, was held today in Eastmore House. Mister Phelps drowned earlier this week while saving twenty-eight-year-old Lauren Donnelly who had fallen through thin ice on the stream near his home. Miss Donnelly attended today's service but was too distraught to comment."

He lowered his glass to the bar. "Shit."

CHAPTER 12

Lauren selected a dried hydrangea flower and glued it onto the wreath's wire frame. Her fingers had finally freed up enough that she could do some fine work. Which was just as well – she was way behind on the spring arrangements.

So it wasn't that she was avoiding the greenhouse; this work had to be done as well. Still, after the miserable weekend she'd had, spending a day alone in the work shop, surrounded by flowers, breathing the fresh scent of eucalyptus, was a balm to her sleep-deprived senses. Last night had been particularly bad, so much so she'd gotten up at three a.m., gone to the kitchen and baked a cake. And she never baked at the best of times.

In addition to her nightmares, her run-in with Josh the Friday before had played on her mind more than she wanted to admit to herself. To say his behavior had been a surprise was an understatement. The more she'd thought about it, the more she'd wondered if something else entirely had been bothering him and he hadn't been mad about being sent to help her at all. Whether it was his job or not, he was still getting paid for his time, so what could he have been angry about?

Whatever the reason, in her current state she didn't want to go anywhere near him. He'd seemed so intolerant of her lapse in control she wanted never to show weakness around him again. Of course he didn't know her very well, and that such outbursts were rare for her. But if he couldn't be bothered getting to know her before passing judgment, well that was his loss.

Still, as much as the incident had bothered her, she wasn't about to fire him for it. Both she and Mel had recognized he was the best person for the job. And in fairness, a misunderstanding wasn't really sufficient grounds. She'd dealt with insensitive people before, and though she was close to Simon and Mel, she didn't have to like *all* her employees.

What's more, if pushed, she'd have to admit, Stedman did have some interesting qualities. Images from their run-in kept flitting back to her – those strong calloused hands, fingers combing through gleaming dark hair, the shadow of stubble on a well-defined jaw...

But, no, she wasn't going there. Workplace romance rarely worked out and would only complicate their situation further. Just as well she didn't like him. She needed to focus all her attention on doing what was best for the business. And right now the best included Josh Stedman. As long as he continued to do his job and never behaved toward anyone else...the way he'd acted...

She lowered the glue gun and looked toward the greenhouse. Mel had a doctor appointment this morning and was coming in late, which meant Josh and Simon were in there alone. Had Mel ever explained to Josh about Simon? If Josh had been short-tempered with her, what would he be like with someone who sometimes got confused, who needed things explained more than once? She set down the gun and rushed from the workshop.

She crossed the yard and started down the side of the greenhouse.

"No. Take it back. Don't you say that!"

Simon's words seeped through the greenhouse wall. She quickened her pace. *Damn it, Stedman, mouthing off to me is one thing, but turning on someone who can't defend himself...* She reached the door and yanked it open.

"You don't know anything. The Sox'll go all the way this year, you wait and see."

She stood in the doorway, halted by the words. The Sox? Is that what this was about?

The two men, up to their elbows in dirt, stood on either side of the potting bench – Josh, tall and lean, Simon short and stocky. A Mutt n' Jeff team if ever there was one.

Simon turned when he saw Josh look up. "Hey Lauren!"

"Hi. Everything okay in here?"

"Yeah. No!" Simon turned to frown at Josh but she could see there was no real anger in it. "Josh doesn't think the Red Sox will beat the Yankees this year."

"Doesn't he?" She started toward them, trying to act as though she'd just happened by. "Those are fightin' words around here."

"All I said was they've got a lot of players injured," Josh protested.

"It doesn't matter. They're still gonna beat 'em!"

Lauren smiled at Simon's vehemence. Her relief that it was nothing more serious lightened her mood. "Well, I'm with you, Simon. I think the Sox'll whoop their asses."

"That's what I said." His expression grew troubled. "Only I didn't say that word. Asses." He clapped a filthy hand over his mouth. "Oh, no, I said it."

"It's okay." She laughed as she brushed the dirt from his face. "No-one else heard you and we won't tell."

Like a switch being thrown, he brightened again. "Hey Josh, bet you can't guess what Lauren has."

"A guessing game, eh. Well now, let's see." Josh glanced over, his look unreadable. "Nice hair? Nice eyes? Beautiful smile?"

Lauren froze. Sexist taunts, his honest opinion, or things he thought Simon wanted to hear?

Simon shook his head. "No. I mean, yes, but that's not it."

"Well, I give up then, what does she have?"

"A baseball signed by Ted Williams."

Josh went still, his expression wiped clean. "You're kidding. For real?"

She couldn't help smiling. What was it about hearing that name that could turn a grown man into a ten-year-old kid? On Josh, the look was definitely appealing. But she still didn't know how he'd meant those comments.

"It was my dad's," she answered cautiously and let it drop. "So are you boys just about ready for a break?"

"I am. I'm hungry!" Simon instantly set down his tools.

"Good, because there's a cake in the kitchen with your name on it."

"There is? What kind?"

"Go and see. Just remember—"

"To wash my hands!" He ran down the aisle and out the door.

Taking a breath, she turned back to Josh, narrowing her eyes as she watched him finish the pot he was on. Had he gone looking for an interest both he and Simon shared? His attitude hadn't seemed condescending. Anyone who was good to Simon had to have some redeeming qualities. Even if he was a sexist jerk. "I thought you were wheeling in the barrows of mix."

"I was. Without Mel, Simon was falling behind with the potting so I thought I'd give him a hand for a while." He shot her a glance. "Checking up on us?"

"Not Simon, just you." Her bluntness drew a faint smile to his lips. She resisted its pull. "Let's just say I wanted to make sure you two were getting along."

"Afraid I might have as short a fuse with him as I had with you?"

"Something like that."

Josh nodded, set the pot aside with the others and turned to face her. "Allow me to apologize for Friday. I was a jerk." He brushed off his hand and held it out. "What do you say we start over?"

She eyed him a moment. He'd given no explanation for his behavior but the apology was something at least. "Sure."

The feel of his hand engulfing hers sent a rush of warmth up her arm. She managed to keep her expression neutral until he released it.

He cocked his head. "Any chance of getting a bit of that cake?"

CHAPTER 13

Outside, they started back toward the office. To his surprise, Josh was finding his situation easier to face today. Discovering what had happened to Lauren – her recent brush with death and dealing with the guilt of someone having died to save her – had no doubt softened his attitude toward her. But he had to admit it was more than that. It was also the woman herself.

When he'd come into work that morning he hadn't known what to expect. After the way he'd behaved on Friday, he wouldn't have been terribly surprised if she'd called him into her office and fired him. He knew a few bosses who would have, plenty of workers who'd been canned for less. And yet she seemed willing to put it behind them.

From the corner of his eye he studied her profile. A sense of humor, the guts to hold her own in a conflict, willingness to overlook mistakes… Good qualities for any employer to have.

He tipped his face to the sun as they walked, its warmth welcome after the weekend storms. "You really have a baseball signed by Ted Williams?"

"I do. My dad got it at Fenway in Williams' last year. What makes it even more special is it wasn't a ball he brought to the game – he caught one of Williams' last homeruns. He took the ball to him afterwards and got him to sign it. Dad was five years old at the time."

Josh smiled at a thought. "I bet you heard that story a few times."

She laughed. "Once or twice."

"Have you ever looked up what it's worth? Could be quite a bit."

"It doesn't matter; I'd never part with it. And if for some reason I absolutely had to, I'd give it to Simon. He loved my dad as much as I did. *Almost* as much as he loves the Red Sox."

Josh nodded. "I thought *I* was a diehard fan. He's really into it, isn't he?"

"Baseball and the beach. Simon's two favorite things in the world."

"And you," he added.

Lauren looked up.

"He spent an hour my first day here telling me how wonderful you are."

She didn't know which she felt more in that moment – disappointed or relieved. His earlier comments about her appearance hadn't been sexist taunts after all, but neither had they been his personal sentiments. They were merely Simon's views he'd been spouting. "I think it's more the job he loves."

"I gather he's been with you a while?"

"When I was a sophomore in high school a rep from Work For The Disabled spoke at our school. I went home and talked to my parents and a week later they hired Simon. He's been with us ever since; it's the only job he's ever had."

"And what about Mel?"

"Mel and I were roommates at college. Every summer she came home with me, stayed in our house, and we worked for my parents. When they died and I took the place over, Mel was the first person I hired."

At the corner of the office, Lauren stopped. Detached from its moorings and nudged by a breeze, the gutter's down pipe banged against the side of the building, a casualty of Friday's winds. She struggled to push it back into place.

"Here, let me." Josh reached over her shoulder and grabbed it. The bracket was simply missing a screw. A stay-tie would hold it until he could get one. He dug in a pocket.

"To be honest, I don't know what I'd have done without either of them all these years," Lauren reflected of her workers. "Mel's been a constant source of support, no matter how much she drives me crazy sometimes. And Simon just brightens everyone's day. The customers love him."

He pulled out a work glove, draped it over the edge of the rainwater barrel beneath the downspout, then retrieved the stay-tie buried below. "Could you hang onto this for a second?"

Lauren pressed her hand against the pipe, holding it in place as he tied it. "I'm glad you two are getting along. Simon can be shy with strangers."

"I wouldn't have picked it, he seems so friendly."

"He's fine once he gets to know you, it's just... Well, as you can imagine he's had a few bad experiences with people. We make sure that never happens here."

With the pipe secured, he stepped back to face her. "Do I detect a note of protectiveness?"

"You bet your petunias. Anyone messes with my boy Simon answers to me." As she lowered her arm, she hit the glove, knocking it into the rainwater barrel. "Oh blast. Sorry." Leaning over the rim to retrieve it, she gasped and jerked back.

"What is it?"

Deaf to his words, she stared at the barrel, backing away.

Josh reached out. "Are you okay?"

At his touch on her arm she actually jumped. For a second she stared at him, eyes wide, then resumed her retreat. "You'll have to excuse me. There's something I forgot I needed to do."

She hurried away. "The cake's in the kitchen. Help yourself."

It was chilly behind the barn, the sheltered spot she'd come to so often as a child, her parents had placed an old stone bench there. Lauren brushed off its mantle of leaves, sat down and pulled her sweater around her.

She just needed a moment to regroup without having to answer questions or give explanations – most of which she wouldn't have been able to provide. More importantly she'd needed some distance from Josh, a man she already knew to have little tolerance for weakness. At least she'd managed to hold herself together until she'd gotten out of his sight.

She wrapped her arms tightly around herself and bowed her head. What the hell was happening to her? She wasn't the sort to go off the deep end like this. Even after her own father's death she'd managed to hold herself together, been surprisingly calm in fact.

Maybe Mel was right. Maybe she did have trouble asking for help. But just at that moment she wouldn't have had a clue what to ask for.

At the sound of someone coming around the barn, she shot to her feet. When she saw who it was, she sat back down and let out her breath. Simon never asked for explanations. He never gave advice or offered suggestions or asked her to be anything but what she was.

He stopped before her, opened the napkin he was carrying, and handed her a piece of the cake she'd made.

Lauren took it but held it on her lap. The image she'd seen in the rainwater barrel – the face of Roger Phelps, staring up from beneath the surface, eyes wide, bubbles escaping his open mouth – had left her barely able to breathe, let alone eat.

"Josh said he didn't know where you went." Simon sat on the bench beside her.

"Yes, I walked away in kind of a hurry. I hope he didn't think I was rude. How did you know where I was?"

"This is where I always used to come."

A smile tugged her lips at the memory. "When you first started working for my parents. Yes, I remember. If something upset you, you always came here."

"I haven't in a while."

"That's good, I'm glad. It means you haven't been upset by anything."

With their backs to the barn, that solid old friend, they gazed across the boundary fence into the wooded acres next door – one of the Cape's many tracts of untouched land forever reserved against development. Though the occasional source of trouble, with larger wildlife – raccoon, deer, even the odd coyote at times – coming across to drink at the pond or raid her rubbish, Lauren had always loved the woods. And the fact no-one else could ever build beside her.

"Who are you hiding from?"

Simon's question drew her back. "Nobody. I just have a little problem and came here to think about it."

"Does thinking help?"

"Sometimes it does." She gave a small laugh. "Sometimes it's greatly over-rated."

"Did it help you this time?"

"No, not really."

He leaned against her, his head coming to rest on her shoulder. "You've been sad."

"I have a bit, yes. But I'll be okay."

"Did I do something wrong?"

"Don't be silly, it was nothing you did." She squeezed his hand. "You're my number one worker, you know that."

"I don't want you to feel bad." He straightened. "That's why I brought you some cake. Cake always makes me feel better."

"Well, thank you, that was very nice of you." She smiled, then looked at the piece in her hand. Dear sweet Simon. For him she could do this. "So, how is it?" She took a bite.

"Not so good."

She tried to chew through her burst of laughter but the taste only made her laugh more. "You're right. This is awful! I think I must've left something out." Which wasn't surprising, seeing as she'd made it at three in the morning.

"I still ate some," Simon assured.

"You're braver than I am." She set it aside, then winced at a thought. "Oh god, did Josh have any?"

"Yeah. But he spit it out when he thought no-one was looking."

She laughed till tears squirmed from her eyes then reached over and hugged him tightly. "You know what? Who needs cake when I have you."

CHAPTER 14

Ada sat in her patch of sunlight. Tuesday afternoon and here she was again, just like yesterday and the day before. Even though she didn't need to be. Even though she could do anything she wanted now, whenever it suited her. She'd never have to set foot in this park again if she didn't want to.

And yet here she was. The spot where her dad used to sit and watch the children sail their boats on the concrete pond. Where he sometimes fed the ducks but never the pigeons because he thought pigeons were dirty. Where the town band played Stars and Stripes on the Fourth of July and vendors sold hot dogs and strawberry shortcake.

So many memories attached to this place. Farmers' Markets. Craft Fairs. The Halloween Jack o' Lantern display. And Christmas, his favorite, with the tree all lit up in the common and skaters skimming around the boat pond. All those things would come again. But she'd be watching them on her own.

And watching was probably all she'd ever do. Because that's what people like her did – sit and watch while others did the things they wanted to do. So many years had slipped away. For so long she had wanted a life. Now that she had one, what would she do with it?

She got up and started back to her car.

Two women sat on the playground bench watching their

children on the swings. For a moment she thought about going over and chatting to them, then saw they were the same two she'd spoken to earlier. Or tried to speak to. They hadn't been very friendly. They probably thought she hadn't noticed their looks to each other, like they were sharing some secret joke. But she'd seen all right. She always did. It was just easier to pretend she didn't.

At the end of the park, she crossed the street and started along a row of shops. Just as she reached the paper store a group of teenage boys spilled out. Too late to avoid them, she scuttled past, cringing at the kissing noises they made. She knew what that meant. It didn't mean they wanted to kiss her. It was the sound you made when you were calling a dog.

She kept up her pace, now keen to get home. But, recalling there was nothing to go home to, she slowed again.

She couldn't get over how fast things had changed. Ten days ago her father was alive. Now the house seemed so quiet. Funny how a man who couldn't talk could've made it seem so full of sound. Probably she just remembered his voice, imagined he was saying things just by the expression on his face.

As she pulled out her keys to unlock her car, a man came out of the menswear store carrying a mannequin. He walked around the side of the building into a laneway and left it propped beside the dumpster.

Ada stared at it as the man walked away. The words came out before she even knew she was going to say them. "Excuse me. Are you throwing that away?"

He waved a hand as he went back inside. "You want it, take it."

CHAPTER 15

Lauren set her arrangement of flowers beside the headstone and took a step back. The narrow patch of freshly turned earth looked like a wound on the otherwise unbroken ground.

She wasn't entirely sure why she'd come. She'd paid her respects last week at the funeral. She'd spoken with Ada, offered her condolences, apologized as best she could. Yet somehow something felt unfinished. She thought she'd come to terms with what happened. But you didn't keep seeing a dead man's face if you'd accepted his passing.

All right maybe it wasn't outright visions she was having. She'd just...catch a glimpse. Always at odd unexpected moments. In windows, birdbaths, rainwater barrels. That horrible image of Roger's face, eyes wide in terror, his pale hand clawing beneath the surface...

When she looked again, it was always gone. But that fleeting snapshot was more than enough to stop her heart, to bring a scream to the back of her throat. That and the nightmares.

Survivor guilt? Is that what it was? According to the website she'd Googled last night it wasn't uncommon in such situations. She hadn't been aware of feeling overly consumed with guilt. Of course she felt terrible about what had happened but the reality was it was an accident. A deplorable tragedy. Still, *knowing* you weren't to blame for something and feeling it at a deeper subconscious level could be two entirely different things.

Then again maybe this wasn't about guilt at all. Maybe it was simply the horror of knowing that, if Phelps hadn't come along when he had, it would've been *her* face beneath that ice; pale, wide-eyed, silently screaming. She shivered at the thought.

Slowed by the weight of unresolved doubts, she turned and walked away from the grave. Sunlight flickered through the ancient maples lining the path. She could almost feel the life force rising from their roots, filling their soon-to-be-open buds. What a difference just one warm day could make at this time of year. It was almost enough to dispel the shadow hanging over her.

Spring. Renewal. A new beginning. Wasn't that just what she had been given? Surely it was how she needed to look at this. Roger Phelps had given his life so she could have hers. What a wasted sacrifice that would be if she spent the rest of it burdened with guilt. What she should be feeling... What she *would* be feeling from this moment on, was the sense of gratitude that act deserved.

She raised her face to the sun and smiled. That was the answer. Rather than focus on what had been lost, she would focus on the gift she'd been given, the selfless act of a total stranger. She would never be able to pay him back, but maybe, one day, she could pay her debt to someone else. That seemed a penance she could live with.

With the weight she'd been bearing suddenly lifted, she continued on. The path veered left and commenced a slow ascent to the gates. Up ahead she could see her car parked in the lot. It had been the only one there when she'd left it but now there was another parked beside it. She hadn't passed or seen anyone so possibly they had just arrived.

As she drew nearer, she noted a silhouette behind the wheel. Another of Roger Phelps's relatives? It seemed most likely, seeing as his was the newest grave. Had they recognized her? Were they waiting for her to leave to avoid a confrontation?

At the top of the rise she stepped through the gates.

The car pulled away and sped from the lot.

CHAPTER 16

She maneuvers the body into the house. Despite its weight – less than half that of its living counterpart – it is awkward to handle. The rigor of its synthetic form gives it an almost contrary purpose, an outstretched hand clutching the door frame, dragging feet curling back carpets.

Inside, she lays it on the living room floor, at once keenly aware of its nakedness. From the nearest box she pulls out trousers, shirt, socks; no underwear required. Diverting her gaze, she kneels before it and, with practiced moves, slides on the pants, pulls socks over toenails she'll never have to trim.

She bends the legs – at the knees, the hips – then stands, and lifts it onto the couch. Painted eyes stare out at the room, taking in the faded curtains, stained coffee table, aging furniture.

Shirt in hand, she threads the wooden arms through its sleeves. As she does up the buttons she notes the rise and fall of his chest. From 'it' to 'he' in five easy steps.

A thought flutters at the edge of awareness. For years she'd longed to be free of this drudgery, the forced isolation, the mindless tedium. Yet the moment she'd been granted that wish she'd wanted him back, as though these soul-devouring labors were the source of all meaning for her existence.

Or was it something else she'd missed?

She leans down, planting her palms on his wrists, pinning his arms to those of the chair. An answer had briefly stirred in her mind but it's gone now. She stares in his eyes.

"You thought you made it this time, didn't you?" She sucks her teeth, shakes her head. "What sort of daughter would I be if I'd let that happen?" She reaches up and caresses his cheek. "I told you, I'll always be here for you. Just like you'll always be here for me. Always."

She straightens, stands back, gazing down at him. "Dinner? Oh, so you're hungry now? Expect me to drop everything I suppose, just like that. Well—"

The phone rings; such an infrequent sound it startles her. She runs to answer, strolls back a few moments later in a state of bemused elation. "That was Lauren. She called to ask me to lunch tomorrow. Can you believe it?"

Catching sight of herself in the mirror above the mantel, she stops and presses a hand to her hair. "She told me she'd call, but I never really expected her to. Not that I thought she was lying about it, it's just that... Well, we're so different. She's tall and slim and beautiful, and I—"

She swings to glare at him, knows what he's thinking. Smiles when he thinks better of voicing it.

"She has an appointment in the morning and asked if I could meet her afterwards at that cafe on Newberry Street. I was so surprised she invited me, I actually said yes."

With the fire that erupts at unforeseen moments, she slaps her palms against her thighs. "Of course I know I can't afford it. You think I need you to tell me that? Well, guess what? I'm going anyway!" She looks back at the red-faced image in the glass. "Somehow."

With the blood still roaring in her ears, she turns and walks off to the kitchen. Maybe she'll feed him. Maybe she doesn't feel like it yet. For now, all she knows is that he is back.

And how she had missed him.

CHAPTER 17

Lauren walked down the park-side terrace, a narrow road flanked with quirky shops that in two months time would be teaming with tourists; for now the domain of contented locals. She didn't know whether to feel good or bad. Should a person feel happy they succeeded at something they never wanted to do in the first place?

With some fast talking and only slightly inflated estimates, she'd convinced her bank manager to give her a loan. Enough to pay some outstanding debts and acquire the new range of products she hoped would boost her flagging sales.

The bad news was he'd insisted on having her house as collateral, so essentially it was a mortgage. That took a good bit of spring from her step. She didn't own her family's home anymore, at least not entirely. But one way or the other she would get it back.

She spotted Ada up ahead, standing outside the cafe where they'd agreed to meet. "Sorry I'm late," she said as she reached her. "You should've gone in, I'd have found you inside."

"It's all right. I only just got here." The woman was dressed in a plain grey skirt and a short-sleeved top revealing powerful arms and shoulders. Muscles developed over years of lifting her father most likely.

"Shall we go in?"

Ada glanced at the cafe door then across the road. "I wonder if you'd mind if we ate in the park."

Lauren took a second. Did she mean she didn't like the restaurant? "We can go somewhere else if you want."

"No, it's okay I just..." She held up a bag. "I brought my own sandwich."

Lauren blinked, then quickly recovered. "The park it is then. I'll just grab something inside and meet you over there."

A few minutes later, lunch in hand, Lauren joined Ada on a bench overlooking a small grassy common. Pleasant enough, but with clouds blocking out most of the sun, not nearly as comfortable as eating in a nice cafe would've been. Still, the woman must have her reasons.

"It's good to see you, Ada. How have you been?"

"I'm managing, thank you. Although, it's funny, I have so much free time now I don't know what to do with myself." As she spoke, Ada opened the sandwich on her lap – margarine and processed cheese on white bread.

Words Lauren had heard at the funeral flashed through her mind. *How will she survive without Roger's disability payments?* Was that why Ada had chosen the park? Because she couldn't afford the cafe?

Lauren slid her slice of warm salmon quiche into her handbag. "I imagine it'll take some getting used to. You looked after your dad a long time."

"I was a freshman in college when he had his stroke." Ada took a bite of her sandwich. "I was doing an education degree. I always wanted to be a kindergarten teacher." She smiled at the memory. "Dad never wanted me to go to college. After Mom died I pretty much ran the household for him so I think he was afraid he couldn't manage without me.

He *said* it was because he couldn't afford it, but when I got the scholarship there was nothing to stop me."

Ada stopped chewing and gazed into space. "Everything was different there. I lost weight without even trying, my skin cleared up. I even made a friend." She blushed. "A boyfriend. John."

The smile faded. "When Dad had the stroke I came home thinking it would just be for a while, that he'd be okay. He'd never been sick a day before that. Then the doctor told me he'd never talk or use his arm again and that he couldn't live on his own anymore. So in the end I had to drop out."

Lauren could sense the effect that had had on her and that it wasn't just the loss of an education. "What happened to John?"

"Oh, we wrote to each other. At least for a while. Then… Well, you probably know how those things work out. Long distance romance."

"So will you go back to college now?"

Ada laughed. "I think it's a bit too late for that. Anyway I've lost my scholarship."

"You never know. There might be others you could get."

The woman stared at her half-eaten sandwich. "And another boyfriend? Could I get one of those?"

Lauren couldn't bear her self-mocking tone. "Of course you could. You just have to go out and meet people. Have you given any thought to getting a job?"

"Oh yes. I've actually started checking the papers." Forced cheerfulness tightened her voice. "I haven't seen anything I like yet but I'll keep looking. What do you do for a living, Lauren?"

Lauren explained about the nursery, how her parents had sent her to college with the understanding she'd come back and work for them when she finished, take over the business when they retired.

"How perfect for you both. So is that what happened?"

"Not exactly." Lauren shifted. It wasn't something she talked about often but seeing as Ada had opened up to her…

"When I graduated I was in a relationship and my boyfriend wanted to travel before we settled down. We took a year and went to Europe to see all the famous botanical gardens."

"Europe." Ada said the word as though it were a dreamland forever and totally beyond her reach.

"Toward the end of our stay, I received word that my father was sick so we cut our trip short and came home."

"Almost like what happened with me and my father."

No, not quite. "Five days after I got back, he died from complications following surgery."

As it did whenever she spoke of them, the horror of those days came flooding back, the worst of it *not* her father's death but the discovery of what had really killed him. Not disease, but stress. Not a breakdown of body, but of mind and heart. Only in returning to live at home had she seen the hell his life had become, the truth he'd kept from her the latter years she'd been away.

Her mother had always drunk 'a bit'. But in the time Lauren had attended college her addiction had taken hold with a vengeance. In her father's last years he'd been little more than a nursemaid to her, trying to preserve a modicum of dignity for the woman he continued to adore.

"And he never told you what was happening?" Ada said. "Never called or wrote and asked you to come home?"

Lauren shook her head. "I only found out after the funeral." A fact she would regret the rest of her days.

Declining any outside help – whether believing he could remedy the situation with love or simply refusing to admit it existed – he struggled alone. Only towards the end had despair overwhelmed him. A fact she'd learned from her Aunt Naomi who'd told her of her father's late-night calls, his tearful confessions.

In that same conversation after his death, Lauren had asked her aunt why her father had never told her. But in truth she'd known before hearing the answer: he hadn't wanted to burden her with it.

Ada shook her head. "That's so sad. At least you got to see him again. What about your mother? You said she died a short time afterwards."

"Yes, in her sleep a few weeks later. A heart attack."

Lauren straightened. She'd come to give Ada support in her grief and here the woman was consoling her. "So after your father had his stroke, he never regained the use of his arm?"

"He got better from what he was initially – at first the whole side of his body was paralyzed. Therapy helped, but… Well, we couldn't afford to keep it up so he never got all of his movement back."

Lauren shook her head. "Considering how disabled he was, it makes what he did for me all the more amazing. He truly was a hero."

Ada sat taller. "He was, and I'm proud of him. That's why I wanted to do the best for him in the end. With the funeral, you know, all the arrangements. I wanted everything to be just right."

"And they were. The service, the flowers, everything was lovely."

"I know they weren't expecting much." Her expression

darkened. "That's why I was determined to show them. They all knew what we could afford. But I wasn't going to scrimp. I wasn't going to let them look down their noses at us. My father was a wonderful man and he deserved it. Even if I couldn't...even if it meant..."

The woman had slowly worked herself up, the 'they' she spoke of clearly her extended family, her financial problem now out in the open. Lauren waited. She didn't want to push, just to support.

Ada smiled and swiped at her eyes. "It's okay, I'll work it out. I did the right thing, that's all that matters."

Lauren unlocked her car and got in. She sat staring out at the lonely figure walking slowly up the street. Ada had things to do, she'd said, in response to Lauren's offer of a lift. But Lauren suspected she was simply embarrassed by her slip, her unguarded revelation of the financial trouble she was in.

They'd sat and talked another half hour and though their conversation had drifted through a variety of topics, Ada's words about her father's funeral continued to ring in Lauren's ears.

How could her family refuse to help her? How could the good people of the world get no assistance? A woman as devoted and self-sacrificing as Ada Phelps deserved more in life than the hand she'd been dealt. A woman who'd done all the things for her father Lauren had been unable to do for hers. A woman who was now totally alone.

Lauren put the key in the ignition and started the engine. She glanced down at the loan agreement on the seat beside her, then pulled from the curb.

CHAPTER 18

Lauren stepped through the office door to find Mel at the desk, scribbling a note. When the woman saw her, she dropped the pen and started toward her.

"Sorry, I'm just flying off home. Peter's been called back for a second interview and needs the car. It's looking good so cross your fingers."

"That's great. Tell him good luck for me."

"I will. Is it okay if I don't come back till tomorrow?"

"Sure."

Mel swept past her then suddenly stopped. "The loan! Did you get it?"

"Every penny."

The woman's arms were suddenly around her. "Great work, kid. I knew you could do it. What a relief, eh? We all have jobs for at least one more summer!" She let go and resumed her dash. "We'll have to celebrate. A few quiet ales. Friday for sure." Her words trailed after her out the door.

Lauren stood with arms at her sides. Slowly she took off her coat and dropped it over the nearest chair. She went to the desk, pulled out the ledger and sat staring bleakly at the columns of numbers.

*

Josh stood wondering if he should knock again, say

something, or simply leave. He'd just stuck his head in to say goodbye for the day, but Lauren was so intent on her paperwork she hadn't heard him.

She was leaning down, head in one hand, eyes glued to the page in front of her. Behind the massive mahogany desk she looked small and vulnerable, the frown marring her lovely features giving her a troubled faraway look.

It wasn't the first time he'd seen her like this. From the day he'd started working there her mood had ranged from preoccupied to downright jumpy. Without really knowing her, it was hard to judge if that was unusual behavior for her and, if so, what might be the cause. But if he had to guess, his money would be on her recent accident.

Still, no need for him to get involved. She was good friends with Mel so surely she'd be getting the support she needed. And the way she'd walked off the last time they'd spoken – two days now and still no explanation on that – he wasn't sure he wanted to offer her any. He'd made an effort and where had it gotten him?

He turned to leave, made it two steps, then stopped and came back. "How's it going?"

She looked up, startled. "Oh. Hi. Sorry, have you been standing there long?"

"Nope, just got here." He folded his arms and leaned a shoulder against the door frame. "You were so engrossed I didn't know whether or not to disturb you."

She dropped her pen and rubbed her eyes. "There's not much I wouldn't rather be doing." Arching back, she stretched her neck.

His gaze flew to the line of her throat, the pulse gently throbbing beneath her skin. He swallowed. "Anything I can help you with?"

She studied him a moment as though deciding. "Maybe there is. Grab a seat."

When he'd taken the chair in front of her desk she cleared her throat. "You said on your application that you used to own a nursery."

The question was the last thing he expected. He felt his shoulders instantly tense. Why her sudden interest in that? "That's right."

"Was it a setup similar to this?"

"Pretty much, but on a smaller scale. We didn't do the florist side as much."

She picked up her pen again, pulled it through her fingers, twisted the cap. "So how long ago did you...did it...?"

"All go to hell?" The words came out harder than he'd intended. Despite his attempts to put it behind him, clearly a bit of venom still lingered. He tempered his tone. "It's okay, you can say it, I've accepted it now. I closed up shop two years ago this September."

She nodded and tapped her pen on the ledger. Her struggle for words had him intrigued. He'd thought she was unaware of what happened, what she'd done to him. If she'd known all along—

"You don't have to answer this if you don't want to, but if you wouldn't mind I'd really appreciate...what I mean is...with the perspective you have now, looking back..." She heaved a sigh and slumped in her chair. "I guess all I really want to know is if there's any strategy I haven't tried."

He stared in surprise. Was she saying *her* place was struggling now? Well, wasn't this a strange development. The woman who'd caused his business to fail, asking his advice on how to save hers. If this was some cosmic test of character he could be in trouble.

She straightened again. "Just tell me this. Was there any one thing you could put it down to? Any one moment you could point to and say, this was the point of no return?"

"Actually there was." He took a deep breath. "Our sales had been down for a couple of years but we were managing. Then that spring, out of the blue, our biggest client cancelled a long-standing contract with us. Seems they found someone who could do it cheaper."

"Gee, that's too bad."

Her expression was one of genuine sympathy. She really had no idea what she'd done. "They'd been our customer for over six years. If we'd been in better shape we might've weathered losing them, but the way things were, it just tipped the scales too far."

"We? So you had a partner then?"

"My fiance. Or she was. She left me when the business folded."

"Oh, Josh, I'm so sorry."

He didn't know why he'd added that last bit. Just one more thing to blame her for? He'd decided he was through with all that, but deep down could he ever be?

He pushed to his feet. "So to answer your question, all I can say from my own experience is, no matter what precautions you take, no matter how things look on paper, someone can still cut the legs out from under you."

Lauren watched as he went out the door. Not a very reassuring message. And certainly not the help she'd hoped for. Yes, despite his insistence he was over what happened, it was clearly still a painful subject for him.

And she couldn't honestly say she blamed him.

CHAPTER 19

The days were getting longer. They had been since December of course, but only now was Lauren beginning to notice the change. Back before Christmas when she knocked off work, she'd be walking up to the house in the dark. Now, even at quarter to six, it was only just growing twilight out.

At a break in the driveway's flanking trees, she looked toward the hollow down near the road – the site for this year's vegetable garden. The last patches of snow had melted, but the earth still lay lifeless and fallow.

Her gaze drifted across to the pond. Just a few small islands of ice remained. The swans would be arriving soon. Yet she wondered if she'd ever again be able to sit with Simon and feed them. To look down into the water without seeing… With a shudder she hurried on up the drive.

At the flagstone patio outside her door, she paused to scan its surrounding flower beds. Overhead, in the cutting wind, the trees' bare limbs rattled like bones. But here beneath them were pockets of green, the first tender shoots of the bulbs she'd planted at the end of last year – snowdrops, hyacinths, daffodils, tulips.

The world seemed poised, trembling on the edge between

winter's death grip and the rebirth of spring. Never in her life had she hungered more for that seasonal change. With it might come her own deliverance. From the lingering nightmares. The visions submerged in every pool. The memories that ambushed without any warning.

She turned for the house and scrambled to get her key in the door when she heard the phone ringing inside. Across the foyer and in the kitchen, she snatched it up.

"Why did you do it?"

For an instant she heard only accusation – forgiveness rescinded. She recovered her voice. "Ada, now listen—"

"I just can't believe it. I went to the funeral home this afternoon to see the director, to make arrangements, work out some way to pay what I owe him. And he told me you had already been there. That you'd already done it!"

Lauren settled into a chair at the kitchen table. "Ada, it's all right." The woman actually sounded distressed. "I did it because it was the right thing to do."

"But all that money! No, it's too much. I can't let you do it."

"Yes, you can. And anyway it's done."

"But...don't you see. Even if what happened hadn't happened, my father was sixty-four. I would've had to pay for his funeral at some stage."

"Yes, that's true. But he didn't just die, he died saving *me*. There's a huge difference, at least in my mind. Which you're not going to change, so don't even try."

The woman stammered a few moments longer then fell silent.

Lauren closed her eyes and whispered. "Ada, after all you did for him all those years..." *Things I never got to do for my dad.* "If anyone deserves a fresh start, you do."

"I...I don't know what to say. No-one's ever done anything like this for me before. I just...I don't..."

"Don't say anything. You don't have to, I'm happy to do it."

The silence was even longer this time. "Do you think you and I met for a reason?"

Lauren was slightly taken aback. To think a person had to die so two others could meet wasn't a scenario she wanted to consider. "I'd just be happy if something good came from the tragedy of your father's death."

"Me too. And I think it has."

Ada slowly lowered the phone and stared at the living room's threadbare carpet. Her debt was paid. How could it be?

"I don't understand. Lauren explained but I still don't get it. Why did she do it? She didn't have to; I never asked her. I hardly know her!"

She started slowly pacing the room; pacing always helped her think. "She said I deserved good things in my life, that I should have a fresh start. But it doesn't explain why she felt *she* had to be the one..."

She cocked her head at a curious thought. "I suppose we do have a lot in common. And you never know – sometimes people, even beautiful people, the ones you'd think would be the most popular, are actually the loneliest."

Laughter suddenly broke from her lips. Her step became buoyant as she swept across the room, fluid and dance-like. Amazing how she could feel so elated, almost giddy, from simple relief and the promise of friendship.

If that's all it was.

She dragged to a stop. But perhaps it wasn't. Perhaps there was something else deeper down. Addictive and primal. The pull of something unspeakably potent. *Look what I got without even trying. What more might I have, what more might she give me...*

Her smiled died as she turned toward the figure seated on the couch. "What are you talking about? It had nothing to do with that."

She started toward him, balling her fists. "You would say that. Everything always has to be about you. No one could ever do something nice just because they liked me. It had to be guilt that made her do it." She stopped in front of him.

"Well, it doesn't matter what it was. This is just the start, you'll see. Lauren and I are going to be friends. Not only that, I'm going to get a job, and I'm going to save money, and I'm going to do the things I always wanted." She opened her arms to embrace their surroundings. "I'm going to get the hell out of this dump. And *then* I'm going to get a boyfriend."

She leaned down and planted her hands on his arms, felt her nails sink into his flesh. "So you just better be nice to me, mister. It could be I don't need you after all."

CHAPTER 20

Nearly two weeks. That's how long it had been since she'd run. Lauren hadn't known a lapse like this since she'd first started running as a freshman in college.

She'd wanted to desperately. Every one of the twelve days she'd missed she'd felt the pull, her body craving the cleansing exertion, her mind demanding a brief spell of peace. Yet every time she'd reached for her running shoes something had stopped her.

No prizes for guessing what that something was.

From the parking lot she forced herself forward along the boardwalk toward the beach. After a break this long, sand would be the easiest surface to run on, less jarring to her joints, kinder on her out-of-shape muscles. Plus the roiling sea, surging with energy and forever linked in her mind to summer, was as far removed from a frozen stream as she could imagine.

At the end of the boardwalk she stopped and took a steadying breath. She stepped from the sturdy wooden planks and felt her foot sink into the sand. With it, something sank inside her. Her breathing doubled, her stomach clenched.

She forced herself on.

Another step and she sank in deeper. The entire beach began to crawl, a surface false and deadly as quicksand. Waiting to open up and swallow her? Spew forth remains of earlier victims?

With a cry she jumped back onto the boardwalk. She was gasping as though she'd just sprinted a mile, yet she hadn't managed a single yard.

She turned and hurried back toward her car. Too soon, that's all, it was just too soon. She'd try again in another few days.

CHAPTER 21

Beer in hand, Mel stood at the nursery's kitchen window staring out into the parking lot. It was the end of a long day, at the end of an ever longer week. Much had happened, some of which they'd promised to celebrate. So why wasn't Lauren in here with them?

Behind her at the table, Josh and Simon sat with their heads together deep in discussion. When Simon finally got up to leave, Josh walked him to the door. "So I'll pick you up tomorrow at three. We'll drive to the station and take the Green line in from there."

They high-fived and Simon ran out. "See ya, Mel! I put the keys in Lauren's desk."

She called her thanks and returned his goodbye.

Josh wandered over to join her at the window. After two weeks working together she was feeling a lot more comfortable with him. His initial reserve had slowly relaxed into an open good nature, and no-one could fault his treatment of Simon. "You two doing something together this weekend?"

"I scored tickets to the Red Sox opening game. Thought Simon would like to go to it with me."

"Like it? You'll be his best friend for life."

Shoulder to shoulder they looked out the window, in time to see Simon rush up to Lauren and say his goodbyes, before getting into the car with his father.

The minute the pair had driven off, Lauren went back to digging the flower bed beside of the archway. Behind her, a strip of freshly-turned earth stretched the entire length of the parking lot.

"I thought that's what the tiller was for," Josh observed, leaning an elbow on the sill.

"Some things she likes to do by hand."

"Good to hear. It was beginning to feel like she was avoiding us."

Mel turned to study him. Had he noticed something amiss as well? "She says working helps her sort out her problems."

"She's been at it all day. Guess she's got a lot on her mind." Sensing Mel's scrutiny, he turned to look at her. "At first I thought it was just the accident."

"You mean with Phelps? She told you about that?"

"I saw it on the news. Never brought it up with her – wasn't sure how she'd feel talking about it. Then she told me of her other concerns, with the business and all." He looked back out at the woman in question. "Enough to keep anyone up at night."

Mel pursed her lips. "In a way I'm partly responsible for the latter. She asked me to buy in as her partner but we couldn't afford it with Peter out of work. I felt really bad not being there for her, but…"

"Nothing you can do. It can't be helped."

"That's what *she* said." Mel looked back out at her friend.

"I'm afraid I wasn't much help to her either," Josh confessed. "She asked me about my old business, what strategies I used to try and save it. There really wasn't much I could tell her." He watched the woman in the yard for a moment. "So when did she start having trouble here?"

"Pretty much right from the time she took over. Her parents got into a hole towards the end and Lauren's been trying to get us out again."

"How long are we talking?"

"Just a few years. This will be our third with Lauren at the helm."

"For some reason I thought it was longer than that. If things were as bad as what you say, she's done well to get you this far."

"Absolutely. The question is, will it be enough?" Mel heaved a sigh. "Thank god she got the loan, is all I can say. Can't imagine what she'd be like if she hadn't. Or what I'd be like, for that matter." She forced a smile. "We can all breath a little easier for a while. That money'll see us through to December."

"A loan, huh?" Josh cocked his head. "Funny, she never mentioned that."

"She's branching out. Investing in a Nowell and Johnson franchise. She didn't tell you?"

"Probably just forgot." He frowned. "Although…"

Out in the yard Lauren drove her shovel into the rock hard soil as frenetically now as when she'd started at nine that morning.

"Although what?" Mel prompted.

"If she got the loan…" His frown deepened. "Why was she asking me for solutions?"

"Exactly when were you going tell me?"

Lauren straightened, still holding the shovel, as Mel

stormed toward her from the archway. "Tell you what?"

"I just checked the log. You never ordered the Nowell and Johnson."

The heat in her voice set Lauren back. She'd hoped to make it through the week without the subject coming up. That would've given her the entire weekend to think of some way to break the news gently. But even having stumbled on the truth herself, Mel's reaction seemed extreme.

"I don't recall ever saying I had," Lauren replied.

"Oh, come on. You knew I'd assume that, that was your plan. So what happened? What's going on?"

"Nothing's going on."

When she said nothing more, Mel dug in. "Look maybe I'm not your partner, but I am your employee. I've got a right to know if I'll still have a job in a month's time."

Lauren sighed. No sense putting it off any longer. "You're right. You do." She took a deep breath. "I can't buy the franchise, at least not yet. I don't have the money."

"What are you talking about? You just took out—"

"The loan money's gone. Most of it anyway."

Five minutes later, when she'd finished explaining, Mel was standing unusually quiet. Lauren reached out and touched her arm. "You okay?"

"I...I don't know what to say. I'm stunned. I can't believe you did it."

"I was hoping you'd understand why I had to."

"Pay for a total stranger's funeral? No, I'm sorry, I don't. Not when..." She clamped her jaw.

Lauren waited, growing more concerned by the minute. Mel was taking this even worse than she had feared. Had something happened she didn't know about?

"How much of the loan did you use?"

"I've got enough left for the usual orders." She hesitated. "Up until June."

Mel put a hand to her head, turned away, then swung straight back. "And you don't think your decision was a little rash? That maybe you should have discussed it with someone first? Like your best friend perhaps?"

She answered softly. "Mel, the only reason I'm here right now is because of Roger Phelps. His death, which *I'm* responsible for, placed a financial burden on his surviving child – a woman who sacrificed everything I've been given in life to look after him for the last ten years. The least I could do was relieve her of that."

When Mel stood simply staring back at her, Lauren went on. "And as for not discussing it first… Even if I had, I'd have done the same thing." She steeled herself. She'd presented her argument as best she could, with far more composure than she was feeling. "Please understand, I had no choice. I was given a gift I had to repay."

Mel shook her head. "You agonized over getting that loan. That money was going to see you through the entire season, maybe put you on top again. What are you going to do now, let one of us go?"

"That's not an option. And even if it was, it certainly wouldn't be you."

"Well, you'll have to cut someone's hours at least. You can't—"

"I'm not cutting anyone's hours either."

"Then how the hell—!" Mel stopped and clapped a hand to her mouth. At the touch of Lauren's hand on her back, she finally lowered it. "Peter didn't get the job he was going for. It came down to him and one other applicant and we found out this morning the other guy got it."

Lauren winced. Talk about your perfect timing. "Mel, I'm sorry."

Her head came up, her gaze accusing. "I know it's your business. I had my chance to buy in and I didn't take it, so technically I don't have a say. But Jesus, Lauren!"

The woman stormed off across the yard.

CHAPTER 22

Leaning against the kitchen counter, Josh digested all he had heard. He hadn't set out to eavesdrop, but with the window open and the two woman arguing right below it, it had been impossible not to overhear.

He sipped his beer. So Lauren had paid for the old guy's funeral. A surprising move. And one he wasn't sure he'd have done himself in her situation, given the problems she claimed to be having. But that didn't mean he thought less of her for it.

He crushed his beer can and tossed it in the bin. He'd been aware his feelings toward the woman had been vacillating lately. His thoughts continually drew him back to her and what she'd done to him two years ago.

Yet if what Mel had told him was true and Lauren had taken over a business already struggling, then undercutting him in the Galway deal would simply have been her desperate bid to get her enterprise back on its feet. Could he honestly blame her for that?

What would he have done in her place? It was part of their business to bid for contracts; he'd outbid plenty of rivals in his time. Had he ever given a moment's thought to what resulting hardships they might've endured? Not once that he could recall. He'd just gone out and celebrated.

And as for her other crime against him – costing him his engagement with Fran… How sound a relationship could it have been if a mere financial setback could destroy it? Plenty of relationships died that way, sure, but it didn't say much that it had happened so quickly, less than a month after the business collapsed.

Maybe with everything else going on, he hadn't wanted to analyze the break-up too closely. It had been simpler, easier – and a lot less painful – to blame someone else, some outside influence. If he'd looked more closely, he might well have seen the signs had been there for a while. In fact, maybe what Lauren had 'stolen' from him had been lost a long time before that.

And now this surprising new development – using the money she'd borrowed to save her business to pay back a debt of a different kind. That wasn't a business choice at all, it was a moral one. And whatever he thought of it, one thing was sure – those weren't the actions of a cutthroat bitch.

Lauren closed the toolshed door and looked around at the sound of Josh driving out of the parking lot. She cringed at the thought he'd overheard her conversation with Mel but if he'd been in the kitchen at the time he couldn't have missed it.

What would he have thought? After learning the business was on the ropes, to find out his boss had spent the money earmarked for investments to make it secure… He probably wondered what the hell he'd gotten into with this new job. And how long it was going to last.

Closing her eyes, she rested her forehead against the door. Had she done the right thing? She'd told Mel she'd had no choice, that she owed a debt she had to repay. But was that the only reason she'd done it? Was it even the primary one?

She turned and started back toward the shop. The fringe benefits of her act of generosity were too conspicuous to ignore. Both her nightmares and visions had eased off slightly since she'd paid her imagined debt. Her sense of relief, even over so slight a remission, was so profound, she couldn't help wondering – had she jeopardized everything her parents had worked for, the trust and livelihoods of her workers...?

For all her lofty words to describe it, had her act been nothing but a bid to buy herself peace of mind?

Inside her office she walked to her desk and lowered herself into the chair at the computer. She stared at the monitor for several moments unable to force her hands to the keyboard. She'd gotten this far twice before, and twice she'd failed to go any further.

What are you going to do, let one of us go?

Not an option. And even if it was, it wouldn't be you.

With her promise to Mel ringing in her ears, she typed in the data and lodged her search. Ten heartbeats later the value of a Ted Williams autographed baseball appeared on the screen. More than she'd imagined in a monetary sense. A pittance compared to its sentimental value.

She hit delete and wiped the page. Sell her memento? No, they weren't to that stage yet. She'd hold off as long as she possibly could, sell it only if she had no other choice, no other way to pay her workers.

As precious as any object was, she couldn't let Mel and Simon down.

CHAPTER 23

Theodore Phelps stood on the porch of the run-down bungalow and rang the bell. After a moment the front door opened and a blocky figure appeared behind the screen.

"Uncle Ted! What are you doing here?" Ada shot a look back over her shoulder.

"I was in the neighborhood and thought I'd stop by to see how you're doing."

"How nice." Another quick look behind her. "I'm sorry, could you just give me a minute?"

"Oh, now don't you go to any—"

The door shut.

Shuffling sounds.

Ted leaned aside, trying to peer through the living room window but the dingy curtain reflected the light.

A moment later Ada returned and held the door wide. "I'm sorry to keep you standing there. Come in. It's good to see you."

From the cramped entryway he scanned the living room as they hugged. Nothing looked amiss. What had he expected? Blood on the walls? Stains on the rug? "I hope you're not making a fuss on my account."

"I was just packing up some of Dad's old things to donate to the secondhand shop." She gestured to the boxes beside the couch. "I never realized he had so much; it's taken me ages. But then I guess I've been putting it off. Every time I start, I find something else I'd rather be doing." She stopped and looked down. "I'm babbling, aren't I?"

"Nonsense. You're doing just fine."

She took a breath. "Anyway, it's all done now so you and I can have a nice visit. Have a seat and I'll get us some coffee." She went to the kitchen.

In her absence Ted looked around more closely, noting the odd gouges on the end table, the discolored floor boards suggesting something hot had been spilled there. At Roger's old chair, he pulled up the seat cushion, felt down the cracks at the sides and back. Nothing. Had she known to clean there?

He was seated on the couch by the time she returned with two mugs of instant. She handed him one and sat down beside him.

"I'm sorry I don't have any cookies. Or milk." She winced. "If you'd only called to say you were coming…"

"Now I told you, don't fuss." He patted his stomach. "I can do without cookies, and black is just fine."

They chatted a while, discussing how they'd both been since the funeral, what her cousins were up to. As always she had little news to impart about herself, so he talked of family vacation plans, gatherings, barbeques, graduations, birthdays – events in which she had never taken part and likely never would.

When the phone rang, drawing her back to the kitchen, Ted went up the hall to use the bathroom. The medicine cupboard contained nothing sinister, but oddly Roger's shaving gear was still on a shelf beneath the sink.

At the thought she might be listening, he flushed the toilet and ran some water over his hands before stepping back out into the hall. He stood undecided, gazing toward the bedrooms further along. Her voice still drifted out of the kitchen. There might just be time.

He'd taken two steps when he heard her call out. "Uncle Ted?" He spun and hurried back to the living room.

"Just checking your plumbing," he said, sitting beside her again.

"That was Lauren."

He shook his head. "Lauren?"

"The woman I was talking to at the funeral."

For a moment the words wouldn't form in his mouth. "Lauren Donnelly? You mean the one…"

She smiled. "Don't look so shocked. We agreed to stay in touch with each other."

"I didn't know. Then…you're okay with…"

"Yes, of course. Like I told Lauren, what happened was an accident, and I'm proud that Dad died a hero."

He nodded, recovering. This seemed an opening on the topic he'd been hedging around all along. "That reminds me, I've been meaning to mention what a wonderful job you did with Roger's funeral. Everyone was impressed with how well you organized things."

"They were?" She beamed. "Thank you, Uncle Ted. I did try hard."

"I know you did. You've always tried hard, haven't you, Ada?"

His smile came easily. Despite how little he really knew her, he'd always felt compassion for his family's black sheep, this ugly duckling niece of his. "Just like you always tried to be the best daughter you could for Roger, to be everything he wanted you to be."

Her expression faltered.

He reached for his mug of lukewarm dregs. "I can't tell you how wonderful everyone thought you were for looking after him all these years. I'm sure it couldn't have been easy for you."

"Really." She huffed. "Well, the fact of it is, there wasn't much choice. No-one else would do it and we couldn't afford to put him in a home."

"You could've walked away."

She laughed at the joke. "I couldn't have done that. He was my father."

"Plenty would have. Your brother did." He lowered his voice. "And your mother."

The muscles tightened around her mouth, twisting her lips. "That was a long time ago. Long before he had his stroke."

"Yes." Ted nodded. "Before his stroke. Things were very different then, weren't they?" He met her gaze. "And then they changed."

He waited but she didn't take the bait.

"I'm not sure what you're saying, Uncle, but the truth is I didn't mind looking after him. He raised me after mom…went away. He loved me, took care of me. How could I not be there when he needed me?"

He studied her a moment. Was that really how she remembered it? "I'm sure he did love you. In his way. As much as Roger was capable of loving. But there was always that other side of him, wasn't there?"

She laughed, bewildered, shaking her head. "I really don't know what you mean."

"Don't you? That other side that was never happy with

anything you did – how you looked, how you spoke, how you made his meals, how you ran the house. That part of him that looked for things to criticize. And found them even when they didn't exist."

He'd watched her smile slowly die, hating himself for being the cause. She swallowed and stared down into her coffee, her jaw working.

"You remember him now, don't you, Ada? The man who looked for any excuse to belittle, to ridicule, to humiliate. Who didn't just believe in discipline but actually seemed to–"

"What would you know?"

The flash in her eyes was gone in an instant, but it was enough to make his breath catch. He gathered himself and answered softly, "I can imagine."

"Can you?"

"Ada, he was my brother. My older brother. I learned firsthand about that side of him growing up. Why do you think we never saw each other much?"

She drew herself up. "Well, as I said, there wasn't any choice. I had to look past all that. I had to remember the good times and forget the bad. Someone had to."

He leaned toward her. "Yes, but did you?"

"Did I what?"

"Did you really look past it? Did you ever truly forgive him?"

"Enough to take care of him all those years."

"When the tables were turned. When he was the weak one and you the stronger." He bent closer. "Was that the difference? Was that what made it bearable, Ada? More than bearable, was that what made it—"

"Stop it!" She clutched her head and shut her eyes. "Uncle Ted you're getting me so confused." She lowered her arms. "I don't know what sorts of things you remember. Maybe Dad was mean when he was young but he changed after that. He was different with me."

"Ada—"

"No!" She shot to her feet. "I won't let you say any more bad things about him. I'm sorry you two didn't get along, but did you ever think maybe that was just as much your fault as his?"

She picked up their mugs and stepped round the table. "It was good of you to pay me a visit. But I think you better be going now."

CHAPTER 24

Outside, Ted walked to his car and climbed in behind the wheel. He sat for a moment staring at the house, noting the shadow behind the curtain – Ada watching him.

He reached in his pocket and pulled out the folded slip of paper, recalling once again the moment Roger had slipped it to him, less than a week before his death. The man had waited until they were alone before clawing beneath the cushion of his chair to retrieve it and press it into Ted's hand. Gesturing for him to keep it hidden when Ada had come back into the room.

Ted unfolded the paper now, feeling the same chill wash over him as he studied the tortuous ill-formed letters. Ada had told him Roger could no longer write after his stroke. Had Roger been hiding the ability from her? Or had she been hiding it from everyone else?

On its own the first sentence wasn't alarming.

Get me away from her!

The statement was totally in character for Roger and expressed an understandable sentiment – the cry of a man long used to having his own way on everything, now forced to live by his daughter's dictates. Sheer frustration. Anyone in his position would feel it at some point.

But the thing that wasn't at all like his brother, what changed these scribbles from a bold command to a desperate plea, were the second and final emphatic words.

Help me. Please!!

Gazing toward the house, Ted folded the note back into his pocket. He could have it all wrong. It might mean nothing. Roger might've simply been angry that day and wanted to retaliate against Ada. Hurt her the only way he could any more.

But the note didn't sound so much angry as desperate, and though he'd tried not to, Ted had to wonder: Was it possible his ugly duckling niece was a whole lot uglier than he or any of them ever imagined?

Ada stood watching through the window until her uncle's car backed from the driveway.

The minute he'd driven off down the street, she turned and stormed along the hallway. He was only one man, the only one who had ever visited. None of the others could possibly know. And clearly he wasn't sure himself or he wouldn't have been so coy about it.

The question was, how did he come to suspect in the first place?

In the bedroom, she yanked back the closet door and glared at the figure sprawled on the floor. "You dirty worm. You told him, didn't you?"

CHAPTER 25

Claudia Weekes, the part-time worker Mel had recruited the same day she'd hired Josh, had a gold stud piercing her upper lip, another in her nose, and short black hair moussed into spikes. The tattoo gracing her slender arm showed a serpent entwined with a human skull, and a dragonfly alighted on her opposite shoulder.

None of that mattered one iota to Lauren. The fact the girl arrived twenty minutes late for her first day of work and offered not the slightest apology, did. But it wasn't till Lauren had shown her around and led her back inside the shop that she got her first inkling there could be an insurmountable problem.

On this, their first day open to the public, Simon was manning his post at the register. He finished serving his current customer and flashed them a smile as they came through the door.

"Simon, I'd like you to meet our new worker. This is Claudia."

His smile died when he saw the girl's face. "Oh. Oh!" He clapped both hands over his eyes.

Claudia jumped back. "What the—"

"Simon, it's all right." Realizing at once what was wrong, Lauren rushed over and took his arm.

"My god, what's wrong with him?" Claudia said.

"It's your studs."

"What?"

"Your studs, your piercings." Lauren turned back to him. "It's all right, buddy. Really, it's okay, it doesn't hurt her."

He peeked out from between his fingers. "It doesn't?"

"No, they're like earrings, see." She showed him the hoops she was wearing. "You've never had a problem with earrings, right?"

"Earrings don't hurt."

"No, of course not. Well, neither do those."

"He's freaking out because of these?" Claudia took a cautious step forward. "What's his problem? He's never seen body art before?"

Lauren bristled – spoken as though Simon wasn't even there. "Just give us a minute please."

"Well, is he all right?"

"Yes, of course. We're fine now, aren't we, Simon?"

He regarded the girl uncertainly a moment, then raised his hand in a hesitant wave.

"Atta boy," Lauren praised. "Good for you!" She patted his arm and stepped out from behind the counter. As she drew Claudia aside, another customer entered the shop and Simon turned to ring up the sales.

"Why'd he go all mental like that?" Claudia whispered.

"Simon doesn't do well when someone gets hurt."

"Yeah, but..." Distaste curled her lip. "Is that *all* that's wrong with him? He looks like maybe he's not all there, if you know what I mean."

The moment had come. As she did with all new

employees, Lauren explained about Simon's disability. When the news only seemed to unsettle the girl further, Lauren felt no inclination to coddle her. "Well, seeing as I have orders to fill, I'll leave you in Simon's capable hands."

"What?"

"You'll be doing mostly check-out work so I'll let Simon show you how we do things."

Claudia blanched. "You want *him* to show me? You're kidding, right."

Lauren stifled her instinctive reply. The girl was new and had probably never known anyone like Simon. "No-one knows the checkout better. He's the best person to show you the ropes."

"Couldn't you show me? I mean what if he freaks out again?"

"He won't. He's fine," she answered tightly. "You'll see that as soon as you get to know him. Now get on with it."

The strains of Beethoven's Pastoral Symphony filled the work room with a joyous energy, just what she needed to lift her spirits and get her mind off all that was happening.

As she worked at assembling her current order – a wreath for the mother of a premature baby on the child's first birthday, commissioned by her husband – Lauren felt her muscles relax, her headache ease, her thoughts unwind. This was her passion, the type of project she most enjoyed – creating a personalized presentation from someone's own treasures and memorabilia.

She straightened when Mel walked into the room. They'd been avoiding each other for most of the day. Though she'd longed to settle the tension between them, she sensed that Mel still needed some time.

"How's Claudia doing?" the woman asked from the end of the table.

Lauren opened her mouth to answer then thought better of it. Things were strained enough at the moment. No point telling her the worker she'd hired was already having issues with Simon. "She should be fine once she settles in."

"Good. Good." Mel chewed her lip then launched ahead. "Look, I'm sorry about Friday. I didn't handle that well at all."

"You don't need to explain, I understand." She paused in her tidying up of the bench top. "How did Peter take not getting the job?"

"With his usual aplomb. Got roaring drunk and slept on the driveway. Woke up with gravel rash on his face."

They shared the laugh, then Mel turned serious. "I'm worried about him. He's been out of work so long, he's getting really down about it. Thinks he's useless and that he'll never…"

When her words choked off, Lauren came over and wrapped her arms around her friend. They stood for a moment, then drew apart.

"You know if you need an advance on your salary…"

"Thanks, but I'm hoping it won't come to that." Mel wiped her eyes. "There is something I wanted to ask you though."

Lauren leaned against the work bench. "Shoot."

"The money for the Nowell and Johnson line."

She slumped, feeling her stomach tighten. "Mel, I told you, if there was any way—"

"What if Peter and I put it up?"

She blinked at her. "What?"

"What if *we* took out a loan, bought the franchise in our name and paid you a percentage of sales as rent. Not only would you get some additional earnings, the range would be bringing in more customers."

"But..." She smothered the excitement that had leapt up inside her. "Mel, that's crazy. How can you afford it?"

"I talked to Peter over the weekend and he thinks we can do it. In fact, he got pretty excited about it, the most positive I've seen him in ages. We figured if sales are as good as you predicted, the profits would cover the loan repayments."

"And what if they're not as good as I predicted?"

"Come on, you said yourself it's a sure thing. Even Josh thinks it's a good investment."

She arched a brow. "Does he?"

Mel stepped closer and took her arm. "Look, I couldn't help you when you asked me to buy in as your partner. But this is something we can afford. Please. Let me do this."

"I don't know." But she felt herself weakening.

"I'm not just being generous here. As soon as the loan's paid off, Peter and I will have that extra income. And by helping you stay afloat in the meantime we'll be securing my current one."

A smile tugged at the side of her mouth. "Guess you've thought of everything, haven't you?"

CHAPTER 26

Sliding the archway gate across, Josh spotted Simon running up the hill from the pond. Every day last week, he'd made the trip down at closing time – hopeful and excited – only to return disappointed. Today his face was lit up with joy. "They hatched, they hatched! Lauren, come see!"

As he ran toward the shop, Mel and Lauren came out the door, Claudia trailing them. From his vantage point across the yard, Josh observed the excited huddle, then the group broke apart, Lauren stepping back into the shop while Mel and Claudia started in the direction from which Simon had come.

"Where's Josh?" Simon spun around and spotted him. "Josh, come see. You have to come see!" Too excited to wait for a reply, he turned and hurried after the women.

Josh stood debating. He had nothing pressing to do after work. Opening day at his old nursery had always been somewhat of an event – full time staff meeting seasonal workers and everyone greeting the influx of new and returning customers. Perhaps Lauren did something special each year to foster relations between her employees.

He wandered over, meeting her as she came out of the shop again.

She smiled sheepishly. "You don't have to come down if you don't want, but you're welcome to."

"All I heard was that something had hatched. I'm just hoping he didn't mean alligators."

She laughed. "Ducklings. Simon waits for them every spring and on the day they hatch we all troop down to the pond and feed them." She held up the bag of bread in her hand.

"Well, he seems to want me there so I can't very well disappoint him." They started down the path together.

"It's sort of become a tradition that all the workers go together." She looked up and shrugged. "Silly, I know, but Simon loves it."

"I don't think it's silly."

"You don't?"

"No. I think it's nice the way you look after him, that you're such good friends."

She nodded. "It is."

They walked in silence to the end of the parking lot, then started down the trail to the pond. The grass was showing its first blush of green, forsythia and dogwood brightening the verges.

Above the sea-scented breeze, the sound of her laugh still rang in his ears. He couldn't recall ever hearing it before. Something had certainly lifted her spirits since her argument with Mel on Friday.

He found himself wanting to hear it again. "So these ducks – I take it they're something special. A rare breed? Endangered species? Genetically modified?"

And there it was again, that musical sound.

"Just ordinary mallards. The only thing that makes them special is that Simon loves them."

"Good enough for me."

"From now on he'll feed them all summer long. They get quite tame by the end of the season; they actually come up the path to meet him."

It was his turn to laugh. "I can picture it – mother Simon climbing the hill with a line of ducklings waddling after him."

"Last year we had a crippled one, born with a clubbed foot. Simon gave it so much food and attention it not only survived, it flew off with the others at the start of winter. Hilda, he named it."

A stone's throw below them, at the water's edge, Simon turned and waved them to hurry. "We need the bread. Quick!"

"Oops, that's me." She reached in the bag, pulled out a slice and handed it to Josh. "See you down there."

He watched her run ahead to the others, hand out slices to Simon and Mel. Claudia declined with a shake of her head and started back up the hill toward him.

"Can you believe this?" She paused beside him and turned to look back. "All this over a bunch of smelly birds?" She shuddered. "Gross!"

She tilted her head, looked up at him from beneath her lashes, and gave an openly inviting smile. "Feel like a beer at Clancy's? I'll buy."

His gaze had already locked back on Lauren; the three friends sharing their yearly ritual. "Thanks but I think I'll stick around here."

CHAPTER 27

Ada shot back the bolt on the door, reached around it, and flicked on the light. From the warmth of the kitchen, she peered down the narrow staircase into the gloom below. With no doors or windows, the basement – little more than a cold cellar really – remained shrouded in darkness and a bone-numbing chill all the year round. Pulling her cardigan closer around her, she started down.

At the bottom, she crossed the concrete floor, nostrils flaring at the stench of lime, rat shit and mold. Beneath the single low-wattage bulb, a figure languished in a stout wooden chair. Silent and hunched. Cowed and contrite. Right where she'd left him.

She commenced a leisurely turn of room.

"So...have you had a chance to think? Are you ready to confess what you did?" As always, the words tasty sweet on her lips. Powerful words. Familiar words. The long-ago words he'd once spoken to her when *she* had been the one sitting in the chair.

She circled closer. Caressing the ropes that secured his arms, the coils that surrounded his chest, she bent and peered in his glazed over eyes.

"Nothing to say? I'm impressed. It's been, what, two days?

You must be hungry, thirsty at least. All you have to do is ask forgiveness."

She narrowed her eyes as she took in the smudges of dirt on his face, the stains on his trousers. "My god, look at you. What a disgrace." Her lip curled. "You're disgusting."

She straightened, turned, and strolled to the workbench against the back wall. She bypassed the hacksaw, hammer and chisel, and selected the file. Holding it up, she pondered its many glistening blades as she wandered back.

She came around behind him this time, bent and brushed her cheek against his. "This is pointless. *You* know what you did. *I* know what you did. All that's left is for you to admit it. Purge yourself. You'll feel better, I promise."

A shiver shot through her. Those glorious words. No need to fear them ever again. So long as she was the one who was speaking them.

Ever so gently, she stroked the file across his cheek, watched in rapt anticipation for the slightest shavings to curl from its blades. Nothing. Not the barest reaction. She straightened abruptly and walked away.

"It's warm upstairs. If you take a deep breath you can smell the soup I had for lunch. Your favorite – chicken noodle. Sadly, I couldn't finish it all, had to throw the rest of it out."

At the workbench again, she turned to face him. "Still nothing to say?" She shrugged, tossed the file aside, and picked up the pliers.

With a heavy sigh she shook her head and started toward him. "Oh Daddy, Daddy, why do you do it to yourself?"

CHAPTER 28

Lauren came out of the work room and spotted a stout middle-aged woman standing at the unmanned checkout counter. "Are you being served?"

"No. And I've been waiting a while. Frankly I was just about to leave."

"I'm so sorry." Lauren rushed over and began ringing up the order. A large one too. On top of all their other concerns, the last thing they needed was to lose sales over shoddy service. Where was Claudia?

"The hydrangea's free. Sorry you had to wait."

The woman grunted and turned from the counter.

After helping load her items into her car, Lauren set off in search of her worker. She found her in the barn chatting with Josh.

"Claudia, can I see you a minute," she said from the door.

The girl wandered over, casting a flirtatious smile back at Josh as she stepped into the yard.

Lauren swung to face her. "What are doing? Why are you here and not inside serving customers?"

The coquettish look vanished, replaced by one of sullen resentment. "I only left for a couple of minutes. There's hardly been any customers all morning."

"First of all, even when there aren't customers, there are

still things you need to be doing. Secondly, *I'll* let you know when you can take a break; that way I can organize someone to replace you. You don't just walk off without telling anyone and leave the register unattended."

"Well, how was I supposed to know?"

By asking? By using your common sense? Granted, it was only her third day but couldn't she work that out on her own? "Well, now you do. Please return to work till I tell you."

The girl stalked off.

When she'd disappeared back into the shop – closing the door none too gently – Lauren slumped. Two days ago she'd been on a high. After her first decent night's sleep since the accident, there'd been the excitement of opening day and the good news that Mel and Peter were prepared to put up the money for the franchise.

Even though the latter wouldn't profit her directly, it would still bring in customers, and in that there was genuine cause for hope. They might just scrape by for another year.

Then later that same afternoon they'd all shared a moment down at the pond. An occasion made all the more pleasant, she had to admit, because Josh and joined them.

For her it had been almost a celebration of sorts. Tensions were resolved between her and Mel, her concerns over financial matters had eased, and the worst of her angst over Phelps's death seemed to be behind her. Though she hadn't dared venture close to the water – she wasn't yet ready to test things that far – she felt she had turned a corner somehow. Things were getting better, returning to normal.

Last night had shown her how wrong she was.

With a sigh she reached up and rubbed her eyes. The image from her dream still lingered behind them, making her jumpy and overly sensitive. Perhaps she'd been a bit short with Claudia. Though her gut was screaming that the girl wasn't going to work out in the position, she ought to at least give her a chance.

She tipped her face up to the sky. Thank God the franchise was going ahead. At least that was one thing she could relax about.

Josh glanced away from the tractor he was fixing and toward the two woman conversing in the yard. He couldn't hear their exact words but from Lauren's brusque tone and Claudia's sulky one he gathered what was going on.

When the younger woman walked off toward the shop, he straightened and stepped to the open door. "Sorry about that."

Lauren turned around. In the barn's long shadow, her eyes were so blue they were almost violet. For an instant he forgot to breathe.

He drew back his thoughts. "I assumed you'd told her to take her break." He nodded in the direction Claudia had gone.

"Don't worry about it. Not your fault." Fingers of warm breeze played with her hair, flicking a tendril across her face. She brushed it back behind her ear. Strange he'd never noticed how slender her neck was.

"So how's it going?" She indicated the tractor behind him.

"Yeah, new plugs was all it needed. Might change the oil too while I'm at it. She'll be plowing up the bottom forty in no time." He stood twisting the rag in his hands.

Simon appeared from around the greenhouse and started toward them across the yard. "Hey, buddy," Lauren greeted. "What have you got there?"

He stopped before her and held out the garden gnome he was carrying – a recent casualty of customer clumsiness.

"You put him back together I see." She turned it in her

hands. "And what a good job too. You can barely see where it was broken."

Josh scratched his ear. Even from where he stood he could see lumps of glue congealed along the seam. She wasn't going to sell it like that, was she?

Lauren cast him a curious look and drew Simon a step away. "So what do you want to do with this one? Take it home?"

Simon shook his head. "Dad won't let me have any more. He said he's tired of falling over them in the yard."

Josh felt a smile tugging his lips.

"Well that's okay, he can live here." She handed it back to him. "Would you like to find a nice place for him?"

"I want him to be with the others. Can we do it now?" He brightened at a thought. "We can show Josh."

Lauren shot another look his way. "I don't really think Josh would be interested."

"Sure I would." He tossed the rag back into the barn. "I'd love to see where you're going to put him."

She straightened with a sigh of resignation. "Fine. Let's go do it then, gentlemen."

They trooped past the greenhouse and through the utility yard behind, until only one building remained before them.

Josh's frown grew as they headed toward it. "Isn't that the old potting shed?"

"Yes." Lauren walked a bit faster.

"The one you told me just the other day wasn't used anymore. The one you said I shouldn't go in because it wasn't safe?"

"*Yes.*"

Her second "yes" had been more emphatic. Clearly she would rather he forgot what she'd said. Had her words been untrue? Why would she lie? What could these two possibly be hiding in this weathered old building?

Ten paces later they stood at the door. Lauren unlocked it and pushed it open.

As Simon stepped in, she turned to Josh and confessed her secret with a crocked smile. "This is the gnome house."

"The gnome house, eh." Brows arched in mounting amusement, Josh moved past her into a storeroom.

The name said it all. Everything from mermaids, to snarling dragons, to squat little men in elfin caps peered from the shelves. Others were positioned about the floor – an angel Snow White with seven gnome dwarves, a dimple-kneed Bo-peep in a dirndl skirt standing guard over a mixed-species 'flock'.

Josh strolled the room scanning the residents, suddenly seeing what they all had in common.

"These are all the figures that have been damaged at the nursery since Simon's worked here," Lauren confirmed as though reading his thoughts.

"Some of these have been here a long time then?"

"This is where they live." Simon pointed to a gnome on the shelf. "This was the very first one. His name's Albert. When he got lonely we brought the others to keep him company. Didn't we, Lauren."

"Yes, we did."

Simon placed the newest addition with care and took a step back.

"That's the perfect spot for him," Lauren approved. "He'll be very happy there I'm sure."

The two friends stood side by side for a moment surveying the display, then Simon nodded. "I'll go water the seedlings now."

"Good, thank you. I'll close up here."

After he ran out, Lauren reached up to one of the shelves, straightened a figure and began brushing dust from his neighbors. Sunlight slanting in through the window warmed her hair to a burnished gold.

Josh cocked his head to improve the view. Stretched to full height, her long frame tapered to a slim taut waist before flaring over sumptuous hips to a perfectly rounded—

"Go ahead, say it."

He straightened. "Say what?"

"Whatever you're thinking."

Request declined – not an option at the moment.

"I know this place serves no practical purpose." She stepped back gazing about the room. "But Simon could never bear the thought of any of them being thrown away. I sometimes wonder..." Her look grew thoughtful, almost troubled.

"What?" he coaxed

She stared out the door, her features softened by loving concern. "Maybe I credit him with more self-awareness than he actually has, but..." She turned to look up at him. "Simon wasn't born how he is, you know. He had an accident when he was five. Hit by a car, suffered brain damage."

"No, I didn't know that." Josh looked back at the shelves with new insight. "So you think he sees himself like one of these figures? Damaged stock?"

"Yeah. Maybe." She shrugged. "In any case what does it hurt to keep them here for him?"

Josh gazed down at this intriguing woman, her capacity to surprise him both amusing and increasingly attractive. "Nothing." He smiled. "Nothing at all."

CHAPTER 29

Business and residence occupied a corner allotment of – at a guess – at least ten acres. On the Cape, an incredibly valuable piece of real estate. Only on her second drive past the grounds did Ada notice the small lane running along one side of it.

She took the turnoff, following the dirt track through the woods with the nursery's pond now on her right. If it turned out this was a private driveway she could always say she'd gotten lost.

Over a slight rise, the trail divided. She could just see a house through the trees to the left. Obviously not the one she wanted. She took the right fork along a fence line smothered in native bramble roses.

The pond hooked further right in an 'L' and on its far side a house came into view hugging its shore – a two-story white Colonial with charcoal shutters and bookend chimneys. She slowed the car and rolled down her window.

An arbor stretched from the building's front door to a wooden pier over the water. Manicured gardens flanked either side, dotted with poplar, dogwood, and spruce. Clearly a much-loved, long established grounds.

A short distance further, a private driveway veered toward

the house. Ada didn't take it. She'd seen enough.

Continuing along the track she was on, she came at last to a public road – part of her original surveillance circuit – and followed it around for one last pass by the nursery's entrance.

Though the gates were open, she didn't go in. She'd only come to look at the place, to see how Lauren Donnelly lived. Looks, money, an education, a gorgeous home, a promising future… Certainly a woman with much to share.

How wonderful they were going to be friends.

Josh wheeled the flat-cart across the yard and pulled it up beside the first bench. He locked the brakes and began unloading the next lot of potted flowers and herbs while Mel arranged them on the display.

"Looking good, guys," Lauren called out, as she came around the side of the shop.

Mel looked up, started to answer, but her friend had already vanished inside. Frozen with a pot in each hand, she stood staring at the closed shop door.

Josh kept working. "So when are you going to tell her?"

Her head snapped toward him. "Tell her what?"

"Whatever it is you're agonizing over."

She stared at him a moment, then her whole body seemed to deflate. "I don't know how."

Josh straightened. He'd only been throwing the comment out there – what man knew the workings of the female mind? – his only clue, that Mel had been strangely subdued all day and several times he'd heard her start to broach a topic with Lauren only to pull back again. By her expression now it was something serious.

"You're quitting," he guessed. "Peter got a job in another state."

"What? No, it's just…" She set down the pots.

"Whatever it is, you can tell her, you know."

She regarded him, amused. "Look who's the expert all of a sudden." When he didn't respond she blew out a sigh. "All right, here it is."

A moment later, when she'd finished explaining, Josh could understand her predicament. "Not to make you feel worse about it but…couldn't you have foreseen this *before* you made Lauren the offer?"

Her laugh was mirthless. "Believe me, this wasn't something I planned."

"Well, fair enough then. She should understand."

"Of course she'll understand, it's just…I don't know how I can do it to her again. She's been through so much lately." She paced a few steps, then turned back. "The worst of it is, I was so sure it would all work out I went ahead and placed the order. Now I'll have to ring up and cancel it."

"Have you told Lauren you placed the order?"

"No. She thinks we're waiting to hear about the loan."

"Well, that should make it a little easier."

She laughed. "You think?"

Mel resumed shoving pots on the bench. "Look, I'm sorry, I don't know why I dumped it on you. This is between Lauren and me."

"It's okay. Any time." An idea popped into his head unbidden. Almost at once it seemed the right course. "Actually… Why don't you hold off canceling the order. And telling Lauren. Just for a bit."

She frowned at him. "Why?"

"I might just have a solution to your problem."

CHAPTER 30

Everything always happened at once. They could go days without any orders coming in and then, on the very morning the place is suddenly swarming with customers, two shipments arrive together.

Out in the yard, Lauren called to Simon who stood watering stock. "Simon, could you please stop that for now and go give Josh a hand unloading."

He shut off the tap and coiled the hose. Head lowered, he hurried away from her.

"Simon, hang on a minute."

He stopped, turned slowly, but refused to meet her gaze.

She wandered over. "Hey, buddy, what's up?"

His head dropped further. "Nothing."

"Sure looks to me like something's wrong. Come on, what is it? You can tell me."

He looked up at last, eyes full of tears. "I don't want to leave. Please don't make me."

"Leave?" She blinked at him. "What are you talking about?"

"I tried but I just can't work any faster. Please don't fire me."

"Fire you!" She'd have laughed if he wasn't so deathly serious. "Where on earth did you get that idea?"

"Claudia said I'm too slow. She said…if I don't work faster you'll hire somebody else instead."

The instant Lauren heard the girl's name her teeth clamped tight.

"Please don't fire me. I can do better. I'll try harder!"

"Simon, listen to me." She took his tear-streaked face in her hands. "No-one's going to fire you, least of all me. You are doing a fabulous job; I am *not* unhappy with your work."

"Really?"

"Really. I don't know why Claudia told you that and I'm angry that she did. As far as I'm concerned you are now, and always will be, my number one worker."

He dragged his wrist across his nose. "Then I can stay?"

"Are you kidding me?" She hugged him tightly. "I couldn't imagine this place without you. You'll have a job here as long as you want it."

He managed a smile. "Forever?"

"Yes, forever." She pulled a tissue from her pocket and wiped his face. "Now why don't you go help Josh unloading the flats and I'll sort things out with Claudia."

The smile broadened. He turned to run off.

"And Simon?"

"Yeah?"

"If Claudia says anything else that upsets you I want you to come and tell me right away. Okay?"

"Okay."

Lauren turned and swept into the shop, never slowing as she passed the checkout. "Claudia, in my office, now."

The girl came in with her jaw set, already in denial mode.

From behind her desk, Lauren fought to govern her anger. "I just spoke to Simon. He was very upset about something you said to him. Apparently you told him I wasn't happy with his performance. That he had to work faster or I was going to fire him."

"What! No way! I never said that. He got it wrong, all I said was..."

She waited. "Yes?"

"I...I just told him what you told me. That we need to look after the customers better."

"Claudia, that conversation we had was about *you* looking after the customers better. Not Simon."

"Yeah, well, I figured it went for everyone."

"Of course it does. But Simon's always been great with the customers. I've never had a problem with his work."

The girl rolled her eyes. "Jeez, you should. He's way worse than me. He's not just slow, he's—"

She shot to her feet. "Simon does his best. And even if he didn't, it's not your place to tell other workers how to do their jobs."

Claudia stared at her, stunned to silence.

"All you need to worry about is doing your job. Now get out there and do it."

The girl walked out and Lauren dropped back into her chair. She sat for a moment catching her breath. That hadn't gone well. Perhaps she'd been right in what she'd said, but raising her voice like that...

What the hell was wrong with her? Was it just the nightmares? The lack of sleep? Last night had been the worst horror yet. The man she'd seen beneath the ice, gasping for breath, clawing for air, hadn't been Roger Phelps but her father. Some treacherous corner of her subconscious mind had mixed the two. What did it mean? Why was this happening? When would this end!

When she looked up, Mel was standing in the doorway.

She straightened in her chair. "I gather you heard my exchange with Claudia."

"I think they heard you down at Clancy's."

Lauren winced. If a customer had been in the shop…

Mel stepped inside and closed the door. "What'd she do this time?"

"She upset Simon. Told him I was going to fire him if he didn't work faster."

Mel simply studied her. In a way it was worse than if she openly challenged her behavior. "I've never heard you lose your cool like that."

"Yes, well, I might've over reacted a bit. You know how I get where Simon's concerned."

"If that's all it is." Mel perched on the edge of her desk. "Sounded to me like maybe there was something more going on."

"Possibly." Lauren shifted. "I haven't been sleeping well."

"Anything bothering you?"

"Just the usual. Having trouble shutting my mind off at night."

"So nothing to do with what happened with Phelps?"

Beneath the desk, Lauren clenched her hands in her lap. How did the woman always know these things?

"Because it wouldn't surprise me if you were still having issues over that."

"It was an accident, Mel. What issues could I still have with it? Now, if you'll excuse me—"

Mel put her hand up. "Sit right there. We need to talk."

Lauren lowered herself with a sigh. Mel in 'mother' mode was a force to be reckoned with.

"If you think I haven't noticed how on edge you've been lately, you're kidding yourself," the woman began. "You keep talking about this 'accident' you had like it was just some little fender-bender. You almost died. That on its own would be good for a nightmare or two for most of us. But on top of that, you saw someone else die – something few of us ever have the misfortune to witness."

Again Lauren started to rise. "What do you say we get back to work." But as she expected, her friend ignored her.

"You tried to save the guy and couldn't. I can't even imagine what that was like. And as if all that wasn't bad enough, there's knowing that the *way* he died was exactly what would've happened to you if he hadn't come along and dragged you out."

Lauren shook her head. "It doesn't have anything to do with that. My leg's been sore so I haven't been running. You stop a regular exercise program and you're left with a lot of excess energy. That's all it is."

Mel studied her a moment longer then pushed off the desk. She walked to the cupboard, pulled out her handbag and rifled through it. After shoving it back, she turned and set a bottle of pills on the desk.

"Those are the muscle-relaxers the doctor gave me when I did my back in. Two of those will knock you right out. It's not going to fix anything long term but at least you'll get a decent night's sleep."

Lauren sat staring down at the bottle as Mel walked past her.

At the door she turned back. "Of course if the thing with Phelps really was an issue, the best solution would be to talk about it. To a shrink, your aunt, a bartender, anyone. A total stranger is sometimes easiest." Mel opened the door. "The worst thing would be to go on denying a problem exists."

CHAPTER 31

The afternoon slowed and Lauren took the chance to get out of the office and see to errands around the grounds. Maybe a bit of hard work in the sunshine would help her sleep better without taking pills.

She tackled the potting shed first. Mel had only done it two days before, but the area always needed tidying. The chore took barely twenty minutes however and she hardly worked up a sweat in doing it.

She moved on to raking the gravel in the yard, but again the job involved little exertion. Working her way through the archway, however, she spotted the perfect solution: three piano-sized crates standing in a row at the top of the parking lot, each containing a portion of the statuary consignment delivered that morning. She fetched the pry bar out of the barn and set to work.

A half hour later, breathing hard and covered in sweat, she looked up when a shadow fell across her.

"Doing my job for me now, eh?"

She straightened and dragged her arm across her brow. "You were busy so I thought I'd get started on this."

Josh cocked his head at the open containers. She'd

removed the planks from the front of each crate, revealing rows of mummy-like figures, shrouded in plastic. "Where do you want these?"

"I was thinking a line across the front here. Customers will have to walk right by them to come inside."

He nodded. Exactly where he would have put them.

They worked in silence at their respective tasks – Josh easing the statues out, Lauren cutting the plastic away – then joined forces to carry the heavier pieces over and arrange them in a new display.

In the warmth of the sun, Josh's T-shirt gradually darkened, his skin growing slick. Lauren was keenly aware of their bodies moving in close proximity, his strong hands manipulating the female figures in ways that raised her temperature further but to which he seemed wholly oblivious.

But as they set the final statue in place and exhaustion finally claimed her, she found herself thinking of the night to come, wondering if she'd make it through unscathed. Or if her father's face would once again appear beneath the ice, gasping, fighting, silently screaming—

"Are you okay?"

The words jolted her back to the present. She straightened and peered at the man who'd spoken them. "Fine. Why?"

"You were making a funny sound in your throat. Almost like groaning."

"Sorry, I wasn't aware of it."

As they started back to the crates Lauren cut him a sideways glance. Talk to someone, Mel had urged. Anyone. Sometimes a stranger is easiest.

While they weren't exactly strangers, her relationship with Josh had thus far been purely professional. It had gotten off to a rocky start with the incident at the funeral home and for some time afterwards, despite his apology, she'd sensed he might have been avoiding her.

But the other day down at the pond, and yesterday in the gnome house, Josh had seemed different. For those few brief moments she seemed to have shared in the warmth he generally reserved for Simon. Or was that just wishful thinking on her part?

She watched him gather up a strip of bubble-wrap, wad it in a ball, and throw it into one of the crates. "Guess I've had a lot on my mind lately."

He straightened and stood surveying the mess around them, considering the best way to tackle the cleanup. "Well, you did say the place was having money problems. That'd cause a few headaches, I'm sure."

"Well, yes, that's partly it, but… Actually, no, that's not it at all. I…You see…" She blew out a breath. Damn it, why was this difficult?

She cleared her throat. "A few weeks ago I had an accident. Well, more than an accident." There, she'd said it. With those four simple words she'd admitted to herself there could be a problem. The first step in any recovery process.

It didn't help. All at once she was quaking with cold, the bitterness of the frigid water knifing her flesh.

She ignored the sensation, blundering on. "I was out running and cut across a frozen stream without knowing it and fell through the ice. A man came along, a total stranger, and–"

"So what do you want me to do with these crates?"

The words she'd struggled so hard to speak crumbled in her mouth. "What?"

"Probably easier to get the fork lift and haul them out back before chopping them up. You want to save these planks or should I toss them?"

She stared, incredulous. Had he even been listening?

For the first time he turned to actually look at her. And there was her answer. Those stunning blue eyes held not the faintest hint of the warmth she'd glimpsed in them the day before. It was as though a different person stood before her.

"There's a recycling dumpster up the back. Simon will show you." She gathered herself and walked away.

CHAPTER 32

Lauren pushed herself out of bed and wandered from her bedroom. She padded along the upstairs hallway, moonlight slanting from the rooms either side guiding her path as she started down the stairs to the foyer.

At the bottom she crossed to and entered the study, opened a drawer of the storage cupboard that lined one wall, and retrieved the fist-sized box it contained. At her desk she cradled the box on her lap – a moment to reflect on all it contained – then opened the lid.

A smell wafted up from the paper swaddling flooding her mind with distant memories. She raised it to her face, the images sharpening as she inhaled – the bleachers, the diamond, spectators on lawn chairs and blankets. Summer sun warm on her face, riding high on her father's shoulders as he jostled through crowds to vendors selling hotdogs and beer.

Gently she parted the wrapping and scooped out the object capable of such wondrous magic. She turned it to catch a shaft of moonlight and read the inscription – To Kenny. All the best! Ted Williams. 1960

Lauren reached deeper into the box and pulled out the newspaper clipping beneath. She unfolded it and stared at the picture she'd long since committed to memory – that of her father at five years old, grinning ear-to-ear as he accepted the autographed ball from his hero. The ball Williams had hit that day, deep into the right field bleachers for one of the last homeruns of his career. A trophy her father had managed to grab simply because the adults around him had been too big to scuttle beneath their seats where it rolled.

She smiled recalling his vivid description of the experience. The story he'd told her so many times it was as though she'd been there herself.

For a moment she sat clutching the treasures to her chest, a desperate need arising inside her as strong as if someone were trying to pull them from her hands. Then she fished the circular stand from the box and set the baseball to one side. For its final days in her possession it would have pride of place upon her desk.

With a flick of the mouse she woke her computer and drew up the website. After entering the required details she sat with her finger poised above the 'enter' key.

Go ahead. Nothing's decided, nothing's irreversible. You're just testing the water. Just in case. If Mel and Peter can't get the loan, or the franchise doesn't earn what you hoped, this will be your fallback plan. A last resort. No-one will agree to the price you've got on it now anyway.

She hit the key, rose from her desk, and headed to the kitchen.

Thunder dragged her from the depths of sleep.

Weak and confused, she sat up on the living room couch and winced at the sunlight streaming through the curtains. Beyond the window was a lovely spring day.

Which meant the sound she was hearing couldn't be thunder.

The TV murmured softly in the corner. She turned it off, threw back the afghan, pushed to her feet, and stumbled from the room. The pounding continued till she crossed the foyer, reached her back door, and yanked it open.

Josh stood with his fist in the air, poised in mid-knock. His brows went up as his arm came down. "Mel was worried. She sent me to check on you."

"Worried?" Lauren looked at the clock. Nine thirty. *Shit!*

Through the pounding still going on in her head she struggled to think. She'd lain awake till after three, the same thoughts chasing endlessly around in her head. The last thing she remembered was coming downstairs, doing some work at the computer, then taking a couple of Mel's magic pills and settling down to watch TV.

She winced and put a hand to her head. "Tell Mel...tell her I..."

"She says there's no rush, we aren't busy. She just wanted to make sure you're all right." A frown creased his brow as he looked her up and down. "Are you?"

Lauren stared back. Was he asking for himself or Mel? Two days ago she'd tried to share her problem with him and he hadn't shown the slightest interest. "I'll be down in fifteen minutes."

Josh watched her go up the stairs – bare legs shapely and impossibly long – and disappear along the upstairs hallway. He'd been surprised at the measure of relief he'd felt when she'd opened the door to him, safe and sound, if a little disheveled.

What had he thought? That in her despair she'd done something rash? Or was it the knowledge that, if she had, he'd have done absolutely nothing to prevent it?

If her clipped reply to his enquiry had contained the slightest note of sarcasm he couldn't blame her. Every time he thought of that day – his lack of response to what had clearly been an appeal on her part for someone to listen – he felt a fresh stab of regret.

She'd simply taken him off guard, that's all, opening up to him like that. He'd known she was about to share some of the details of her experience and in all likelihood some feelings as well. Hearing them would've almost certainly involved comforting her. Which could all too easily have led to...other things.

The bottom line was she was his boss. A boss he'd hated not all that long ago but things had changed a bit since then. And perhaps that was the heart of the problem.

No, he'd done the right thing. Best to play safe. Keep things strictly professional between them.

So why did he feel like the world's biggest louse for letting her down?

He stood gazing up at the second floor. She said she'd be down in fifteen minutes, but did that mean downstairs or down to the shop? Did she want him to wait, or leave and close the door behind him?

With no way to know, he chose the latter. But as he turned to go, his gaze strayed into the nearest room and fixed on an object sitting on the desk.

Excitement quickly built inside him as he realized what he could be looking at. Like a child drawn to a shiny new toy, or in this case an old one, he moved to the doorway.

A private study. Normally he wouldn't dream of entering, but the lure of the object – the very one Simon had told him about? – was simply too great. He might never get another chance to see it and it was sitting right there! Besides, the shower had just come on upstairs so he knew where Lauren was for the moment.

He stepped through the door and picked the object up from its stand.

Awe engulfed him as he turned it in his hands, built to elation as he read the inscription. Damn. Not that he hadn't believed Simon and Lauren but *the* Ted Williams? Double damn!

Beside the stand lay a newspaper clipping. He picked it up, read it, then set it back. Caressing the baseball he shook his head. To think the man with a lifetime average of over .340, who'd hit over five hundred homeruns and ended his career as player of the *decade* had once held this in his hands. Just seeing it was a thrill few fans would experience, that the legend himself had actually written a personalized message to Lauren's father...

For an instant his fingers tingled with a less than admirable urge. Then he heaved a sigh and set the treasure back on the desk. It slipped from the stand and rolled a few inches before he stopped it and set it back.

In returning it this time, his hand bumped the mouse and the computer screen flashed to life. He glanced up in reflex, then looked again at seeing the website that had last been viewed.

The thrill he'd been feeling drained away, leaving his body heavy as lead. "Aw no, you can't."

At hearing the words he'd unwittingly spoken, he looked toward the door. Upstairs the shower had just shut off.

Casting a last longing look at the treasure, he eased from the room and left the house.

CHAPTER 33

Showered, dressed, and having gulped down a few bites of breakfast, Lauren hurried down the driveway. She didn't know what rankled her more, that she'd overslept or that Josh had been the one to come and find her.

Only when she'd gone upstairs and seen her reflection in the bathroom mirror – bloodshot eyes, hair sticking out in all directions – had she realized the vision that had greeted him when she'd opened her door.

Bad enough he'd had to see her that way, that he'd actually inquired about her state only made it worse. Why had he bothered? No-one could blame him for not wanting to hear her problems but don't turn around and *pretend* to care just because… Well, she hadn't quite figured that part out yet.

Rounding the last bend into the yard, she was confronted with a delivery truck backed up to the shop's main door. At the sight of the name printed on the side, relief swept through her.

Since offering to put up the money for the franchise, over a week ago, Mel hadn't mentioned the subject once. As the days passed Lauren had begun to fear she and Peter hadn't been able to get the loan, but she hadn't wanted to press Mel about it. Now it appeared she'd had no cause to worry.

With a burgeoning smile she rushed through the door. Crazy Mel. It was just like her to make this a surprise.

Inside she found her friend wielding a Stanley knife, opening boxes. When she straightened, Lauren wrapped her in a hug, then stepped back. "You could've told me, you know."

"Told you what?"

"That you'd gone ahead with this." She gestured to the merchandize piled around them.

"Oh." Mel shifted. "Well, you see…"

Lauren cocked her head when she failed to go on. "What?"

"Things didn't work out exactly how we planned. Something came up and… Peter decided…"

Her meaning dawned but it didn't make sense. "You couldn't get the loan?"

"Actually in the end we didn't even try; we couldn't. I was going to tell you but—"

"Well, then where on earth did all this come from?"

Mel slumped, then lifted her head.

Lauren followed her gaze to the man who stood overseeing the order's delivery. She swung back to Mel. "You've got to be kidding."

"Lauren, wait—"

In ten quick strides she was across the room, standing in front of him. "Would you mind telling me what you're doing?"

Josh reached out and pulled her aside, clearing the way for the two men carrying a large shelving unit through the door. "Over there," he said, pointing to a space that had been cleared along the wall.

"Just a minute." Lauren stepped in front of them again.

"I'm sorry, there's been a mistake. I'm afraid you'll have to take all of this back."

Straining under the weight of their burden, the men looked from Lauren to Josh.

"Over there." He jerked his head, sending them on, then took Lauren's arm and steered her toward the office hallway.

"What are doing? Take your hand off me!" She pulled her arm free.

"Relax, would you, I want to explain."

"The time for that would've been *before* you did this. You think it's okay to just spring this on me? I had an arrangement with Mel, not you."

"Fair enough. And once you hear the explanation, if you're not on board, we can send it back. I'll even pick up the tab."

"You're damn right you will. And you'll do it right now."

Mel was suddenly on her other side. "Lauren, would you just listen a minute."

"No, this is simply not on. I can't imagine what either of you could possibly say that would make this all right."

Mel gave a huff. "How 'bout 'I'm pregnant'."

CHAPTER 34

Lauren stood looking from one to the other. She couldn't say she was over her anger but Mel's revelation had stunned her to silence long enough for them to go on.

"The thing is, I'd already placed the order," Mel explained, "and I didn't want to let you down. Again."

Her friend's confession pricked at her heart. "Oh, Mel…"

"You still have final say on this," Josh assured. "You can send it all back at the end of the month. If you decide to keep it and want to buy in, we can do it together. If not, I'll pay you rent, just like you arranged with Mel."

From the door, a delivery man waved to Josh and held up the papers that still needed signing.

Josh nodded, then turned back to Lauren. "How about dinner tomorrow night?"

She blinked at him. "What?"

"Dinner. You and me. To talk this over. You're right, I should have done that first. The meal will be my way to apologize."

"She'd love to," Mel kick-started her.

Lauren found her voice. "Yes. Fine. Good idea. But strictly business."

He shrugged. "Of course."

As they watched him walk off, Mel leaned closer. "What difference does it make who holds the franchise? The products will still be here in *your* shop, drawing in customers. That's the most important thing, right?"

Lauren stared across at Josh. What difference indeed? Was she letting the sting of the man's brush-off blind her to a genuine business opportunity? "I'll think about it." She turned back to Mel. "So you're really pregnant?"

"Really and truly. I'll pee on a stick if you don't believe me."

"How far along?"

"Just a few weeks."

"You could've told me. I would've understood."

"I know. I was going to but…Josh made the offer and…well like I said, I didn't want to let you down again."

Lauren reached out and rubbed her arm. With Peter out of work this wasn't going to be easy for them. "What will you do?"

"Have it, of course. We always planned to start a family one day. We would've preferred it wasn't right now, but we still want it."

Lauren finally let herself smile. "Then it's okay to congratulate you?"

Mel opened her arms for a hug. "I wanted you to be the first."

Josh looked over at the women embracing, Lauren's heated words still burning his ears. Bad luck the shipment had come in the morning after she'd had a rough night. It would've been a shock in any case, but at least if she'd been in a better mood…

Still, even discounting her ragged nerves he could

understand her anger toward him. He hadn't exactly been Mr. Nice Guy in the time he'd worked there. And maybe that accounted for – in a very small way, of course – his springing for the franchise.

And that was okay. He could live with making amends for his shortcomings. But taking her to dinner? What was that all about? Surely they could find a few quiet moments at work during the day to discuss the arrangements. What had he been thinking?

He *hadn't* been, that was the problem. His invitation had been purely spontaneous. As much of a surprise to him as to her. Still, it didn't mean anything other than business would come of it. They were both adults. They could handle a bit of informal negotiating.

Yeah, right.

His gaze lingered a moment longer then, shaking his head, he walked out the door. So much for keeping things strictly professional.

At the end of the day Lauren walked Mel out to her car. The sun warmed their faces as they stepped through the archway into the parking lot. Despite the obvious hurdles ahead, Lauren couldn't help feeling uplifted. Her best friend was pregnant. A new life was on the way.

"Starting tomorrow things are going to be different for you around here," she said. "No more heavy lifting, no more spraying, you're not to go into the greenhouse when the temperature gets over eight-five—"

"I'm only six weeks!"

"Hey, if I'm going to be this kid's auntie, I'm going to look after him from day one."

"Fine. I'll let my doctor know you're in charge." A few

steps further Mel arched a brow. "So. Dinner with Mr. Stedman tomorrow night. Interesting."

"He'd just better be ready with some fast explaining or this deal with the franchise is off."

Mel cocked her head. "What is it with you two?"

"What do you mean?"

"Every now and then I pick up this vibe like maybe something's happening there. And then, like that, it disappears."

"That's because it's all in your head. There is no *vibe*."

"You wouldn't be mistaking that cool exterior of his for indifference."

Lauren frowned. Indifference? Try outright dislike. There was no denying she found him attractive. Hell, she even liked him at times. Occasionally. But even at his most receptive, she could never quite shake the niggling sense he had something against her. And she couldn't for the life of her figure what it was.

"You want me to drop a few subtle hints? Let him know you're interested?"

Mel's words reached her from far away. "What? No! You stay out it."

"Boy, talk about ungrateful. I was only trying to help."

"I'll ask you to remember the last time you played matchmaker for me."

Mel winced, then let out a laugh. "Wendell Dietz. Will you ever forgive me?"

CHAPTER 35

Lauren raised her hand, saw that it was trembling slightly, and lowered it again without knocking. The last time she had stood at this door she'd been all but frozen and nearly incoherent with shock. How could she have agreed to come back? Meeting in a park or cafe was one thing, but to return to where it actually happened was like stepping into one of her nightmares.

She closed her eyes, focusing on the chorus of birds in a nearby tree, feeling the sunlight warm on her back. *It's spring, not winter. The ice is gone. Everything's changed.* And still the images strobed through her mind: gentle hands guiding her into this house, a blanket draping about her shoulders, words of comfort from a total stranger…

She jumped when the door swung open in front of her.

"Lauren! How wonderful to see you; come in. I'm so glad you decided you could make it."

She took a deep breath and stepped up into the small entryway. "It's good to see you too, Ada. Thank you for asking me. I'm sorry I can't stay very long. We're having a few issues at work."

"Yes, I imagine now that the weather's warmer you have

lots of customers."

"Yes, exactly."

Lauren said the words with conviction but in truth that was only part of the problem. When Ada had called the day before to invite her for lunch, her first reaction had been to decline, and not because of memories linked to her experience.

That very morning she'd overheard Claudia being rude to a customer and had been forced to have another talk to her. With the girl failing to perform as she should, Lauren was reluctant to leave her unsupervised. But Ada had sounded so disappointed when she'd tried to bow out, in the end she'd accepted the invitation.

"Well, I better not keep you waiting then," the woman said. "Come this way, lunch is all ready."

Lauren swallowed. Her stomach tightened as Ada led her into the house. How was she going to be able to eat sitting at the same kitchen table, staring out at the very stream…

She stumbled to a halt at the sight of the plates arranged on the coffee table. The coffee table.

Here, in the living room. Not the kitchen.

She slumped in relief.

"Please, sit down."

Lauren perched on the couch and surveyed the feast. Cheese sandwiches cut into wedges – just like the ones Ada had brought to the park that day – a bowl of potato chips, another of carrot and celery sticks. "Why, this looks lovely."

"What would you like to drink with this? I have iced tea, diet Coke, cranberry juice—"

"Diet coke, thank you."

"Coming up."

Lauren sat gazing about the room – the threadbare carpet,

the yellowing wall paper, the aging sofa on which she sat. Beside her, a stack of week-old mail covered the end table, the red Final Notice stamp on one envelope catching her eye. Gently she reached out and inched it aside, only to find a similar notice on the one beneath.

Ada bustled back into the room. "I'm sorry, the soda isn't quite cold. I didn't realize I'd run out of ice."

"However it comes is fine with me."

The woman set their glasses down, scanned the table and threw up her hands. "I knew I forgot something!" She turned and marched straight out again. "Go ahead, dig in. Don't wait for me."

Lauren took a sip of her drink and grimaced. Luke warm. Even without ice, in the fridge it should've at least been…

She lowered the glass and peered toward the kitchen. Her host was hunting around in a cupboard. She reached out and switched on the end table lamp. It didn't come on.

Lauren's heart sank. The final notices… Was one of them for her electricity bill? Was that why the woman had no ice?

"Here we are." Ada returned with a folded paper towel for each of them and sat down beside her.

As they ate, they spoke of everyday matters – their health, the weather, what flowers to plant at this time of year.

Then Ada shyly set down her plate. "I have to confess I had another reason for inviting you today. I'm applying for a job."

"That's wonderful, Ada. I'm glad you feel ready to take that step."

"The thing is, I need a reference. I know I've never worked for you but… Well, I've never worked anywhere so that makes it hard. I thought maybe if you could just say you know me and that I'm not a thief or a murderer or anything."

Lauren struggled to word her reply. She didn't want Ada to think she could find nothing nice to say about her.

"I didn't realize how important they are," the woman rushed on. "See I've already applied for a dozen jobs and they've all said no, and the man at the agency said it was probably because I didn't have one. A reference I mean."

She stopped and looked down. "To be honest I was embarrassed when he asked me for one. Not many people my age have never had a job."

"Don't feel embarrassed. You were looking after your father all those years. If you explained that to him I'm sure he'd understand."

"Oh, *he* understands. It's the people doing the hiring who don't." She looked at her hopefully. "So would you? Write one?"

"Ada, I'd be more than happy to, but I'm not sure how much good it would be. You see, when you write a reference for someone, you have to say how long you've known them, and when I say that it's only been a few weeks..."

The woman slumped. "They'll think you don't know me well enough to tell."

"I'm sorry, I really wish I could help."

"That's all right. I guess I could always...maybe ask Uncle Ted I suppose, or..." Her face crumpled. She pressed her napkin to her eyes.

"Ada?"

"I'm sorry. It's just that I don't know what they want from me." She pushed to her feet, took a few steps and swung back to face her. "Sometimes I just want to call them and tell them."

"Tell them what?"

"That I'd do any job they wanted me to. That I'd work

really hard, no matter what it was. I'm used to doing things no-one else will. If they'd just give me a chance I'd prove it to them!"

Standing in the driveway a short while later, Ada waved her guest goodbye. When Lauren's car had vanished from view, she turned and headed into the garage. She opened the fuse box, flicked the main switch, and turned the power back on in the house.

The end table lamp was burning brightly when she returned to the living room. She smiled and switched it off again. In a strange way it gave her great comfort being able to predict another person's behavior so well. To know the sticky threads of self-recrimination were already bonding this woman to her.

Oh sure, things would have progressed on their own. She'd just wanted to speed them along, make absolutely sure. Her future with Lauren was too important to leave to chance. And really what did it matter how or why their friendship deepened? As long as it did.

On a rush of excitement she raced to her bedroom, opened the closet. Inside she sorted through the meager contents, rejecting most with a scowl of disgust. Only her prettiest outfit would do. She started her first ever job in the morning. Working at Lauren Donnelly's nursery.

CHAPTER 36

"You don't have to watch me every second, I know how it works."

The words drifted out the open shop door as Lauren walked toward it from the parking lot. She recognized Claudia's petulant tone and quickened her step.

"Yeah, but you're not doing it right," Simon protested. "Lauren wants us—"

"The hell I'm not! This isn't my first job, you know."

"But Lauren said—"

"Look, will you bug off, I'm not a retard! And the day I need help from one is the day—"

"Claudia!"

The two workers spun toward where Lauren now stood in the doorway.

Claudia slumped and rolled her eyes. "Time for another talk I suppose."

Not trusting herself to say another word, Lauren walked on. She went to her office, strode to the desk and turned as Claudia came through behind her.

"You're fired," she said as calmly as she could.

The girl's jaw dropped. "What? *Fired?*"

"I'll forward your check plus two weeks severance. Collect your things from the kitchen and go."

"But what did I do? I don't get it."

"Then I'll explain. You're slow, lazy, you come to work late, you're rude to customers. I've made allowances up to now – more than I should have – because you were new. But the one thing I will not tolerate here is anyone being disrespectful to Simon."

Her brows shot higher. "Is *that* all I did?"

"Is that *all*?"

"God, you'd think I robbed you or something. You mean this is just because of what I said to him out there? *He* didn't care, why should you?"

Lauren's jaw was starting to ache.

"Well, I'm *sorry* if I hurt his feeling." The girl's sneer said she was anything but. "He just drives me crazy. He's always watching me, always telling me what to do."

"It's part of Simon's job to train new staff. I explained that to you your first day here."

"Well maybe you should get someone else to do it. Someone who isn't—"

Lauren put her hand up. "Claudia, I'm warning you; in a moment I'm really going to lose my temper. Please leave now."

The girl stepped toward her, suddenly contrite. "All right, look, I'll apologize to him if that's what you want. It's just… Man, my folks'll freak if I'm fired again."

"I'm sorry, Claudia, you had your chance."

The pleading look dissolved in an instant. "Fine. The season's already started. Good luck finding someone to replace me."

"You mean someone with your sensitivity, good nature

and eagerness to please? I'll take my chances."

For a moment Lauren thought the girl would lunge at her. Then she spun on her heel and marched from the room.

"What are you looking at!" The words, followed by the crash of shattering crockery, resounded from the shop.

Lauren rushed out to find Simon, Mel and a woman customer staring at shards of a ceramic pot spread across the floor.

"I was going to buy that," the woman said, stunned. "That girl came past and deliberately pushed it off the counter."

Simon looked shaken. "She broke it! Claudia broke it on purpose!"

"It's all right, Simon, I'll take care of it. Would you see if there's another pot like that one and bring it down to the register please?"

"Does that girl work here?" the woman called after Lauren as she rushed out the door.

"Not any more."

Outside, Lauren reached the archway in time to see Claudia speeding from the parking lot. She watched her car roar down the driveway, forcing the driver of an in-coming van to slam on his brakes and veer to the side. At the bottom, the car turned onto the road and drove away.

Lauren balled her hands into fists. The cost of the pot – and anything else the girl had damaged – was coming out of her first, last and only pay check. She turned to find Mel standing behind her.

As she started inside, Mel fell in step beside her. "She's right, you know. This late in the season the high school kids will all be hired. You'll struggle to find someone to replace her at minimum wage."

"I already have."

"You already— Who?"

"Ada Phelps."

Mel stopped dead. "Ada Phelps? You mean the daughter of the man…"

"That's right. I just came from having lunch with her. She needed a job so I gave her one."

"You hired her *before* you fired Claudia?"

"Like I said, she needed a job."

"Right." Mel studied her a moment longer. "Guess everything worked out perfectly then."

CHAPTER 37

"Rushing the season a bit, aren't we?" Lauren leaned her head back against the front seat of Josh's Sierra and gazed at the stars through the open sun roof.

"If you get cold, I'll close it," he said.

But she wasn't cold. The drive to the restaurant was exhilarating. Within a few blocks the wind had blown the stagnant thoughts from her head, her worst concerns briefly forgotten. It did limit conversation however, but even that she took as a blessing. She was a long way from understanding this man and uncertain what she wanted to say to him.

As they drove the darkened forest-lined roads, she tried to ignore his presence beside her, to break her fixation with his hands on the wheel, his thighs flexing as he worked the pedals.

She couldn't deny she had strong mixed feelings about tonight – as she seemed to have acquired for the man himself.

She didn't for a moment imagine he'd forked out for the Nowell and Johnson in a selfless act of generosity, or to do her any sort of favors. What he'd done, he'd done in his own best interests. And fair enough; business was business. It was the *way* he'd done it that had bothered her. She could understand

Mel not wanting to let her down again but they should've cleared the new arrangements with her before going ahead with them.

Or was she just being pedantic about it? She'd never liked being forced into something, even if it would ultimately benefit her. If that was one of those only-child traits Mel was always razzing her about, she didn't care. Bottom line: she wasn't going ahead with this unless Josh Stedman was clear on the rules.

Twenty minutes after leaving her house, they pulled up to a barn-like structure at the edge of a wharf where a tidal channel met open sea. Brine-scented air filled her head, balmy with just a kiss of moisture. As he led her to a sheltered deck out back she took in the tables lit with candles, the flaming torches that lined the railing.

He selected a spot overlooking the water. Distant lighthouses winked along a suggested horizon; the running lights of a night-cruising yacht drifted by a bit closer to shore.

The waiter came as soon as they sat, greeted Josh by name and handed them menus. He pointed out the daily special, took Josh's order for a bottle of wine, and left a basket of bread on the table.

"You've been here before," Lauren said, perusing her menu.

"My favorite restaurant on the Cape. Even nicer before all the summer vacationers get here." He set down his menu and looked across at her, his attention all the more disconcerting for the fact he rarely bestowed it so fully. "I hear I missed some drama this afternoon."

Lauren exhaled. Josh had been up the back at the time and hadn't witnessed the scene with Claudia. "Who told you? Mel?"

"Simon actually. According to him, Claudia put on quite a display."

"You can say that again." She filled him in on what took place – her reasons for dismissing the girl and that she'd already hired a replacement.

"Well let's hope the new one gets on better than the old one did."

Lauren frowned. "Did Simon seem upset when you talked to him?"

"Not really. Though he's certainly happy Claudia's gone." The ghost of a smile turned his lips. "He gets in under the wires, doesn't he?"

"I'm sorry?"

"Simon. He's very disarming, not a hurtful bone in his body. I can see why you protect him so fiercely."

She studied him a moment, intent on this glimpse of his other side, the part that made him such a mystery to her. How could he be so distant with her, yet so warm and thoughtful where Simon was concerned?

"It took a long time for Simon to come out of his shell initially. The first summer he worked for us he was painfully shy. Wouldn't speak, wouldn't look you in the eye. It was my dad who finally got through to him."

Josh leaned forward onto his arms. "And something about that makes you smile."

She couldn't help it. She always loved recalling this memory. "One day, not long after Simon started with us, a family came in – mother, father and their two sons, one of whom was in my class at school. Nathan Marks, our tenth grade bully." Her smile broadened. "Nathan went home with a fat lip that day."

Josh raised his brows. "Ms. Donnelly, I'm shocked."

"Not me. My dad. Caught him and his brother taunting Simon behind the greenhouse. They were playing 'keep it away' with his hat and had him worked up into a frenzy. To Nathan's credit, he never told his parents what really happened, otherwise we probably would've been sued."

She shook her head in fond remembrance. "My Dad was the sweetest most gentle soul – except when it came to defending someone he cared about."

"I see where you get it from."

She looked up to find him taking her in, his expression unreadable. After a moment, perhaps in befuddlement, she let out a laugh. "I've never smacked anyone in the mouth before but I admit I came close to it with Claudia today."

When they finished their meal – a choice selection of seafood for Lauren, a prime rib and baked potato for Josh – Josh surprised her by suggesting they walk along the beach before heading home. They'd already discussed the terms of their agreement – a surprisingly painless process as it turned out – so Lauren didn't really see the point. But after three glasses of wine she conceded a stroll might help clear her head.

They walked in silence for several minutes, then Josh said softly, "I hope I didn't scare you yesterday."

"Scare me? When?"

"When I came up to the house to wake you. You looked a bit stunned when you opened the door. I got the feeling you weren't quite with it yet."

"No, not quite." She winced at the memory of her image in the bathroom mirror. "Just so you know, I don't make a habit of lying around in bed all day. I've been having trouble sleeping lately. I guess it caught up with me."

As soon as she said them she wished the words back.

Without thinking, she'd strayed onto the subject she'd tried to broach with him the other day. She waited for him to change it again.

"A lot on your mind?" he said instead.

She glanced at him. "Yes."

"But nothing to do with your business problems."

"Why do you say that?"

"I didn't, you did. When we were unloading the statues. You said there was something else on your mind."

So he *had* been listening. If he'd cut her off then, why bring up the subject now? "Yes, something else."

"The same thing that upset you outside the funeral home that day."

Not a question, a statement. It appeared he'd learned of her accident with Phelps. She swallowed. "Yes."

He walked with his hands jammed in his pockets, shoulders hunched. Why was he asking her about it if the subject made him so uncomfortable?

"And your vanishing act at the rainwater barrel when you knocked in my glove."

She stopped to gape at him, stunned he had made that crucial connection. She hadn't told anyone else this side of it, not even Mel.

"There've been other times, haven't there?"

The words wouldn't come.

"I watched you at the koi pond one morning. A paper wrapper had blown in the water and you went to fish it out, only you stopped and jumped back as though..." He lowered his voice. "As though you'd seen something. Just like with the barrel."

She'd unwittingly lifted her hand to her mouth, closed her eyes against the image now burning her eyelids.

"You left the wrapper floating there even though you could've easily reached it." She felt him move closer. "Something in the water frightened you, didn't it?"

"A face. His face." She looked up at last.

He nodded as though he knew what she meant. But how could he? How could anyone?

"I keep seeing it. Those huge frightened eyes. That gaping mouth. His clawing hands…"

"The man who saved you."

"I see him in anything that casts a reflection – ponds, barrels, windows, birdbaths, even puddles. Just like when he was under the ice. Just like my nightmares. Just like—" Her throat closed over.

Josh reached out and pulled her against him. In the chill air rolling in off the water, his arms were a haven of warmth and solace. "Don't look away."

His words were a murmur on the wind, spoken so softly she didn't dare ask him what he meant.

She waited, intent, till he whispered again.

"Every time you can look in those eyes, the next time gets easier."

CHAPTER 38

Halfway up the drive to the nursery's entrance, Josh spotted Lauren at the top of the hill – a lone figure standing with hands on hips, attention focused on something at her feet.

He slowed his approach. He hadn't expected to face her this soon. The fact he'd come so dangerously close to crossing the line at dinner last night, and had pulled back only with the greatest effort, had left him unsettled. Deeply conflicted.

His decision to keep his distance from the woman was proving more difficult than he'd imagined. Twice in the last week he'd managed to evade the topic she clearly needed to discuss, only to bring it up himself last night. He was torn between wanting to help her through her crisis and needing to forget it ever took place.

Steeling himself, he steered his car up into the parking lot. He was counting on their new franchise arrangement to provide him the extra incentive he needed. If he wanted to avoid any complications *and* maintain his peace of mind he needed to keep things purely professional.

He pulled up beside her, buzzed down his window, and got his first glimpse of what she was staring at. "Looks like Claudia threw herself a good old fashioned tantrum last night."

"You think it was her?" Lauren gazed grimly at the pallet of twenty-pound bags of fertilizer, each one slashed and spilling its contents onto the ground.

"Guess it depends. You get much of this sort of thing?"

"No. In fact I don't think we've ever been vandalized. This far from the road and with the gates locked down there, a person would have to come up through the woods next door and hop the fence."

"Well, after the scene you said Claudia made when she left yesterday, she certainly tops my suspect list. I'm not a big fan of coincidence."

"No, me either. I was hoping for some other explanation but so far I haven't come up with one."

He studied her as she surveyed the damage. She seemed to be handling the setback well enough. "Have you called the police?"

"What good would that do? We can't prove she did it."

"You didn't hear anything last night after I dropped you off?"

"Not a thing." She smiled for the first time since he'd pulled up. "I actually slept very soundly last night."

"Glad to hear it."

The smile lingered. "Thank you again for a lovely evening. And for listening."

He tipped the brim of an imaginary hat and drove the remaining yards to his parking spot. As he climbed from his car, another pulled up and Lauren exchanged a wave with the driver.

The car cruised past him and parked beside his as he walked back to join her. "That the new girl?"

"Yes, that's Ada."

He consulted his watch. "Ten minutes early. She's already scoring better than Claudia."

"Cross your fingers it stays that way." Lauren nodded at the mess at their feet. "You think you could clean this up straight away? I don't want any customers falling over it."

"I'll get the wheelbarrow. I'll salvage what I can to the potting shed, and pick out all the empty bags later."

Footsteps behind them and Lauren turned. "Ada. Welcome." She gave her a hug.

When the pair drew apart Ada presented herself for inspection – a chunky figure with stove pipe legs extending from beneath a shapeless dress. "You didn't say what I should wear so I hope this is all right."

"It's fine. But if you find you feel more comfortable in pants, that's okay too."

Josh bit his lip. With those legs, pants were the better choice.

Lauren introduced them.

Ada smiled shyly as she shook his hand, then noticed the stack of damaged bags. "Goodness, what happened?"

"A little problem with a former employee," Lauren bit out.

"You know, it might not hurt to call the cops," Josh thought aloud. "Even if they can't pin it on Claudia, if they question her, it could scare her enough not to do it again."

"Or goad her into doing something even worse. No, I'll leave it and just hope she's gotten it out of her system."

Ada's eyes widened. "You mean it wasn't an accident?"

"Look, you might as well know." Lauren faced her. "Claudia worked here up until yesterday when I had to fire her. She wasn't very happy at being let go and—"

"Oh, no, you didn't fire her because of me. I'd feel terrible!"

"No, it had nothing to do with you. I'd had problems with her from the day she started."

Ada looked down at the ruptured sacks. "So you fired her and she got mad and did this?"

"We don't know for certain she did it, we just think she's the most likely suspect. In any event, it's nothing you need to worry about." Lauren brightened. "So, are you ready to have a look around?"

Inside the shop, Simon was manning the check-out. He beamed a greeting as Lauren and Ada came through the door and approached the counter.

"Simon, I'd like you to meet our new worker. This is Ada. She'll be taking Claudia's place."

Like a sun eclipsed, his beautiful open expression closed over. When Ada put out her hand in greeting, he shrank back several steps.

The sight of him cringing raised Lauren's hackles. What else had the hateful Claudia done that she'd never witnessed?

"I'm sorry," Ada said. "What did I do?"

"Nothing. It's okay, just give us a minute." She came around the counter and took Simon's arm. "Hey, now, what's this all about?"

"She's gonna work here instead of Claudia?"

"That's right. Remember I fired Claudia yesterday."

"I remember." He eyed the stranger. "She's gonna do check-out? With me?"

"Is that okay? You'll be able to show her how to do it, won't you?"

He turned away. "I don't want to."

"But Simon I need you to. Ada needs you to. You're the only person who can help her."

He shook his head.

"How come? Are you afraid she'll yell like Claudia did?"

"Claudia was mean. She broke Mrs. Cravitt's pot on purpose."

"Yes, she did and that's why she's gone. One of the reasons." Lauren gently turned him around. "But Ada's not like that. Ada's nice. She won't yell like Claudia did."

"Or break things?"

"No."

"Well, unless it's an accident." Ada shrugged as she took a step closer. "I drop things sometimes. Or knock them over. I can be pretty klutzy actually. My Dad used to say I was like *two* bulls in a china shop."

Simon slowly lifted his gaze. "That's okay. Everybody has accidents."

"Sure they do." Lauren slid her hand from his back. Either Ada had sensed the right thing to say or simply fluked it.

The woman peered over the checkout counter, her look growing troubled when she spotted the register. "Is that the machine I'll be working with? Oh God, it's like a computer, isn't it. I don't know anything about computers."

Lauren stepped aside and let Simon answer.

"It's not so hard. If I can do it, you can."

"But so many buttons. I'll never remember what they all do! What if I can't?"

"Sure you can." Simon waved her around to join him. "Come on, I'll show you."

Josh stuck his head through the office door and found the room empty. He moved down the hall but Lauren wasn't in the kitchen either.

Out in the shop, Simon was showing Ada how to work the

register so he didn't disturb them. He rounded the corner to the workroom door but stopped short of stepping through it.

Lauren stood at the table, intent on her latest creation – a spectacular dried flower arrangement in a huge pewter bowl, the pinks and golds of roses, peonies, statice and larkspur offset perfectly with spikes of acacia and eucalyptus. By the smile on her face she'd recovered from Claudia's spiteful payback.

Josh stepped back, choosing to watch and not interrupt. He'd grown to have great respect for her work. The hanging baskets she arranged for cafes had some of the most interesting and unique plant combinations he'd ever seen, and the wreaths and personalized frames she created were heirloom quality.

Before commencing her current project she'd gone to the hotel that had ordered it and photographed the room where it would be displayed. Not many florists would have gone to that much effort but she'd wanted a firsthand look at the setting so she could gauge her scale and colors accordingly.

Yes, it was obvious she loved this side of the business, just as he loved the landscaping side. And like many creative types, she hated bookwork; whereas he had always found working with numbers soothing. From a business stand point they made a good match.

He turned from the door and headed back to the greenhouse. He hadn't needed to tell her anything. After Claudia's stunt he'd simply wanted to make sure she was okay. On a purely professional level, of course.

CHAPTER 39

Stepping out into the afternoon sun, a coffee in each hand, Lauren crossed the yard to where Mel stood watering. They hadn't spoken since the previous day when Ada had arrived, and Lauren was sensing a lingering tension. Time to get things out in the open.

She set the extra mug on the stone bench beside her friend.

"Thanks," Mel said, glancing down at it.

"How'd you go delivering those orders this morning?"

"Yeah, no problem."

"Then you're feeling okay? No morning sickness?"

"Nothing yet. Just a little more tired than usual."

"Well, take it easy. Stop and rest whenever you need to." She sipped her coffee. "So nothing else bothering you?"

"Like what?"

"Could be my imagination but you've seemed a bit cool with Ada so far."

"Haven't had much to do with her yet. She's only been here a couple of days."

An explanation but no denial. Enough with beating around the bush. "Look, I just want to make sure you don't feel that what happened with Claudia was in any way your fault."

"How would it be my fault?"

"I mean, with her not working out. Hiring workers isn't easy. Even with the best credentials on paper there's no way to know what a person will be like in a job until they're in it. Who knows, I might've hired Claudia myself."

"*If* you'd done the interviews."

Lauren had been all but ready to walk away, the subject closed, but the sentence stopped her. She studied the woman. "You were wonderful to do them for me and I appreciate it. Don't think for a minute I don't."

Mel kept watering.

"Claudia might be perfectly fine in a different situation. It's just that she's young and probably never dealt with anyone like Simon before. Ada, on the other hand, has had some experience with the disabled."

Lauren looked toward the shop. "You know, Simon wouldn't even shake her hand when I introduced them, he was that scared. Somehow Ada picked right up on it. I hadn't even told her yet about Simon and she seemed to know exactly how to draw him out, put him at ease. I think she's going to work out fine."

"I'm sure she will."

Lauren frowned and blew out a breath. "I can't believe you're miffed about this. I'm trying to tell you it's no reflection on your judgment that Claudia didn't—"

"On *my* judgment?" Mel laughed. "Is that what you think this is about?"

"I have no idea what this is about because you won't tell me."

"Okay, fine." Mel shut off the hose. "It's about whether or

not you're thinking clearly. It's about whether you're making critical business decisions – decisions that will affect all of us – based on logic, or purely out of..."

"Yes?" Lauren couldn't fathom the look on Mel's face – not so much anger as deep concern. "Purely out of what?"

"All right. Guilt. Because, girl, from where I'm standing, that is exactly what this comes down to. You feel guilty over causing Phelps's death so you paid for his funeral and now you've given his daughter a job." Mel shook her head. "I just can't help wondering what these decisions will end up costing you. And the rest of us."

Ada watched the dollop of mustard quiver at the corner of Simon's mouth. With each word he spoke it oozed a bit further down the side of his chin. Couldn't he have wiped his face after lunch? She'd already watched a few specks fall and land on his shirt – even this was more interesting than listening to his faltering explanations – yet Simon went on, totally oblivious.

When Lauren came in from the yard unexpectedly, Ada straightened and tried to look attentive. But her boss rushed past without giving her so much as a glance and disappeared back into the workroom.

Ada felt the same prick of irritation she'd experienced at other moments since yesterday. The first was when Lauren had introduced her to Simon and gone to such lengths to assure him about her. Why had she lavished so much time and attention on *him*? It had been *her* first day, *her* first job, *she* was the one who'd needed support.

She'd never dreamed she'd be so nervous. After all, this was what she'd wanted for ages – a new life, the opportunity to meet people. But after the initial thrill of being offered the job, a near-paralyzing uncertainty had gripped her. She'd hardly slept at all that night, hadn't managed a bite of breakfast, and been dressed and ready an hour before she was due at work.

When she'd stepped from her car in front of the archway she'd smiled at finding Lauren there. But instead of waiting to greet her as she'd thought, Lauren had simply been inspecting some stock damaged by a former employee.

The minute she'd finished sorting that out, Mel had come along – a woman who'd made her feel anything but welcome when Lauren introduced them – asking her about some flower arrangement. And then that customer, demanding even more of Lauren's attention with her stupid questions about some plant she'd bought.

Ada glowered at their insensitivity. All she'd wanted was to have Lauren to herself for a while. Long enough to feel the woman's support for the enormous new undertaking she had begun. Couldn't any of them understand that? Were they all as thick and blind as Simon? Didn't they know how much Lauren owed her!

So far the only bright spot about her new job was Josh Stedman. Her face grew warm at the thought of his hand engulfing hers, his sparkling blue eyes smiling down at her. Clearly he'd felt the same about meeting her.

Yes, Josh would've been more than enough to offset her other disappointments. Except for the fact that, like Lauren, she'd hardly seen him since. He was always working outside somewhere and she was stuck in the shop all day.

Still, the issue with Lauren irked her the most, and was a matter about which she needed to take great care. Each time her envy had flared, she'd tamped it down hard, but she hadn't snuffed it out entirely. It glowed like an ember deep in her chest, threatening to ignite at unguarded moments. Something she couldn't allow to happen.

With a deep breath she looked back at Simon and nodded as though she was listening to him. For some reason Lauren cared about this twit, and perhaps that's what made her angriest of all. She'd only been there a day and half and already she could do his job practically as well as he could. And still Lauren had him explaining things to her!

When the spark flared, she clamped her teeth, swallowed the fire. Simon was someone important to Lauren so she'd have to be nice to him.

At least for now.

CHAPTER 40

That night, in her study back at the house, Lauren stared at the computer screen and felt her heart sink.

She couldn't believe it. She'd put a ridiculously high price on her treasure, secretly hoping no-one would buy it, and someone had. Or at least they'd agreed to. No money had as yet changed hands so it wasn't too late, she could still back out.

She picked the baseball off its stand and held it. Did she really have to part with it? The new product line had been in the shop for less than a week. So far sales hadn't lived up to expectations but it was possible, as Josh believed, that that was simply due to lack of awareness. Once word got around, maybe with the help of a little advertising, things might improve.

But what if they didn't?

I can't help wondering what your decisions are going to cost you. And the rest of us.

Could she afford to take such a gamble without having some sort of safeguard? Even if franchise sales did improve, she'd soon be facing the added expense of Mel's maternity leave, plus the salary of her replacement. The money she'd get from selling the baseball would leave nothing to chance. Unless they were hit with some outright catastrophe, the livelihoods of Simon and Mel, not to mention Ada and Josh, would be secure into the foreseeable future.

Rubbing her thumb along the baseball's stitching, Lauren stared at the computer screen. She could always wait and see what happened, hold off selling, and if things improved… But only one buyer had agreed to her price, no one else had even put in a bid. If she let them get away, and then changed her mind, who knew if they'd be interested next time.

Her decision made, she gazed one last time at the object in her hands. When the memories started flooding back, she pushed them away and quickly returned the ball to its box. The longer she took to do this, the longer she would prolong the torture.

She wrapped the box and wrote the buyer's address on top. Funny that, of all the people who could have bought it, the person lived right here on the Cape. Maybe she'd even run into them some day. Bleak comfort seeing as it was more than the object itself she was parting with.

"I'm sorry, Dad." She set the package back on her desk, ready to mail as soon as the funds were in her account.

CHAPTER 41

Josh crossed the yard with the energy of a decision made. In the end it had been surprisingly easy. He'd come to it without his usual debating, fact assessment or to-ing and fro-ing. Since his dinner with Lauren – a week ago now – he'd managed to keep his distance emotionally, proving to himself he was in control. So really what was there to hold him back?

The next step now was to make his proposal. It wouldn't commit him to follow through, just give her a chance to think it over. Then they'd discuss it and see where it led. Unlike the franchise, this time he would do things right.

He reached the door to the nursery shop just as Ada was coming out. They exchanged apologies for nearly colliding. By the keys in her hand he judged she was heading home for the day.

"I'm sorry we haven't had more of a chance to get to know each other yet," she said.

"Yes, it's been a busy week, hasn't it?"

"Maybe tomorrow we'll have a moment or two."

"Yes, maybe."

Her eyes came alight. "That would be wonderful. This is my first ever job, you know."

"No, I didn't know that." He cast a longing glance toward the office, then pulled his attention back to the woman.

As he'd noted before, she wasn't so much overweight as powerfully built, especially through the arms and shoulders. She either worked out or was used to a lot of heavy lifting. "So how are you liking it here so far?"

"I love it! The flowers, the people. Lauren's so nice." She looked down shyly. "I know what you're thinking. I'm old for never having worked before, but there's a reason. I had to take care of my father you see. After his stroke."

His gaze swung back to her. Her last three words had snagged his attention. "I imagine that was a full time job."

"It was. He couldn't do much for himself any more. Still, I didn't mind looking after him. That's what good daughters do, isn't it?"

"So, your father…he isn't…?"

"No, he died about five weeks ago. That's how come I could take this job."

Five weeks. Josh struggled to mask his unease. "I'm sorry for your loss. I hope he didn't suffer."

"Oh no, it was quick. Nothing at all to do with his stroke. He had…an accident. Still," she brightened, "as sad as that was, it wasn't all bad – that was how I got to meet Lauren."

He found himself standing in the office doorway a few moments later. But the momentum that had carried him here had been replaced by confusion and disbelief.

He stared at the woman behind the desk unable to comprehend her reasoning. However certain he'd been before, her actions in regards to Ada had changed things.

Before he could make his presence known, Simon swept past him into the room. Reciting the words he said every night, he laid the keys on the desk before her. "I locked the barn and the potting shed and the greenhouses. I'm going home now. See ya. Bye."

"Simon, hang on a minute." Lauren looked up. "How'd you go working with Ada this week?"

He grinned. "She's nice. I like her a lot better than Claudia."

"Good, I'm glad. You let me know if you have any problems, okay?"

"Okay."

Josh said goodbye as Simon ran out. When he looked back, Lauren was staring at him, her expression wondering.

He blurted the first thing that entered his head. "It's good you give Simon responsibility."

"You mean locking up? He's done it for years. Does a pretty good job of it too." She cocked her head. "Something on your mind?"

He opened his mouth, then closed it again. "I just wanted to say good night. See you tomorrow."

He left the room and headed for his car. The decision he'd been so confident about only moments ago would need a bit more consideration.

CHAPTER 42

Ada let herself into the house, rushed to the living room and threw out her arms. "Oh what a wonderful week this has been! I never dreamed working could be like this."

She tossed her handbag onto a chair and started taking off her sweater. "I know I've complained about Simon a lot but I realized today he's simply not worth it. I'm pretty sure Lauren sees that too now. I knew it was only a matter of time. She's already giving me more responsibility. She must see how much more potential I have."

With her sweater removed she threw it aside. "But that's not the only thing that's happened, Daddy. The really big thing, the most wonderful of all, is that I've met someone."

She pursed her lips in exasperation. "Yes, of course, a boy. Well, a man really." She felt the color rush to her cheeks. "He's tall and handsome and he knows so much about plants and flowers. Oh, I just can't stop thinking about him."

She frowned toward the couch. "Now why do you have to talk like that? Plenty of men are interested in plants. And it's not just flowers. Josh does landscaping and vegetable gardening. He's more like a farmer really. It's mostly Lauren who does the flowers."

Her smile returned. She wouldn't let his comments upset her. Not today. Today nothing was going to deflate her. "You should see the wreaths Lauren makes. People come from all over to buy them. She makes them special, using little objects the customers give her. Every one is unique and personalized. They're works of art, really."

She marched to the kitchen and flicked on the kettle. "I've decided that's what I want to be. A floral designer. Lauren said she'd train me if I wanted. When we're not too busy in the shop."

She bustled about, setting out the sugar, coffee and milk. "So how have you been getting along by yourself?" she called to the living room. "Have you missed me much?"

The kettle boiled. She took down two mugs and assembled their coffees. "Well, you better get used to it. Lauren says I'll be working more hours soon. In a few weeks the nursery's going to get really busy. Then they'll need me just about every day. Not that I mind. I'll get to spend more time with Josh."

A mug in each hand, she stopped in the doorway and cocked her head. "I know I've only known him a week but there was this instant connection between us. Even the others felt it I'm sure. You just can't hide that kind of thing."

She started slowly across the living room, encased in her dream, feet fairly skimming the carpet. Passing the hearth, she caught her reflection in the dingy mirror and stopped to stare.

Sometimes it scared her to look in the mirror. Sometimes the image wasn't quite right. How it happened she didn't know. Something wrong with the glass she supposed. Like now. The face staring back at her was that of a stranger's. And not a very attractive one. Certainly not the sort of face a boy like Josh would be interested in. Scowling, she turned away from the image.

With the sudden movement coffee sloshed from one of the mugs. She winced when a drop of scalding liquid landed on the back of her hand.

Her step now leaden, she moved toward the couch. The joy she'd been feeling since leaving work was starting to fade, her world rapidly collapsing to normal. *No, please, just a little bit longer.*

"Did I tell you Josh reminds me of John a bit?" she tried desperately. "Josh is better looking of course, but there are other things they have in common. Even their names are alike, aren't they? Josh and John. You remember John, don't you, Daddy? My friend at college?"

Her struggling smile finally died. "Yes, of course you remember. That was the whole reason you got sick, wasn't it? To get me away from him." The words felt thick in her tightening throat. "You never wanted me to go away. And when I finally did, you found a way to bring me back."

She continued toward him, clutching the mugs as though they could stop her hands from shaking. "Poor Daddy. Can't do a thing for yourself any more. Brush your teeth, cut your nails – Ada has to do it all for you."

Standing before him, her tremors grew worse. Coffee splashed from the rims of both mugs, staining his trousers like blotches of blood. "Oh dear, another spill. Look what you've done."

She bent down over him. "You never wanted me to get this job either, did you? Well, you know what? You can get as sick as you want this time. Heart attack? Cancer? Another stroke? Go right ahead. Nothing you do will ever make a difference to me again."

She straightened and held up the mugs before her,

watching the steam in its sinuous dance. "What's that? I'm taking too long? That's right, you like it really hot, don't you?" Her smile returned. "Well here it is."

Dressed for bed in her slippers and robe, Lauren entered her home study, opened the cupboard door, and stopped. After a moment she slowly lifted her hand to the shelf, the empty space where her father's baseball had once resided.

She'd felt so strangely hollow this week since letting it go. Knowing it was now in the hands of some stranger, someone for whom its sentimental worth meant absolutely nothing.

It's just an object, a thing. Get over it. You'll always have your memories of him.

Yes, the important thing, the thing to remember, was that the livelihood of her friends and workers was now more secure for what she had done.

She shuffled items around on the shelf, moving them across to fill in the gap. She grabbed the notebook she'd come in search of, closed the cupboard and shut off the light.

CHAPTER 43

Lauren wiped a palm down her track suit pants, returned it to the steering wheel, then did the other. *Pretend you have a different destination in mind, a different purpose. Think about something else entirely. Someone else...*

Okay, someone. That was easy. Josh had been on her mind so much lately she could conjure his face in a heartbeat. He was quite captivating when he smiled, yet he seemed to engage in the act too rarely.

It wasn't that he was cold, she had come to realize, but simply reserved. Thoughtful. Discerning. And perhaps, beneath that calm exterior, a little bit troubled. Yet even with the insights she'd gained about him, he was still as much of an enigma as ever.

After their dinner the other night, she'd felt they'd made strides toward a genuine friendship, if not the relationship she was hoping for. She'd been touched by his gesture of support for her problem, even if she hadn't understood his words. *Don't turn away. Every time you can look in those eyes, the next time is easier.* What on earth had he meant by that?

But then yesterday when he'd stood in her office door, she'd been certain he'd wanted to say something to her, ask her something, yet he'd walked off again without a word. What had stopped him? What had she done to put him off? No, the strong silent type, as Mel described him, didn't tell the whole story where Josh was concerned. Not by a long shot.

As she pulled into a seaside parking lot, all thoughts of the man at once dissolved. Her heart was jumping as she climbed from her car. She ignored it, strode through the open gate and down the boardwalk over the dunes.

Though the sun was shining, a brisk on-shore breeze whipped her hair, driving line upon line of thundering breakers against the shore. This early in the season she had the entire beach to herself – the spectacular setting still insufficient to draw her completely out of herself.

At the end of the boardwalk, she stopped and did a few stretching exercises. Her muscles protested, a stiffness to be fully expected after so long a break. She'd have to take things gently at first. Just a light jog to ease herself back. But that didn't matter. The important thing was to make a start.

After another sleepless night – her third this week – she'd grown more convinced than ever that her problem was largely lack of exercise. Selling her father's treasured baseball had gone a way toward relieving their financials worries for now, so, really, what else could it be?

She did what chores she could at the nursery, but none amounted to the sustained aerobic effort of running, workouts that had long held mind and body in balance. She needed this. More than pills, more than work or talking to friends.

With her stretching complete, she swallowed and stepped to the end of the planks – a diver preparing to throw herself from the highest cliff. Before the fear could stop her, she leapt.

The loose sand clutched at her feet. She struggled forward against the pull. Before she'd gone a dozen strides her breathing was labored far worse than any lack of fitness could account for.

Ignore it. It'll pass. Just keep going.

She forced herself on, refusing to quit, knowing at some deeper level the importance of smashing through this barrier, of taking this step whatever way possible. She'd crawl the beach on her knees if she had to!

With a strangled cry she fell to the sand. Clutching her calf, she massaged the angry knot of muscle but couldn't get it to loosen up. After several fruitless minutes she gave up trying, pushed to her feet, and hobbled back to the boardwalk.

The moment she reached that solid foundation her pain disappeared.

When she unlocked the nursery's archway gate an hour later, Lauren found Josh and Mel standing in the parking lot deep in discussion. Something about the way they were huddled suggested more than a light conversation.

"Hey, what's up?" she called as she slid the gate open.

The pair swung toward her and again she sensed the topic was something they'd rather not share. She started over.

"Someone graffitied your sign," Josh said as she reached them.

"What, down by the road?" She looked toward the entrance but couldn't see anything amiss from their current distance. "Graffitied, how? What did it say?"

Josh opened his mouth to reply but Mel got in first. "You couldn't really read it, just a lot of splashes of paint. Nothing to suggest who might've done it. We were just working out the best way to clean it off."

As they spoke, another car came up the drive and pulled in the lot. Ada got out and hurried over. "My god what happened to your sign?"

"We were just discussing that," Lauren said.

Ada took her arm. "I saw what they wrote. What a terrible thing to say about you! I hope you weren't too upset."

Lauren shot Mel a look before answering. "I'll survive."

"So you think it was Claudia again?" Ada scanned their faces in turn.

"We don't know. Probably just kids." Lauren was happy to leave it at that but frowned at a thought. "Ada, you never said anything to Simon about the fertilizer bags, did you?"

"You mean the ones that got slashed? No. Why?"

"Probably be better if you didn't mention it. Or this. We're not sure Claudia was responsible in either case but..."

"That's right, Simon was afraid of her, wasn't he? He'd be scared if he knew she was hanging around causing trouble."

"And when Simon's upset he sometimes has trouble concentrating, doing his job."

Ada nodded. "Don't worry, I won't say a word."

"Thank you."

Josh jerked his head toward the road. "I better get to work on that sign before it dries. Shouldn't take long." He headed to the barn to get what he needed.

Ada toyed with her mug of coffee debating whether or not to speak. Mel had just swept into the kitchen, walked right past her without a word, and now stood at the open fridge swigging from a bottle of water.

In the week Ada had worked at the nursery, the woman had deflected all her overtures of friendship. Had she sensed the lack of sincerity behind them? Had she detected Ada's growing aspiration to take her place as Lauren's top worker and primary confidant? No, she couldn't have. It had to be something else that was bugging her. Still, until she *had* replaced both Mel and Simon as Lauren's most valued, it would be wise to appear to keep trying.

"Thirsty work out there in the sun."

Mel wiped her brow. "Warmer than they forecast, that's for sure. And a good twenty degrees hotter in the greenhouse."

Ada bit her lip. Another of the woman's smug references to the difference in their current standing. Mel did so much more important work than a lowly check-out girl.

Before Ada could speak again, Lauren came in. She stopped briefly when she spotted Mel – as though she hadn't expected to see her and maybe wouldn't have come in if she had – then continued to the counter and switched on the kettle.

Casting her a silent glance, Mel took another swig of water. Ada could sense the tension between them. From what she'd observed other times this week, their friendship already had a crack or two in it. Chinks into which she might be able to drive a wedge.

"You have such a great figure, Lauren. How do you do it?"

Lauren looked over, startled by her words. "Just too busy to eat I guess."

"Lauren's a runner, that's how she does it," Mel volunteered. "She can eat twice what the rest of us do because she burns it right off again."

"Really? I've always wanted to take up running. Unfortunately I'm just not built for it. Not streamlined like a runner should be."

"You don't have to be thin to run. Right, Lauren?"

Their boss took a moment to answer. "Anyone can run if they want."

"There, you hear that. Anyone can run if they *really* want

to."

Ada looked from one to the other. Mel's eagerness and Lauren's reluctance suggested she'd stumbled onto a charged topic. "I've heard it's addictive, once you get into it."

"Well Lauren's certainly proof of that. Rain or shine, sleet or snow, she's out there running. Never misses more than a day or two." Mel shoved the bottle back in the fridge. "At least she never used to."

As the woman walked out, Ada looked over to find Lauren staring at the counter, her jaw working. She rose from the table and wondered over. "Are you all right?"

"Yes, fine." She took down a mug from the cupboard but simply set it on the counter before her.

"What did Mel mean? Don't you run any more?"

"I've been having a little trouble with my leg."

"What's wrong with it?"

"Nothing serious. Just a persistent cramp is all." She shrugged. "Sometimes when you stop for a while, it's hard to start up again."

A piece of the puzzle was starting to take shape. "Why did you stop?"

Lauren looked down.

The puzzle piece clicked into place. "It's because of what happened with my dad, isn't it. You were running when you fell through the ice, so now every time you try to do it..."

Lauren closed her eyes. "Possibly that has something to do with it."

"Oh please." Ada took her arm and turned her. "Don't let what happened change your life. It wasn't your fault, it was an accident. You have to move past it."

"I've been getting that advice a fair bit lately."

Ada sighed and lowered her hand. "Easy for others to say,

isn't it?" She thought for a moment. If ever she'd wanted a way to endear herself to this woman, a way to move deeper into her life… "Lauren, would you teach me to run?"

"I told you, you don't need anyone to teach you. You just do it."

Her laugh was genuine. "I'll bet you've never been out of shape a day in your life. Well I'm about as *un*fit as you can get. I never had a chance to exercise with dad, apart from lugging him around. Plus I'm an oaf, as you can probably see."

"No, you're not."

"Well the bottom line is I wouldn't have a clue how to start. How fast, how long, how hard, what to wear, nothing. If you could maybe just get me started…" She leaned forward slightly. "It would be such a help."

Lauren looked up and forced a smile. "If you want me to, of course I'll help you."

CHAPTER 44

"I don't think she's home."

Ted looked toward the sound of the voice that had just called out to him. A man in shorts and a tattered T-shirt – years' worth of beer sunk into the belly peeking out from beneath its hem – stood watering the scrappy lawn next door. Ted let Ada's back door close and wandered over.

"Don't think she's home," the neighbor repeated as he approached.

"No, it doesn't look like it. Nobody answered at the front door either."

"Yeah, I'm pretty sure she's at work today."

"Work?" Ted had been ready to say thanks and leave, but the news stopped him. "Ada didn't tell me she got a job."

"Only last week. Think my wife said it was at some nursery."

Ted frowned then quickly recovered. "Well, that's terrific. She'd sure be relieved."

The man took a drag of his Marlboro light. "You a friend of Ada's?"

"Her uncle. Ted Phelps." He put out his hand.

"Greg Kauffman." The man shot a glance across his back

yard. Beyond the fence, the stream flowed serenely through a copse of trees. He cleared his throat. "So you'd be related to Ada's father? The one who…"

"Roger was my brother, yes."

"Hey, man, I'm sorry. Really, his death was a terrible thing. A real freak accident."

"Yes, it was."

The man aimed the hose at a clump of pansies, pinning the tender shoots to the ground. "My wife thinks the world of Ada, looking after Roger all those years. Hope you don't mind me saying it but he could be a real handful at times."

Ted gave a laugh. "I'm sure he could. He relied on Ada for practically everything."

"It wasn't just that. She had to watch him every second, day and night. Make sure he didn't wander off."

"Wander off?"

"You didn't know? Hell, Roger strayed all over the place. Some days he was fine. He'd go for his walk around the block and come straight home. Others he'd just disappear, be gone for hours. Ada'd be frantic. Next thing she'd get a call from some neighbor three blocks over telling her to come and get him, he'd shown up at their place."

"No kidding."

"He actually turned up at our place a few times." The man jerked his head at his house. "Mostly at night. Don't know where he thought he was, but he sure as hell didn't want to leave. Ada had a terrible time getting him to go home." He shook his head. "Awful what dementia does to a person."

At seeing Ted's frown, he quickly added, "You know, from his stroke. Ada explained it all to my wife. Couldn't even recognize his loved ones sometimes, the people who cared about him the most."

Ted stretched his memory back ten years. From what the doctor had told him personally, Roger had been lucky. Aside from losing the ability to speak and partial paralysis down one side, his memory and reasoning had been little damaged by the stroke. When had dementia come into the picture? He'd seen no evidence of it himself on the few occasions he'd come to visit. Even at the end.

"As if that wasn't bad enough, the poor guy was always falling down. Every time I saw him he had a fresh lot of bruises." Greg gave his flowers a final blast then glanced toward the stream and shook his head. "Between you and me, I don't know how he managed to pull that woman out of the water. Must'a been one of those things like you read about. You know, some kid gets pinned under a car and grandma comes along and picks it up."

"That must've been it."

Kaufman looked back at the stream and nodded. "I hope you don't mind me saying, but in a way thing's worked out for the best. Poor Roger's out of his misery and Ada finally gets to live her own life. After all those years of looking after him, it's about time she got some payback."

Ted pulled his gaze away from the stream. "And possibly no-one deserves it more."

CHAPTER 45

"I thought you couldn't read what was on the sign?"

Lauren's words stopped Mel in the archway, as she had hoped. Even though the incident had happened that morning and it was now closing time, Mel knew at once what she was referring to.

She turned and shrugged as Lauren came toward her. "I must not have gotten a good enough look at it."

"Yeah, right. More like you just didn't want me to know." Lauren stopped before her. "Look, for the record, I don't give a hoot what Claudia Weekes graffities about me. I'm not living on a knife-edge here."

"No-one said you were."

"I get the impression you think I'm one step away from the funny farm."

"No more than usual." When her attempt at humor went unappreciated, Mel got serious. "I'm concerned about you. Is that so bad?"

"Concerned? Then why...?" Lauren looked away, then back again. "Why did you bring up my running with Ada? Of all people."

"Same reason."

"Because you're concerned? What sense does that make?"

"I was trying to get you to see that you *do* still have a problem with what happened. If you didn't, what I said to Ada wouldn't have bothered you so much, would it?"

Lauren exhaled, shaking her head. Her friend's logic could be truly confounding. But whether she agreed with her view or not, she could see the caring sentiment behind it.

"You have the most convoluted way of making a point." She put out her arm. "And what really worries me is, I get it."

Ada came out the shop door in time to see the two women embrace. The ember inside her kindled at once. She hurried over.

As the pair drew apart, she held up the keys she'd taken from the top drawer of Lauren's desk. "Would you like me to lock up the outbuildings for you?"

Lauren looked over. "Thank you, Ada, but that's Simon's job."

"I can do it. I don't mind."

"No, it's okay. He expects to do it. You better put the keys back so he can find them."

Ada stood silent, wanting to protest, wanting to slap the gloating smirk off Mel's face.

"Oh, and Ada, please don't go in my desk again unless I ask you to." Lauren waved. "You have a good night. See you tomorrow."

Ada glared as the two walked arm in arm through the archway. Beside her at the edge of the walk, one of Simon's hideous gnomes perched on a rock. With the burst of fire flooding her veins, she snatched it up.

Idiot Simon. Couldn't Lauren see she could do a better job than him?

She swung the statue up over her head, took aim at the

flagstones beneath her feet. Couldn't any of these idiots see!

She stood for a moment, a living statue, then slowly lowered the figure to its rock.

No, clearly none of them understood, but that was okay. They'd see soon enough what she was capable of.

CHAPTER 46

Josh left the kitchen, a mug in each hand, a small box clamped beneath one arm, and strode up the hallway for Lauren's office.

Five days had passed since he'd made up his mind – or thought he had – and only now was he ready to commit to his plan. He'd taken that long to reconsider and had decided it was none of his business who Lauren Donnelly hired or fired. At least not yet.

Granted, Ada appeared to be fitting in well and was certainly doing a better job than her predecessor. So on the face of it, Lauren had been right. *Or* just plain lucky.

Had it been him, he never would've hired the woman. What had she been thinking? Hard enough to get over what she'd experienced. To willingly create a situation where you'd come face to face with the one person who'd remind you of it day after day… Well it sure wouldn't help her sleep any better. Or maybe it would. What did he know?

In any case, it hadn't been his choice to make. And since this was purely a business matter, the emotional upshots of Lauren's decisions had nothing at all to do with him. As long as they didn't jeopardize sales, he could live with whatever off-the-wall scheme she came up with.

He reached the office and stopped in the doorway.

"Coffee?"

Behind her desk, Lauren looked up. "You're a mind reader. I was just coming to get one."

Stepping forward to hand her a mug, he spotted the catalogue she'd been perusing. "Ramsey's. We used to order from them."

"Great place, isn't it? I'm heading up there on a buying trip next week. Thought I'd get a preview of what I'll be seeing." She sipped her coffee and arched her brows. She'd never told him how she liked it but he'd obviously been paying attention. "Thanks. This is perfect."

He stood gazing down at her, the same thoughtful look on his face as the other day. Maybe this time he'd speak his thoughts.

"Something on your mind?"

"Actually, there is. You got a minute?"

"Sure, have a seat." She leaned back as he settled before her.

"I've been hashing something over since the night we had dinner and I just want to run an idea by you; get your reaction. Seeing as we've settled on a working arrangement with the Nowell and Johnson, I was wondering how you'd feel about maybe taking things a step further."

She fought to keep her expression neutral. What sort of step did he have in mind?

"Mel told me that at one stage you'd asked her to buy in as your partner but it didn't work out. I was wondering how you'd feel about me investing a bit more in the business? Depending on what you wanted up front, I might even manage an even split."

Lauren blinked back at him, for a moment unable to speak.

"I take it the idea doesn't appeal to you."

"Oh, no, it's not that. It's just of a surprise, that's all." She straightened in her chair. "You're serious about this?"

"Absolutely. As I think I told you, I've got some money in a term investment. Well, I *did* have the money up until recently. I can still liquidate the assets if necessary, but I thought, instead…if things go ahead and I do buy in…" He reached out and set the box on the desk. "Perhaps you'd accept this as part payment."

Lauren stared at the familiar shape, unable to move. It couldn't be.

Slowly she set down her coffee mug, drew the box toward her and opened the lid. "Oh my God." Her eyes widened. "I don't believe it. *You* were the buyer?"

She sat staring at the man across from her, her joy at seeing her father's baseball briefly overshadowed by a puzzling thought. "But…how did you know I was the seller? My name didn't appear on the website."

"How many autographed Ted Williams baseballs could there be on the Cape?" He nodded at the object in her hands. "I know how much it means to you and that you wouldn't have parted with it unless you felt you had no choice. I thought maybe this was a way for you to both keep it *and* save the business."

For an instant tears stung her eyes and she blinked them away. She set the ball gently back in the box. *Let's not get carried away, this is business.* Still, however you looked at it, it was a thoughtful gesture. "I don't know what to say."

"No need to give me an answer right away. I just wanted to lay the offer on the table and give you a chance to think it over."

"Oh, I promise you I'll certainly do that." She slid the box back across to him. "In the meantime keep that in a safe place."

"Will do." Josh picked it up and rose to face her as she came round the desk.

Something in her eyes raised his heart rate a notch. He cleared his throat. "As I say, there's no rush. Get back to me when you've thought it over."

She stretched up and planted a kiss on his cheek. "Thank you."

"For what? Nothing's been settled."

"Thank you any way."

Transfixed by the lips that had just brushed his skin, he felt himself leaning in closer. His hand was reaching to cup her face when cries from the shop jolted them apart.

"Lauren! Lauren!" More commotion, then Simon burst through the door. "Oh, Lauren, they're dead! They're all dead!"

Lauren led the way down the path to the pond. After the description Simon had given, she was less willing than ever to go near the water. Still, they had to check out his story, see if they could determine what happened.

Past a break in a row of yews, the grisly scene spread out before them. A half dozen tiny feathered bodies, bloodied and broken, littered the clearing at the water's edge. The very spot where Simon stood to feed them each day.

Josh stepped past her and knelt to examine the nearest body. Picking it up in one gloved hand, he turned it over, studied it a moment, then laid it in the box he'd brought for the purpose. The gesture was mindful, almost reverent. But by the look on his face he was angry more than upset.

"It was probably an animal." Lauren stepped into the circle of bodies. Such a pitiful sight. "A cat or a dog; a coyote even."

"If a predator was after a meal why didn't it carry the bodies off?"

"I don't know. All I know is, I remember it happening once when I was little, before Simon came to us. Just a shame he had to be the one to find them."

Josh straightened beside her. "Then again, maybe it wasn't an animal."

Her gaze swung toward him. Clearly he'd been thinking the same thing she had. "Oh god, she wouldn't, would she?" Lauren surveyed the scene again, wincing at the thought a young woman could have wrought such cruelty. "She'd have to be truly sick to do something like this."

"But Claudia knew they were here, didn't she? She knew Simon came down to feed them every day."

"Yes, of course, but…what sense would it make for her to kill them? Her beef is with me, not with Simon."

"Unless she blamed him for getting her fired."

Lauren placed a hand to her mouth. The thought was sickening. She bent to scan the ground more closely. "There's nothing here. No footprints, no weapon, nothing to prove—"

She cut off abruptly at seeing the figure standing nearby. "Simon. I asked you not to come down here."

"Claudia did it? Claudia killed them? Why would she do that?"

"Simon, please, we don't know for sure—"

"I hate Claudia! I hate her, *I hate her!*"

Clenching her fists, Lauren watched him run back up the hill. "That girl better pray she and I never cross paths again."

CHAPTER 47

Lauren strode across the supermarket parking lot, smiling at the pleasant ache in her legs. Not the dreaded stab of cramp, but of muscles taxed by unaccustomed exercise. After weeks of trying to get back into running, she'd finally broken through her resistance.

Yesterday morning when she and Ada had met on the beach, Lauren had suffered vast misgivings about following through on her promise to coach the woman in running. And sure enough, they hadn't gone a dozen strides when she'd fallen to the sand, helpless in the grip of agonizing cramp in both her calves.

Only with Ada's goading encouragement had she gotten to her feet. And with the woman lumbering along beside her, puffing and red-faced yet egging her on, the cramp had finally yielded its grip. For the first time since the accident she'd been running freely.

The feeling had been so exhilarating, akin to flying, she'd finished off their jog with a full-out sprint of the last fifty yards. A burst of enthusiasm for which she was paying dearly now. Yet she didn't care. It was worth every twinge! This was the kind of pain that would fade.

Whether her previous resistance had been due to what happened with Phelps seemed an answered question now. Why else would Ada's encouragement have made all the difference, enabling her to push past the pain that had been crippling her for all this time? Who knew, maybe with the progress she'd made in this, her nightmares might finally stop as well.

Yes, Ada was a remarkable person, a truly selfless individual. To not only put her own feelings aside but to help Lauren do the same with hers. And to top it off she was a fabulous worker. Unlike Claudia, she got along with all the customers and Simon loved her. Surely even Mel would come around eventually once she got over her reservations.

With a joyous if painful bounce to her step, Lauren pushed her shopping cart toward her car. Her spirits deflated when she got within sight of its driver side door.

"Damn!" She bent and examined the dent. A blue late model Datsun sedan was parked barely two feet away. If she visualized the arc of its door swinging open it would strike her door at about where the dent was.

Of course that didn't prove anything. It could've been the car parked there before that had done the damage. And that's no doubt what the Datsun's driver would claim if she ever tried to pursue the matter.

She looked more closely, hoping to spot a hint of blue paint on her car's silver finish. Not a speck. Cursing whoever the culprit had been, she loaded her groceries into her trunk and drove from the spot.

At the parking lot exit she checked her mirror one last time, but couldn't see anyone approaching the Datsun. With her last chance gone to confront the owner, she turned from the lot and started for home.

Early morning traffic was light on the highway; she'd be back in plenty of time to open the nursery. She'd wanted to pick up something special for coffee and had splurged on cannoli and scones from Elroy's. Much had happened the day before and not all of it good.

On the down side there'd been the incident with Simon's ducklings, Ada breaking that expensive vase, and Mel insisting she be made to pay for it. In that regard they could all do with a bit of a boost.

On the bright side however there was Josh's proposal, and, in her own mind at least, the treats were also a celebration, if a touch premature. Even if he bought in as a quarter partner it could totally revitalize the business. Plus she'd have her Dad's baseball back.

All that was left was to make the decision and give him her answer. But it seemed she had one reservation. How would she manage in partnership with a man she had such mixed feelings about?

Pulling up at a traffic light, Lauren gazed in the rear-view mirror and noticed the car in the far right-hand lane. It looked like the Datsun from the parking lot, but of course it couldn't be. The driver would've had to leave right after her in order to be trailing her now. How could she have missed seeing them get into their car?

Unless they'd been in it all along.

The thought sent a shiver of disquiet through her. She'd been so intent on the dent in her door, had she even looked in the other car? Had someone been in there? Slumped down to avoid detection so they wouldn't have to pay for the damage they'd caused?

Or had that someone caused the damage deliberately and stuck around to witness her reaction?

The shiver got worse.

No, that was nuts. After the recent vandalism at work she was just being paranoid. It wasn't impossible for the Datsun to be behind her now. The driver could've been speeding or taken some short cut she didn't know about. Yet she couldn't shake the feeling she was being followed.

She put on her blinker and took the next left. The car behind her made the turn too. Which again proved nothing; the driver might simply have been going this way – they were both main roads. But were they to follow her down one that wasn't…

At the next corner she turned again. A residential street. Yards with fences, and sidewalks between their gates and the road. Halfway up the block she looked back and saw the Datsun turn the corner. What were the odds?

She hit the brakes and pulled to the curb. If this was Claudia they were going to have it out right here and now. Not for the lousy dent in her door, but for all the heartache the girl had caused Simon. She shut off her engine and leapt from the car.

The Datsun sped past her without slowing down, its interior too dark to make out the driver, even whether it was a man or a woman. Lauren caught only the first three digits of its license plate number before it vanished behind a parked car.

As her heart rate slowed, she took a deep breath. All right so maybe it hadn't been Claudia. Claudia probably would've run her over! Maybe what happened at the pond yesterday had simply left her a little jumpy.

Back in her car, she sat thinking a moment. Other things could be contributing to her sense of paranoia. Though she hadn't yet mentioned it to anyone, she'd found something else damaged at work this week – a large cement bird bath knocked on its side, its basin shattered. Customer mishap? Or had Claudia paid them another visit?

Shaking her head, she started the engine. Add to the mix her lack of sleep... "Little wonder I'm imaging things."

CHAPTER 48

Lauren paused in the kitchen doorway enjoying the sound of Simon's laughter. His anguished cries over the ducklings yesterday had been proving difficult to blot from her mind. Yet seeing him now, sharing a secret joke with Ada, she could almost believe the incident had never happened. How good of the woman to try and help him forget about it.

As she watched them, Ada took a napkin and wiped some cannoli cream from his face. Again she felt the profound relief that the woman was fitting in so well. How different Simon was with her than he'd been with Claudia. Thank God for Ada.

Stepping forward, she caught Simon's eye. She didn't want to dampen the mood but perhaps that's what made this the perfect moment. "Simon, can I talk to you for a second?"

Still laughing, he got up and wandered over.

She led him out into the hall a few steps. "Simon, I noticed the potting shed door wasn't locked this morning when I came down to open up. Did you remember to lock it last night?"

"Yes. I did. I always lock it."

Lauren nodded. The slip had been minor; she didn't want him to get upset. "Yes, you usually do. But do you think maybe because of what happened yesterday you might've been a bit distracted?"

The smile faltered. "No, I locked it. It's my job. Someone must've opened it again."

"Well, no-one else was here when I came down this morning. I hadn't even opened the front gate yet. Who could've opened it?"

A frown appeared on that cherubic face.

"Look, it's okay," she quickly assured. "It's not a big deal. Everybody forgets sometimes."

"But..."

"It's just that with the trouble we've been having with Claudia it's extra important we lock all the doors and gates at night."

His eyes grew round. "Oh yes, Claudia. We have to be careful, we can't let her in." He nodded vigorously. "I won't forget again. I promise."

"Thank you, Simon. It's good to know I can count on you."

From the kitchen she wandered out to the barn where Josh was loading hay into the trailer. The scent of alfalfa and aged wood greeted her as she stepped through the door. At the sight of him hefting the heavy bales, she paused to admire the way he moved.

He stopped when he saw her and accepted the bottle of water she handed him. "Thanks." He popped the tab and tipped it back.

A thin stream escaped the side of his mouth and trickled down his chin. Lauren tore her gaze from its winding course down the contours of his throat and forced her mind back to why she was there.

"I've been thinking about your proposal," she said. "It's a big step and there's a lot we'd need to discuss if we're to go ahead with it. That buying trip I'm taking next week – if you came along it'd give us a chance to talk on the drive, see if we're on the same wavelength with this."

He wiped his mouth and handed her back the empty bottle. "Think the others can manage with both of us gone?"

"I do this trip every year so Mel's used to holding the fort. Besides she'll have Ada and Simon and it's only a couple of days."

He nodded. "Sounds good. Count me in."

From the shop's front window, Ada watched Simon watering the stock in the yard. When he glanced up unexpectedly, she waved and smiled. The idiot flashed her his idiot grin, then returned to his chore.

Wearing a look of intense concentration – the expression he acquired doing anything more complex than scratching himself – he worked his way slowly around each table, and, when the job was done, shut off the hose and left it coiled beneath the tap near the shop's back door.

As he vanished up the path beside the greenhouse, Ada scanned the yard in all directions. Lauren had gone to the barn a short while ago, Mel was out making a florist delivery, and there were no customers currently in the shop. She was alone.

She moved quickly, slipping outside and positioning the hose so its nozzle was aimed at the door. With a last look to make sure no-one was watching, she locked the nozzle in the 'open' setting, turned on the faucet and ducked back inside.

Almost at once, water started seeping in under the door. Smiling, she backed from the spreading pool and returned to the window. She picked up the towels she'd left on the sill and stood poised to enact the rest of her plan.

The instant Lauren emerged from the barn, Ada set to work. By the time her boss came through the front door, the water was off again and Ada was on her hands and knees mopping up the mess with the towels.

Lauren spied her at once and came over. "What happened?"

Ada feigned surprise at her appearance. "Oh. I... Nothing. Just a little accident. Someone left the water on."

Lauren opened the door and surveyed the area just beyond. Ada watched her gaze move from the puddle to the hose to the faucet and back again.

She let the door close. "Wasn't Simon just watering out here?"

"Um. Well, yes, but... You know I saw some kids hanging around after he left. I think maybe one of them..."

Lauren shook her head. "Ada, you don't have to cover for him. I know Simon can forget sometimes." Her brow furrowed. "Though he's normally pretty good about shutting off faucets."

Ada bowed her head. "I didn't want him to get in trouble."

"I know you didn't. And I thank you for cleaning up after him. I think this business with Claudia has really upset him."

Ada nodded. Yes, Claudia. Cruel, vicious, scheming, Claudia – the monster who'd killed Simon's precious ducklings.

She frowned in anger. "Claudia doesn't sound like a very nice person."

"No, she wasn't. Anyway thank goodness you were here to shut off the water. Otherwise we'd have had a real mess on our hands."

CHAPTER 49

"So you're sure you'll be all right on your own then?" Standing at the nursery's work room table, Lauren clipped the end from a sprig of eucalyptus. On this, the morning before she and Josh were due to leave for their trip, she was still debating whether to cancel. Any other time she wouldn't have hesitated to leave Mel in charge. But with the woman pregnant and the trouble they'd been having with Claudia recently…

"Simon and Ada will be here of course, so you'll have back-up in case it gets busy. The problem is Thursday's supposed to get warm so you'll have to do some extra watering." She lowered her hands and let out a sigh. "Maybe I should skip the trip this year. I don't have to go. I can do a lot of my browsing on-line."

She peered around the arrangement she was making to see why Mel hadn't yet responded. Across the table, the woman was smiling to herself as she worked.

"What's so funny?"

"You. Making all this fuss over me. Last I heard, pregnancy wasn't a debilitating illness."

"Well no, but you have been tired lately."

"So I'll rest if I need to."

"And the morning sickness?"

"I found an herbal remedy that helps." Mel paused in writing out the card for her order. "Look, will you stop worrying. You've done this trip every year since we started and we've always muddled through fine without you."

"Good to know I'll be missed." Lauren smiled at the good-natured slight. After the tensions that had arisen between them in recent weeks, it was good to have things back to normal. "Still, it's not exactly the same this time. Josh is coming with me so you'll be two men short instead of one."

"Like I said, we'll manage."

Mel went back to writing her card. For a moment Lauren let herself hope the woman wouldn't say what she had to be wondering. But of course, she did.

"You two sharing a room on the trip?"

Lauren threw a handful of ribbon at her. "None of your business." Still, she was pleased. Mel's mood had definitely lifted since she'd learned of Josh's offer to buy into the business.

"There is one thing I wanted to mention." Lauren cast a glance toward the door and lowered her voice. "I need you to check that Simon locks up every night."

"Hasn't he been? That's not like him."

"No, it isn't and I'm not sure what's going on. It started the day the ducklings were killed so I figured he was just upset. But it happened the next two nights as well."

"Did you talk to him about it?"

"I did and he swears he didn't forget, but I've been checking myself and I know he has." Lauren frowned. "Although these last two days he's remembered again so whatever was wrong, he might be over it. Still, with the trouble we've been having, the vandalism and all..."

"Don't worry, I'll make sure we're locked up."

Mel's phone rang and she reached in her pocket. "Hey, Babe, how's it going?" She listened a moment. "That's fantastic. I've got all my fingers and toes crossed for you; I'm sure you'll do great. Call me as soon as you hear."

Frowning, she returned the phone to her pocket. "That was Peter. He's in Portland for that job interview. Said they want him to stick around for a meeting with the CEO tomorrow. He's staying overnight."

"That sounds encouraging. He must be excited." Lauren glanced up when she didn't respond. "So why is it you don't look very happy?"

"I'm just hoping it finally happens this time. He's gotten this close more than once and he didn't take it well when he missed out. In a way it's worse than if he got axed in the first round." Mel transferred her finished arrangement to the bench and turned back. "He's so stressed, Lauren. I honestly don't know what he'll do if this falls through."

"Hey, come on. I've got a good feeling about this one." Lauren leaned over and gave her a hug. Only after they drew apart, did she notice the figure standing in the doorway.

For an instant Ada's expression seemed so dark Lauren wondered if something had happened. Before she could ask, the woman's face cleared. Obviously just a trick of the light.

"Sorry to interrupt, but a customer asked for a bit of string to tie up a box. Five feet should do."

Lauren pulled two yards from the spool, cut it off and handed it over. "There you go."

"Thanks." Ada started to turn then stopped. "Lauren, I just want to say again how much I appreciate you're teaching me to run."

"Don't mention it. You're very welcome."

The woman glanced toward Mel then back again. "We had a great time yesterday morning, didn't we?"

"We certainly did."

Ada beamed. "You were so patient. Bet you never guessed what you were letting yourself in for, me being so klutzy and all."

"You'll get the hang of it, I'm sure. Now you better not keep your customer waiting."

"Oh. No, of course not." With a last look at Mel, she turned and left.

Ada stalked back up the hall toward the shop, shoving the wad of string in her pocket. There was no customer needing string. She'd made up the story as an excuse to check what Mel and Lauren were talking about. And it hadn't been what she had hoped.

As far as she knew, Lauren hadn't yet said a word to anyone about their shared running experience. At the time, Lauren had been so pleased with her breakthrough, she'd given Ada a spontaneous hug. Had she forgotten that incident so quickly? Were hugs things she gave out so freely they meant virtually nothing?

Ada clamped her lips at the thought. *She* certainly hadn't forgotten. Lauren's unbidden show of affection had moved her in a way she'd never expected. Yes, she'd been trying to ingratiate herself for personal gain. Yes, she'd been hoping to get closer to Lauren; closer even than Mel herself. But never had she dreamed she'd be moved by that closeness once she had it.

It had struck her in that moment, as Lauren had stood with her arms wrapped around her, that for the first time in her life she had a real friend. The wonder of it had stayed with her since. But if the friendship mattered as much to Lauren, why hadn't she mentioned it to anyone else? Why did the woman continue to treat her like nothing but a lowly employee? Especially in front of Mel? Why did these people go out of their way to make her feel so unimportant?

Fists clenched, she stormed round the corner at the end of the hall. And froze at the sight of the customer standing at the check-out counter.

CHAPTER 50

"Uncle Ted?"

The man's face lit with a smile. "Ada. How good to see you. How have you been?"

She hurried over to join him at the counter, surprised at her sudden rush of panic. She hadn't been doing anything wrong. Why should she feel he'd caught her at something?

"What on earth are you doing here? You don't like flowers. You don't even garden."

"Well, I'm thinking of taking it up, how's that. A man should have a hobby at my age. Who knows, I might have a real green thumb."

Unlike herself, he seemed wholly unfazed at their meeting. Suggesting it wasn't just a coincidence? "Really, uncle, why are you here?" She couldn't help feeling he'd come to check up on her.

"I heard you got yourself a job. Congratulations. I thought I'd stop in and see how you're going with it."

"I'm doing just fine, thank you very much." She frowned. "Who told you I was working here?"

"Your next door neighbor. I came by one day when you weren't home and he and I had a chat in his yard."

So much for this being a random encounter. "Well it's very nice of you to come and see me but I really have to get back to work."

Ted looked around at the empty shop. "There's no-one here. Surely you can spare a minute to chat."

"We might not be busy but there are still things I'm supposed to be doing." Taking his arm, she started guiding him toward the door. "I'll walk you to your car, we can talk on the way."

Outside, Ted stopped to examine the herbs on display near the door. She tried to coax him on toward the archway but he wouldn't budge. Was he being deliberately difficult?

"I didn't even know you were looking for a job." He bent to sniff a pot of rosemary. "Did you apply for many before getting this one?"

"Yes, quite a few." She tugged his arm and managed to turn him, then found herself staring into his eyes. Eyes too familiar and far too knowing. A shiver swarmed over her. For a moment her father stood before her.

"Isn't it strange that of all the places you could've found a job you ended up here? Working for the woman who caused Roger's accident."

Ada swallowed. What was he saying? What had he guessed? Nothing. He could know nothing at all. "I needed work, Lauren had an opening. What do you find so strange about that?"

"Then it doesn't bother you?"

"Of course not. I told you, I've forgiven Lauren. We've both moved on from what happened. In fact we're becoming quite good friends."

"Is that right."

"The fact is, I love this job. Which I'm not going to have

for very much longer if you don't let me get back to doing it."

Lauren stepped from the kitchen hallway, mug in hand, and stood taking in the empty shop. No-one at the counter? There weren't any customers waiting to be served but she hoped Ada hadn't strayed far. Through the shop's side window she could see a young couple, arms laden with pots and seedlings, heading up the path to pay for their purchases.

"Ada?" she called toward the back of the shop. When the woman failed appear, Lauren continued toward the front door. With her gaze on the coffee she was bringing to Josh, she stepped out into the morning sun.

The mug dropped from her hand and exploded on the flagstone pavers. For a heart-stopping moment she was sure she was having another episode. Then reality slammed her with equal force – this was no apparition, no trick of the mind. The face before her was that of a living, flesh-and-blood man. A face she'd last seen wide-eyed, twisted and silently screaming beneath a barrier of ice.

Ada was suddenly at her side. "Lauren, it's okay. This is my uncle. Theodore Phelps."

"Your..."

"That's right. My father's brother."

"I'm sorry Miss Donnelly, I didn't mean to startle you." The man nodded.

Lauren stood mute.

"Uncle Ted just stopped by to see how I was doing in my new job." Ada glared across at the man. "And now he's leaving."

When she returned from escorting Ted to his car a few moments later, Ada found Lauren sweeping up the pieces of broken mug.

"Lauren, I'm so sorry. That must've been a terrible shock for you. I never realized how much Uncle Ted looks like my dad."

"Don't be sorry. It wasn't your fault." Despite her protests, the woman still looked like she'd seen a ghost.

"Look, you don't have to worry. I've explained things to him and he understands. He won't be back."

Ada put an arm around her shoulders and turned her for the door. Guiding her back inside the shop, she was struck by her second surprise of the day – discovering she not only *had* a friend, but that she could *be* one.

CHAPTER 51

Ada left the shop at the end of the day and headed across the yard for the greenhouse. She was feeling much better about Uncle Ted's unannounced visit that morning. Surely she had nothing to worry about. His suspicions over how she'd treated her father couldn't possibly extend to her relationship with Lauren. And even if they had, after witnessing how concerned she'd been over Lauren's distress, he'd have changed his mind.

Yes, her caring behavior would've made it obvious to him she hadn't merely forgiven Lauren, she'd actually come to care about her. Most convenient of all, he'd accepted that Lauren's distress at seeing him was the reason Ada didn't want him to come back.

Her only regret regarding the incident was that Mel hadn't been there to witness it, that she'd missed seeing how much Lauren relied on her – the way Lauren had clung to her arm as she'd led her inside, the woman's whispered yet heartfelt thanks over Ada's continued selfless support.

Smiling, she started up the path by the greenhouse. She'd been wrong to have doubted her boss. Clearly their burgeoning friendship meant every bit as much to Lauren as it did to her. What had started as a scheme to get all she could from this woman was fast becoming an experience more rewarding than anything she had ever known.

At the end of the path, she stepped out into the utility area and spotted Josh loading pavers into the trailer. All that could further brighten her mood would be for *their* relationship to move forward as well. Something that would surely happen in time but, as with Lauren, might need a push to get started.

She wandered toward him. So far he'd been overly cautious in revealing his feelings for her. But if he knew how important she was becoming, he might be inclined to declare them more openly.

"Lauren sent me to look for Simon," she said in greeting. "Have you seen him anywhere?"

Josh hefted a stack of pavers and placed them neatly into the trailer. "He was up the potting shed, last I saw him."

Ada glanced in that direction, then looked back. She paused for a moment as though weighing her words. "How has he seemed to you lately?"

"Simon?" He straightened. "Fine. Why?"

"Lauren's a little worried about him. Actually, so am I. All this business with Claudia, you know." She shook her head gravely.

Josh dragged a gloved hand across his brow and went back to work. "What happened with the ducklings certainly upset him, but I thought he'd pretty much gotten over that."

"Well, if it's not the ducklings it's something else that's bothering him. He's been really forgetful lately."

"I hadn't noticed."

"Didn't Lauren tell you? He forgot to lock up two nights this week." She glanced around them and lowered her voice. "Actually it was *four* nights. He forgot the other two times as well, but I did it for him. I didn't tell Lauren because I didn't want him to get in trouble."

"Maybe you should." Setting the last stack of pavers in place, Josh turned to face her. "If he's having trouble doing his job, Lauren should know."

"Oh no she's happy for me to look after him. It's a full time job though, I can tell you. This morning he left the hose running outside the shop. Water started gushing in under the door. If I hadn't seen it and shut it off the whole shop would've been flooded."

She stopped to find him regarding her intently. In an instant her heart was pounding, her stomach twisting itself into knots.

"Good thing you were there then." He studied her a moment longer then pulled off his gloves. "Well, I better get this order delivered."

"Oh sure," she croaked. "I'll see you later. Thanks for the talk."

Ada walked on, barely feeling the ground beneath her. Her exchange with Josh had been everything she'd hoped for and more. He still hadn't proclaimed his feelings, but in that rapturous moment their gazes had met, it had been obvious what he was thinking.

After relaying Lauren's message to Simon, Ada started back toward the shop. At the sight of Mel watering in the yard she veered toward her. Technically she was through for the day but, filled with the joy of her new importance, she couldn't pass up such an opportunity.

"How's Lauren? Is she feeling any better?"

Mel kept watering, as usual declining to meet her gaze. "Didn't know anything was wrong with her."

"Oh?" Ada infused the word with surprise. "Perhaps she didn't want you to know. Forget I said anything. She's obviously happy just confiding in me."

Mel smiled faintly and shook her head.

"I guess I'll go see if she needs anything else before I head home. Is she still doing orders?"

"As far as I know."

She glanced toward the shop, reluctant to leave. "I'll probably be doing them too pretty soon. Orders, that is."

"And why would you imagine that?"

"Lauren said so. She's been training me."

"It does take a bit of time to learn. Which is why she and I spent four years at college studying design."

Ada's jaw clenched. Mel always had to bring that up. "Lauren says I'm picking it up really fast. She's been giving me lots of instruction. We're spending heaps of time together, both here and outside of work."

"I guess you're going to miss her tomorrow and Wednesday then."

She gave a laugh. "Miss her? Why, is she going somewhere?"

"Her buying trip. She goes every year."

Ada had asked the question in jest. Mel's reply axed any humor she'd felt.

The woman glanced over and read her expression. "Didn't she tell you? Guess she didn't think you needed to know."

Her nails were suddenly biting her palms. "Of course she told me, I just forgot. She...she asked me to give Josh a hand with the unloading while she was away."

"Well now I wonder why she would've said that." Mel shut off the hose and faced her. "Seeing as Josh is going with her."

CHAPTER 52

Lauren rolled the roto-tiller up the ramp and along the barn's central aisle. The smell of hay, aged wood and dust rose from the floorboards, light from the overheads forming pools at regular intervals and banishing shadows to the recessed corners beneath the loft.

She set the tiller to one side and surveyed the row of tools and equipment now neatly lined up along the walls.

Since shutting the gate at closing time, she'd cleaned, dusted and rearranged every component of this, her largest storage area. A pointless exercise, some would say, yielding a misleading sense of control. Yet on this day of shocks and setbacks she'd employ whatever strategy helped. She could impose no order on the rest of the world – on the rest of her *life* – but here in the barn, neatness would rule.

Her encounter with Theodore Phelps that day was going to cost her, she could already feel it. At best it was going to slow her recovery; at worst, undo what progress she'd already made. The thought that, in a few short hours, she'd be climbing into bed, closing her eyes and seeing that face in one of her nightmares…

She stifled a shudder. Her best hope was to utterly exhaust

herself before that time came.

Taking hold of the trailer's tow bar, she hauled the massive unit forward, then swung it aside as she pushed it back, trying to create a space for the tiller. For some reason it only rolled halfway before stopping and refusing to go any further. She bent to peer under it, trying to see what was in the way. But even with all the inside lights on, the area beneath the hayloft was dim.

At a sound from behind her she straightened and turned.

The cone of light shining outside the door lit up the ramp and a circle of yard. Beyond that, darkness. Nothing moved. The sound she'd heard had been a kind of rustling. Most likely a bird.

She was turning to resume her struggle with the trailer when another sound came – a faint scratching along the wall. With a thrill of disquiet she marked its progress from the rear of the building toward the front. A branch scraping the side in the wind? Or a person moving down the side of the barn?

She braced, waiting for that person to appear in the doorway.

Ten heartbeats later nobody had.

"Hello? Is someone there?" The sound of her voice and the silence that followed only made her feel more alone. Time to knock off and head up to the house.

Still clutching the heavy bar, she tried again to maneuver the trailer into place. In her haste she slammed it into a post, part of the loft's supporting framework. Grain and dust sifted down over her.

She took a deep breath. *Don't be an idiot. They were sounds you probably hear everyday. Sounds that would never bother you otherwise if not for your current state of mind.*

But all at once she'd had enough. She could finish her

rearranging in daylight.

She dropped the tow-bar, feeling the floorboards quake with the impact, and turned for the door. Before she'd taken a single step she felt a movement of air on her neck, and a second thud jolted the soles of her feet. She spun around.

With a hand to her mouth, she stumbled back. She tore her gaze from the object before her and looked to the hayloft. "Who's there?"

Trees rustled faintly out in the yard. A cricket chirped.

"Answer me, damn it! I know someone's up there."

But of course there was no-one. If it had been deliberate, whoever had done it would hardly stick around and wait to be caught.

Reluctantly she lowered her gaze to the pitchfork that had missed her by inches, its handle still quivering from the force of the impact that had imbedded its tines deep in the floor.

CHAPTER 53

They got an early start the next morning. Josh had suggested they take his car and, because hers was overdue for a service, Lauren agreed. A decision for which she was quickly grateful. Watching the scenery streak by her window she felt almost drugged, tired to the point of disorientation. She'd paid a high price for her dreamless night by staying awake for more than half of it. Thank God she didn't have to get behind the wheel.

Ten miles past the bridge to the mainland they stopped for breakfast at a shopping mall diner. After a meal and two cups of coffee she felt a bit better. Though the images flitting at the edge of her mind constantly tried to get her attention.

While Josh used the rest room and grabbed a paper, she went outside to wait in the car. She'd been sitting undecided for several minutes when he finally joined her, but by then she was sure enough to voice her thoughts.

"This may sound crazy but I swear I've seen that car before."

Josh looked across at where she was pointing – the late model Datsun sedan parked two aisles over at the edge of the lot. "Yeah, where?"

"Back on the Cape. Following me."

His gaze swung back to her. "When was this?"

She told him about her car getting dented the week before, that a blue Datsun just like this one had been parked beside her at the time and that she'd later noticed it tailing her along the highway.

"You don't think it just happened to be going the same way as you?"

"I took a few turns and it stayed with me. When I finally pulled over, it drove past, but I'm pretty sure I saw it a couple days later."

"And you're sure it's the same car?"

"Same make, same color, same first three numbers on the license plate. Pretty long odds if it isn't, wouldn't you say?"

He looked back out. "There's someone in it."

Lauren sat forward. Through the glare on the Datsun's windshield she could just make out a silhouette behind the wheel. She hadn't seen anyone get into the car so they had to have been there when she came out. "Why are they just sitting there?"

"Maybe waiting for someone, like you were."

She clamped her jaw. She'd had enough of being afraid. Of jumping at shadows, hearing noises, seeing faces that weren't there. If this was her imagination running riot then damn it all, she wanted to know.

"Let's find out, shall we?" She opened her door.

She'd barely touched her foot to the ground when the Datsun's engine revved to life. It shot from its space and maneuvered out of the diner's sector. She watched it drive the length of the parking lot and exit onto the mall's side road.

"Guess they weren't waiting for anyone," Josh said when she got back in.

Lauren sat thinking. "What kind of car did Claudia drive?"

"A Ford XL. But that doesn't mean that wasn't her." He nodded after the receding Datsun. "Could be her parents' car or a friend's."

She slumped in the seat. Her jolt of adrenalin was already fading, leaving her even more deflated than before.

"Are you okay?"

She lifted her head. "Look, I don't know if it's related or not but…"

Five minutes later when she'd finished relaying the incident in the barn the night before, Josh was sitting staring back at her. "Pardon my French but *Jesus Christ.*"

She laughed. "That was pretty much my reaction."

"Well, what the hell was it doing up there? The pitchfork, I mean."

"I don't know. I can't even remember the last person to use it. It could've been there for weeks. Months. I figure it must've been lying right on the edge and when I banged the post I knocked it over."

She stifled a shudder at the memory of the object falling past her – close enough to feel it stirring her hair – and hitting the floor boards right behind her. Where she'd been standing not two seconds earlier. "At least that's what I want to believe."

"Not to point a finger, but did you ask Simon?"

"Simon never goes up in the loft. He's afraid of heights." She waved a hand. "Look, now that I've told you, I feel a bit foolish. It was a accident. Nobody's following me, no-one's out to *get* me. I've just got a bad case of nerves, that's all."

When he didn't respond, she looked over at him. His reluctant expression twisted her gut. "What?"

"I found something else damaged at work. One of the statues out front by the fountain had its arm broken off."

She pushed herself up. "When did that happen?"

"Can't be sure. I saw it last night when I was leaving. But it could've happened any time and we just didn't notice."

"A customer?"

"Probably."

"But you don't think so."

He blew out a breath. "I found the arm in the bushes twenty feet away. Either the person threw it there or hit it with such force it flew that distance." He gave her a moment to take in his words, then reached down and started the engine. "So are you ready to call the cops yet?"

She studied the side of his face for a moment, the muscle working in that clean-edged jaw, the way his hands were gripping the wheel. Could it be he was actually worried about her?

"This could impact the business, you know," he pointed out. "What if Claudia sets up some ambush and a customer gets hurt?"

She let out her breath. So much for caring. "You're right. I'll do it as soon as we get home."

CHAPTER 54

With her key inserted in the shop door, Mel paused to fumble her phone from her bag. "Hello?"

The voice that responded was barely audible.

"Sorry, can you speak up, I can't—"

"It's Ada. I'm not coming in today."

"You're not..." Mel clenched her teeth to staunch her reaction. The woman couldn't have picked a worse day. "Why? What's wrong?" She checked her watch – fifteen minutes until they opened. "If it's your car, I can come and get you."

"No. I'm sick."

Mel took a breath and counted to five. The woman didn't sound all that sick. She'd been perfectly fine closing time yesterday. "Ada, you know Lauren and Josh are away both today and tomorrow. If you don't come in, it'll just be me and Simon here."

Silence from the other end.

"Look, we really need you. Lauren needs you. Is there any chance you could make it in later, even for just—"

The line disconnected.

Mel fought the urge to hurl her phone down against the

pavers and instead returned it to her bag. She couldn't help feeling Ada's refusal to come to work had less to do with some suddenly acquired illness and more with the conversation they'd had about Lauren yesterday.

Clearly she resented not having been told that Lauren was going away on this trip. For some reason Ada seemed to think she should be privy to Lauren's every move, her every thought. And the look on her face when she'd learned Josh was going as well… Well, it seemed someone had a serious case of the green-eyed monster.

Mel unlocked the door and pushed it open. Of course if she related her feelings to anyone else they'd think she was simply being uncharitable. Was she the only one who could see how peculiar Ada Phelps was?

It wasn't just her original misgivings over Lauren's motives in hiring the woman. It was more than that now. Something she couldn't quite put her finger on. Yes, Ada got along well with Simon. Yes, she was hard working and good with customers. But somewhere deep down, beneath that earnest, caring veneer…

Shaking her head, Mel stepped to the security alarm and disarmed it. Yes, something was definitely wrong with the woman. And the worst of it was – there was no way to prove it.

CHAPTER 55

Lauren inhaled the warm perfumed air. The restaurant where they'd eaten dinner was three blocks down a tree-lined boulevard from the bed and breakfast where they were staying. As they strolled from the hub of the sea-side village, quaint shingled homes replaced craft studios and touristy shops. Sweet Gum and Locust lined the sidewalk, lilac and crab apple dotted the lawns.

At a foot bridge she slowed to take in the view of a tidal channel flowing out to sea. There was nothing waiting for her back in her room – nothing but dreams and a big empty bed. She was more than happy to prolong their walk, admiring the gardens and enjoying the slowly gathering dusk. And the company.

She glanced up at Josh walking beside her, darkly compelling if a little pensive. Their discussion over dinner had been mostly business. They'd rehashed their day of perusing stockists, discovering to their mutual relief they had compatible views on what products to carry. Then they'd moved on to Josh's proposal.

They'd agreed the best way to organize things would be for each of them to manage separate parts of the business. So, *if* they went ahead with the deal, Josh would take over control of the perennials. His initial outlay would buy him all the existing stock and he'd be in charge of every aspect of its management thereafter. Not the full partnership they'd spoken of initially – more of a one quarter/three quarter split – but a place to start and see how things went.

"We should probably talk about staff a bit too."

Lauren looked over, surprised by the statement. She'd hoped they were finished with business for the night. She hadn't considered he might want a say in who they hired and wasn't sure his quarter share would entitle him to one. Still, she was willing to hear his thoughts. "I'm listening."

"I just want to make sure we're on the same page as far as hiring." Perhaps sensing her reservation, he quickly added, "Mel's terrific."

"Yes, she is. I couldn't manage the place without her. She knows how everything works and can step in for me at a moment's notice." *At least until the baby comes.* "I couldn't make this trip every year if it wasn't for her."

He nodded, then fell strangely quiet.

"And?" she prompted.

"Ada seems to be doing okay."

"I agree. She's great with Simon, goes out of her way to make him feel important. She's always patient and never talks down to him."

He pulled at his ear. "Just so I'm clear – that's not your only criteria for hiring workers, is it? Whether or not they're good with Simon?"

"No, of course not, but it is important." She frowned. This seemed to be heading somewhere. "If there's something on your mind, please, just say it."

"All right, here it is then. Why Ada?"

She blinked at him. "Sorry."

"I get where you were coming from firing Claudia. I'm just not sure why you hired Ada instead."

"You just said she was fitting in well."

"She is. But you have to admit that's due more to luck than careful evaluation on your part. I mean isn't the usual process to advertise a position and then choose the best qualified applicant?"

"This late in the season there wouldn't have been any, at least none that I could afford. I can't pay more than minimum wage and the high school kids get snapped up quickly."

"Yes, possibly there was that chance, but you didn't even try. You just hired a woman you hardly know who's never worked a day in her life."

Lauren stopped. "What is everyone's problem with this? Ada's doing a terrific job. What does it matter *why* I hired her?"

"Look, I'm not challenging you on this..."

She laughed. "I'd hate to hear it if you were."

"It's just... Okay, fair enough, Claudia was screwing up left, right and center. But Ada's had some mishaps too – that broken vase, the day her register didn't tally. Why are you prepared to make allowances for some of your workers and not others?"

"I made plenty of allowances for Claudia. More than I should have. But you can only do that up to a point. When it comes right down to it Claudia was a nasty vindictive person. You really want someone working for you who could do what she did to Simon's ducklings?"

"No, I don't."

The answer cut the wind from her sails.

"Look, I didn't want to argue over this," he said. "It's not a big issue. At least not for me."

"What does that mean?"

"It means until I actually am your partner, I've got no say in who you hire and fire. I was just trying to understand your reasoning."

"Yeah?" Mollified, she gave a slight smile. "How's that working out?"

The corner of his mouth lifted slightly. "Haven't heard anything I can't live with." He went on staring, his dark eyes holding her as warmly and closely as if his arms were tight around her. "What do you say we forget about work for the rest of the night."

"Sounds good to me." They'd reached the steps of the bed and breakfast. Lauren looked ahead and spotted a marquee just up the road. "Feel like a movie?"

"Thanks but, I can't. I'm meeting someone."

Her jaw dropped. "Sorry?"

"An old friend of mine lives near here. I gave him a call. We're going to catch up."

It was hard to hide her stunned disappointment and just as maddening that she felt it.

"Don't worry," he said. "I'll be ready to leave in the morning when you are. Just bang on my door when you go down to breakfast." He cocked his head when she didn't reply. "That's okay, isn't it? You didn't have more you wanted to discuss."

"No, I think we've pretty much covered it." She started up the steps. "Have a good night."

CHAPTER 56

"You going to sit in that chair all night or you going to get me something to eat?"

Ada heard the voice as though from a distance. It reached through the darkness pressing around her as it had on and off through most of the day. For stretches the blackness would overtake her and there would be nothing. Blessed silence. But always that unwanted voice would return.

"What the hell are we doing sitting in the dark for? Turn on a light. And while you're at it, go have a shower. Think I want to smell your stink?"

Despite the warning edge to his tone she couldn't stir herself enough to respond. She'd sat unmoving, his words raining down on her like blows, as the hours slowly slithered by.

"If you think this is how it's gonna be from now on, you can forget it. There's things that need doing around here, girl, so get up and do them. Bad enough you didn't go to work today."

"I'm sick."

"Sick, my ass! That bitch, Mel, has you pegged all right. Lazy as shit and twice as ugly."

She closed her eyes. Praying for the blackness to return.

"Aw, are we feeling sorry for ourselves? Poor little fat girl. Lover boy went off with someone else."

Her eyes flew open. How did he know? How did he always know just the right words to use as weapons. These verbal clubs to bludgeon her with.

"Don't know what you're surprised about. The surprise would've been if he *hadn't* gone. You think he'd ever choose you over that?"

She gripped the arm rests, heard the scrape of her nails on the fabric as she balled her fists. Only slowly did the thought fill her mind: this was the way he *used* to talk. Back in the days when she had to listen.

But she didn't have to listen any more.

"Be quiet." She looked toward his silhouette seated on the couch.

"So the guy didn't run when you bent his ear. So he put up with all your mooning over him. You didn't really think that meant anything, did you? More like he lost a friggin' bet."

She reached beside her and flicked on the light, pushed to her feet, and started toward him. "I said, be quiet."

Moments later, catching her breath, she reflected that he'd actually done her a favor. His taunts had goaded her to move past her pain, to choose to fight back. And reminded her the many ways she knew how.

Josh steered the car around the corner and pulled to the curb beneath a street light. Consulting the paper he took from his pocket, he confirmed he was on the right street, then drove on, checking the numbers on mailboxes.

With each house he passed, the knot in his gut pulled a bit tighter. By the time he spotted the one he was looking for, he was just about ready to lose his dinner – what little he'd managed to eat in the first place. Knowing he'd be making this side trip afterwards hadn't exactly whetted his appetite.

Pulling to a stop across the street, he felt his heart rate slow to normal. The lights were off inside the house. Too early for them to be in bed, they had to be out.

He laid his head back against the seat and took a deep breath. Why he'd felt the need to do this after all these years he didn't know. Though he did have a vague understanding *who* might've inspired the urge. And perhaps that was all the answer he needed. If Lauren could face her demons head on and survive her ordeal...

But was she surviving? That was the question. Anyone could see what she was going through – lack of sleep, nightmares, waking visions.

Didn't she realize she had a measure of control over that? Couldn't she see there were things you could do, ways to block out the worst of the horror? To stop it endlessly eating away at you until there was nothing of heart and soul left?

Headlights flashed in his rear-view mirror – a car turning the corner behind him. He gripped the wheel as it came up the street, braced himself as it turned beside him and pulled into the driveway opposite.

The garage door opened, the car pulled in, and beneath the lights that came on inside, a man and woman emerged from the front. The couple stepped out onto the driveway, gazed for a moment in his direction, then proceeded up the path to their door.

Josh sat frozen, clutching the wheel. Despite the changes the years had wrought, he knew them at once. Her raven hair now ghostly pale. His once-proud stride, now stooped and slow. How they had faded. How they had aged.

If only his memories would do the same.

CHAPTER 57

She woke in the dark, gasping for breath, fighting the arms wrapped tight around. "Lauren, it's all right, it's just a dream. It's over, I've got you." A voice she knew.

The light on the bedside table snapped on, revealing the man, the four-poster bed on which they sat, and surroundings only vaguely familiar. She fought to remember.

The buying trip.

Adjoining rooms in a bed and breakfast.

Another nightmare.

"Josh, I'm so sorry. I didn't mean to wake you."

"You didn't. I was just coming back to my room and heard you yell out."

He whispered the words against her hair. She felt the warmth of him through her night gown, caught the faint scent of beer on his lips.

"I thought your nightmares had settled down."

"They had. For a while."

"Something happen to trigger them again?"

She swallowed. Her breath was returning to normal, but composure was still a fair way off. "Yesterday. I ran into Ada's uncle at the nursery – literally ran into him, outside the shop.

He looks so much like Ada's father, for an instant...it was like..."

"Yes, that would do it."

She curled herself into him. "The thing is, the nightmares have changed since I first started having them. I'm still on the ice, on my hands and knees, trying break through. But the face that rises up below me isn't Roger Phelps, it's my father."

"Your father. Why would you dream about him?"

"I think in some way I feel as responsible for what happened to him as what happened to Ada's dad." She explained about her mother's drinking, her father's futile struggle to manage it, the years he'd kept it all secret from her, hoping to spare her.

"But how does that make you responsible?"

"I doesn't, I *know* that. Still a part of me thinks...because I wasn't there when he died. Because I didn't come home like I promised. If I had, I would've seen what was happening and been able to stop it."

"Lauren, how could—?"

"By getting my mother the help she needed, the help they both needed. Don't you see? All my dad cared about was the two of us, and in our separate ways we both deserted him."

He drew her close, held her until her shudders subsided. "Well, at least you know what you have to do now. How to finally end this." When she looked up puzzled, he frowned right back. "You still don't see? How can you not? I'm talking about Ada."

"What about her?"

"What about her?" He gave a slight laugh. "Lauren, every day you see the woman is contributing to what you're going through? *She's* the reason you can't move on and forget what happened. If you want this to ever be over, you're going to have to put some distance between you."

"What kind of distance?"

"Letting her go would be a start."

She pulled from his arms. "Fire Ada? You can't be serious."

"You fired Claudia easily enough." He swung his legs off the side of the bed.

"Claudia was a terrible worker. Ada is..." Suddenly their conversation earlier took on new meaning. His issue wasn't about workers in general, it was about her hiring one in particular. "Josh, I can't."

"Can't or won't?"

She steeled herself, knowing somehow, for a reason she didn't yet comprehend, she would be losing him with her answer. "All right, won't."

He stood for a moment gazing down at her. Then, as she'd feared, he turned away, crossed to the door between their two rooms. "Then I guess you'll just have to get used to nightmares."

CHAPTER 58

Braced against the check-out counter, Ada bent to massage her calves. It was the first quiet moment they'd had all day. She'd been on her feet since early that morning and her legs were killing her, her headache much worse.

She should never have agreed to come into work. Though she certainly felt better than yesterday, having to wait another whole day before Josh returned… Well, this was the worst place she could be. Everywhere she looked she saw evidence of him, reminding her how much she missed him. And how furious she was that he had left.

To make matters worse, Mel was being an absolute cow. Not that she'd ever been overly friendly. But this morning when Ada had first arrived, she could've sworn she'd heard Mel mutter 'good of you to join us' under her breath.

Since then the woman had spent most of her time outside watering, claiming that on a warm day like this the seedlings needed constant moisture. That left Ada and Simon to do all the *real* work of dealing with customers. And whenever Mel had come inside, she seemed to watch everything Ada did like she was hoping to catch her making a mistake.

Ada grabbed the box from under the counter and walked

around to the seed carousel. In her spare moments she was supposed to sort the packs on display and fill in any that were running low. But handling the vegetable varieties only made her think of Josh on the tractor, plowing the garden.

She jammed a fistful of packets on the stand and turned away. She couldn't decide who she was angrier with – Lauren for inviting him to go on the trip, or Josh for accepting the invitation.

He shouldn't have gone. Not that she doubted him. Well, she might have for a moment or two, but that was just foolish insecurity. He would never be untrue to their love, she could see that now. What they had was too special. His trip with Lauren was purely business. Still, it could give people the wrong idea. Didn't Lauren see that? What was wrong with her? This woman who called herself a friend.

Ada slammed the seed box down on the counter. Josh was hers. She'd waited so long. What had Lauren done to deserve him? What had she done to deserve any of what she had? Wasn't it enough she had looks, a great home, caring friends, a thriving business? Wasn't that enough for one person!

"I brought you something."

The words startled her and she spun around. Simon held out a mug of tea then set it on the counter beside her. Idiot. She hated tea. And even if she liked it, her headache was so bad she felt a bit woozy; she couldn't put anything in her stomach.

"Thanks," she muttered, praying he would just leave her alone. The only good thing about having been busy was that she hadn't had to put up with him much.

He followed as she started back around the counter. "You're sad today."

"It's just a headache."

"No, you're sad, I can tell. And I know why."

She stopped in her tracks. Though Josh, in his own way, had made his feelings clear to her, he hadn't yet proclaimed them openly. Had he confided them to Simon? "You do?"

"Because Lauren's not here. It's lonely when your friends go away."

Even as she slumped, she clenched her teeth. What did a moron know about loneliness? "That's it, you guessed it."

He beamed at having solved the puzzle. "We should do something to make you happy. I know, let's sing!"

"Oh no, I'm not a very good—"

"Row, row, row your boat...!"

Ada winced at the off-key rendition. She tried to interrupt, but he just kept singing. He started waving his hands in the air, urging her to join him by conducting the beat.

"Simon, I don't—"

"Merrily, merrily, merrily, merrily...!"

She turned and continued around the counter. Simon followed right behind her repeating his refrain. The sound went through her head like a mallet. "Simon—"

"Gently down the—"

"Stop it!" In whirling to face him her arm caught the mug he'd left on the counter.

Mel came through the shop door in time to see it crash to the floor. She never broke stride as she walked toward the office. "Get to that quickly, there's customers on their way to check out."

"It was an accident." Ada stared at the mess, incredulous.

Mel paused at the seed carousel and straightened the packets she'd just put out. "Not saying it wasn't. Just get some paper towels from the kitchen and make sure you pick up all the pieces."

"But if it wasn't my fault, why should I have to clean it up?"

"I can do it!"

"No, Simon, you stay right there." Mel spoke the words while keeping her gaze locked on Ada. "Ada had the accident, she cleans it up. That's how it works."

Mel held her gaze a moment longer then turned and walked off.

Ada slipped into the nursery office an hour later and moved quickly to the window. Outside she could see Mel watering, giving the seedlings a thorough soaking to counter the heat of the afternoon sun.

Keeping the woman in sight the whole time, she grabbed the address book from the desk, looked up Mel's home telephone number and called it using Lauren's phone.

After two rings her call was picked up. "Peter Haynes speaking."

She adopted her most formal 'secretary' voice. "Mr. Haynes, this is Karen Thompson calling. I'm ringing to advise you that, after careful consideration, the directors have decided you aren't quite right for the position."

Silence from the other end. "But I...I thought Mr. Letterman was planning to get back to me himself."

"Yes, he had intended to, but unfortunately he's been called away. You'll be contacted by mail, of course, but he asked me to let you know in the meantime."

Another pause, then, "Right. Fine. Thank you for calling. Please tell Mr. Letterman should he ever—"

Ada set the phone gently back in its cradle. The precaution of silence was hardly necessary. She could still see Mel outside watering and Simon was busy in the shop with a customer. And even if he did come into the room she could always give him some excuse why she'd needed to use the phone. Simon was so easy to fool.

She smiled as she stared out at Mel. Her husband had answered after only two rings, suggesting he'd been sitting by the phone. Clearly every bit as anxious about landing this job as Mel had told Lauren in the workroom the other day.

As she turned for the door, Ada's smile grew. Even if the real people contacted him later and offered him the job, her call would no doubt serve its purpose.

Knowing the nursery's gates had been locked at closing time, Lauren directed Josh to drive up the private lane at the back of her property. Her house lights winked on as they pulled to a stop in front of the garage; the ones inside, set on a timer, had come on at dusk.

Beside her, Josh made no move to get out of the car and simply sat with the motor running. On this, their second and final day of the buying trip, he'd been somewhat subdued. Courteous enough, yet subtly distant, keeping the door firmly closed on what had almost happened last night. Or at least what she thought might have almost happened.

She'd been stunned, grateful and deeply moved when he'd come to her room to comfort her. In his arms she'd found more than solace, in his touch, the desire she wished they would share. Yet moments later when he'd returned to his room, he'd left her thoroughly confused.

On the surface his words had been plain enough, but she'd sensed there was something more beneath them, something he was reluctant to confide. Pressing him about it didn't feel right. She could only do her best to keep channels open and hope he'd trust her enough to tell her.

"Would you like a cup of coffee before you head off?" It wasn't that she needed him to walk her inside, more the selfish wish to prolong his company.

"Thanks, but it would only keep me awake. I assume we're putting in a full day tomorrow."

She smiled. "As much as I'd like to give us both the day off, it wouldn't be fair to the others."

"No. Better make it an early one then."

"Yeah. Me too." With her hand on the door, she stopped and looked over at him. "Thank you."

"For what?"

She hesitated. So many things she wanted to say. "For coming along. Doing all the driving. It was nice to have company for a change." Cautiously neutral. Grossly inadequate.

He nodded. "You're welcome."

CHAPTER 59

Blades of sunlight slanted through the trees, gilding the headstones in the first glow of dawn.

He had to be out of his mind to come here. Yet from the moment he'd opened his eyes that morning – perhaps even sooner, if his dreams were any indication – he'd felt the pull. He had an important decision to make and somehow this seemed the appropriate place to think it over.

Josh walked slowly among the rows. At the grave he stopped and stood staring down at it. Lichen had grown across part of the name but the dates were clear.

His stomach clenched. So short a life.

He squatted and pulled a weed from the paving, straightened the vase of plastic flowers. In a pile of leaves he found the drumsticks, bleached as bones from their years in the open, and set them back on top of the stone.

How could Lauren have managed to wake this ghost he'd worked so hard to bury? What she was going through – what she insisted on putting herself through – was all so horribly, if distantly, familiar. Through her striving to make amends, she was forcing him to question again whether he'd done enough in his situation.

How could he feel what he did for the woman when she brought back such wrenching memories? How could he ever reconcile two such strongly opposing needs?

The answer was, he couldn't. Not any more.

When he'd initially made Lauren his offer, he'd been certain he'd be able to keep his distance. But the more he got to know her, the harder that became. Holding her in her room that night, touching her skin, breathing her scent... The bare fact was, he was falling in love with her.

Which left him with only one alternative.

Lauren headed down to the nursery at seven, determined to get an early start. Though she'd only been away two days there was sure to be a dozen emails to answer and new orders for arrangements to fill. Key in hand, she rounded the building and stopped at the sight of the shop door standing slightly ajar.

She stood for a moment then took a step closer. No sounds from inside. The yard around her looked intact, nothing disturbed. Had Mel come in early? If so, why? In payment for the two days she'd held the fort, Lauren had given her the morning off. The woman's one and only text hadn't mentioned there'd been any problems.

Lauren leaned to peer through the crack. The lights weren't on, so unless Mel had arrived only seconds ago this couldn't be her. She grabbed a garden gnome from the flower bed, stepped through the door, and flicked on the lights.

A sea of debris stretched before her clear to the opposite wall of the shop. Wind chimes and the frame that had held them lay in a hopeless tangle at her feet. To her right, the glass display case and all its contents had been smashed, and on the shelves to her left, plastic containers of liquid fertilizer leaked their contents through multiple stab wounds.

She could only imagine the destruction awaiting her deeper inside – the office, the workshop, the flowers in the fridges... She winced at the thought.

Fearful of destroying evidence – or worse, that the culprit was still on the scene – Lauren slowly backed from the room. She pulled out her phone and called the police.

With the break-in reported, she scrolled through her contacts, pausing briefly at Josh's number. She couldn't deny there was no-one she wanted more to see in that moment, no-one's voice she wanted more to hear.

She scrolled back and dialed Mel instead.

Josh spotted the police car the minute he turned in the nursery entrance. Lauren had said she was going to call them regarding the on-going trouble with Claudia but he hadn't expected her to do it this soon. Unless something else had happened last night.

At the thought it might have been more than vandalism – another pitchfork incident or worse – he skidded to a stop in his parking space, jumped from the car and ran through the archway.

Lauren stood to one side of the yard, deep in conversation with a plain-clothed officer. Seeing her safe, he reined himself back before starting toward them.

In passing, he looked through the open shop door, his relief dissolving at the sight of the destruction within. A second officer stood taking photographs of the wreckage – an extreme show of temper even for Claudia.

A chill slithered over him. A woman capable of this much hatred... Even with all he'd gone through with his business, he'd never come up against something like this. Had Claudia been the one they'd seen in the mall parking lot on their trip?

Was she stalking Lauren outside the nursery? The thought was more than a little unsettling.

He looked back at Lauren, trying to judge how she was coping. On top of all her other concerns this couldn't be easy. By outward appearances she seemed to be doing reasonably well. Yet outward appearances could be deceiving.

"Josh, this is Detective Olsen," she said as he walked over to join them. "Detective, this is one of my employees, Josh Stedman."

Josh shook hands with the tall, thin, middle-aged man, and submitted to a short bout of questioning.

As Olsen recorded the answers he'd given, Josh reached over and touched Lauren's arm. "Are you okay?"

She gave a brave smile.

"I assume we're thinking this was Claudia again. You give him the story?"

She nodded. "I have."

"The pitchfork in the barn? The car you've been seeing?"

"Everything, yes."

Frowning, Josh looked back toward the shop. "The door's intact. No windows are broken." He turned to Olsen. "How'd she get in?"

"That's about the only thing we do know right now." Olsen finished and closed his notebook. "There was no forced entry. Whoever did this simply walked in."

CHAPTER 60

Ada stood in the shop doorway, feigning a look of shocked dismay as she surveyed the carnage. She was getting quite good at producing the proper reaction on demand.

She wove a course through the debris to where Lauren stood sweeping up broken glass. "You poor thing, you must be devastated. Why don't you come and sit down for a while."

"I can't, I have to get started on this, otherwise it'll take forever."

"Well just sit down for a little while and then you and I can do it together."

Lauren let the broom be taken from her hands. The police were just finishing up outside and had given her the okay to start the clean-up. Between answering their questions, searching the grounds for further damage, and the job ahead of her – not to mention the conversation with Mel she was dreading – she wouldn't mind some time to regroup. "Yes, all right. Just for a minute."

In the kitchen she sat at the table while Ada busied herself at the counter. The woman returned, took the seat next to her and set two steaming mugs in front of them.

"There. Just like when I dropped that vase. You brought

me in here and made me a nice cup of coffee to settle me down. You remember that?"

"Yes, I remember."

"You were so nice. More concerned that I might have cut myself than with the damage I caused." Ada rested a hand on her arm. "You've always been nice to me. Nicer than anyone else ever has. I want to be nice to you for a change."

"Thank you. I appreciate it."

Ada sipped her coffee to hide her surprise. She'd spoken her words intending to deceive, but as they left her lips she realized she meant them. She *did* still want to be close to Lauren, to believe in this magical thing called friendship, a treasure she knew so little of. If she could only be sure the woman hadn't tried to steal Josh away from her...

"Why don't you tell me about your trip, get your mind off things."

Lauren took a moment to focus. "It was okay. A nice drive at this time of year."

"Did Josh enjoy himself?"

"As much as possible I suppose. After all, it was business, not a vacation."

Ada brightened. "Yes, of course."

"Usually I make the trip alone, but since Josh had talked about buying in, I thought it might be a good opportunity—"

"Buying in?"

"Yes, he's thinking of investing in the business. We're still discussing it."

Ada felt her hopes dissolving. She'd been starting to think her fears were ungrounded, only to be struck by this new possibility. "You mean...the two of you would be partners?"

"Like I said, nothing's definite. There's still a few things we need to sort out. Neither of us wants to rush into anything."

"No, that's wise." Ada took another swallow of coffee and pushed to her feet. "Well, I'll go get started on that mess. You sit here as long as you like and if there's anything else you need, just call me."

Lauren reached out and squeezed her hand. "Thank you, Ada. You're a good friend."

Before she could answer, another figure swooped into the kitchen, face streaked with tears. "Oh, Lauren, I am so sorry."

As Ada walked out, Mel took the empty seat beside Lauren. Though the police had just taken Mel's statement, Lauren hadn't yet heard her explanation for why the shop door hadn't been locked.

"What happened?" she asked gently. As bad as things were, there was no point hurling accusations.

"The first night you were away, I did what you said and checked that Simon had locked up everything – which he had. But then…last night…" The tears got away from her and she bowed her head.

Lauren leaned closer. "It's okay. Don't worry we'll get past this; just tell me what happened."

The woman straightened. "I was closing up. Simon had already left and I was about to go around after him when I got a call that Peter was arrested."

"What? *Peter?*"

"He found out he didn't get the job in Portland and I guess he just snapped. He went out and got drunk, drove into a telephone pole coming home, and got arrested for DUI."

"My god, is he all right?"

"Physically, yeah. Emotionally…" She shook her head. "Anyway when I got the call, I didn't even think, I just ran out."

"Of course you would, so would anyone. How bad is your car?"

"It was towed away. I haven't even gone to look at it yet." A frown creased her brow. "Lauren, I could swear I locked the archway gate at least before I left, but in the state I was in… Please, don't blame Simon. It wasn't his fault, it was—"

Lauren gripped her hand to silence her. "Checking on Simon is something we never have to do ordinarily and there's only one reason we're having to now. The only person I'm blaming is Claudia."

CHAPTER 61

Oh, Lauren, I am so sorry.

Ada couldn't keep the smile from her face as she strode from the shop out into the yard. All afternoon, through the tedious hours of cleaning up the mess, Mel's stricken words had rung in her ears.

Peter's reaction to her bogus phone call the day before had accomplished all she'd hoped for and more. What had started as simple payback, a way to get even with Mel for her bitchiness, had turned into a chance to make both Mel and Simon look bad.

The timing had been perfect. Mel had gotten word of her husband's arrest just as they were finishing for the day and Ada had seized on the woman's distraction by taking the keys from Lauren's desk. She'd returned hours later, unlocked all the doors Simon had locked and indulged her every grudge and frustration trashing the shop, leaving everyone to think Claudia had done it.

But of course the real guilty party was Mel. Though the drama had yielded the additional bonus of making Simon appear incompetent, Claudia would never have gained access if Mel had remembered to check on his actions.

Ada stifled her delighted laugh at recalling the conversation she'd overheard standing outside the kitchen door: Mel trying to explain her failure, Lauren pretending she understood, when surely she must hate the woman. Yes, hearing Mel's tearful confession had kept Ada smiling to herself all day.

Still, it wasn't enough. Not after the way Mel had treated her. Making her grovel, making her feel so second rate, so inadequate. Not even destroying that abiding friendship, not even getting Peter arrested, was enough of a payback for that.

But the *next* part of her plan surely would be.

Her smile returned as she headed for the archway. The only thing detracting from her current mood were her lingering uncertainties regarding Josh. And even that couldn't dull her hopes entirely. They just needed to sort things out.

She found him out front loading statues into a wheelbarrow. "Welcome home. First chance I've had to say that to you. Sorry it's not under better circumstances."

"Thanks. Me too." He straightened with a mermaid cradled in his arms. "Everything going okay inside?"

"Well, the mess is cleaned up. We loaded it all in that trailer you left outside the back door. Lauren's still calculating the damage bill."

"That could take a while." He laid the statue gently in the barrow. "How are things otherwise? Everyone okay?"

She felt her cheeks redden. It was so like him to ask how she was. "Yes, thank you. It was tough work though. And I suppose, technically, I didn't have to help since it isn't my job. But I couldn't let Lauren do it alone. Still, I'm pretty exhausted now."

"I don't doubt it. But Lauren's all right otherwise you think?"

She bristled at hearing the name on his lips. "She's fine."

"And Simon and Mel?"

"Simon's pretty quiet. He's upset about what happened but I don't think he understands he was to blame. Lauren hasn't explained it to him yet. Or that she's given his locking up job to me."

His gaze swung toward her. "She has?"

"Well, you can hardly blame her. She can't very well let him keep doing it; not after this. She needs someone responsible, someone she can count on."

He turned to the next of the row of statues. "I suppose."

"As for Mel, she feels just awful and isn't saying much. In a way, she's more to blame than Simon. Still..." She brightened. "We'll get through this together, won't we. After all, we're a team."

"Yes, we are."

She smiled at his confirmation. Like most things, they were on the same wavelength. She watched him pick up another statue. "So what has she got you doing out here?"

"Lauren wants to move these inside the gate."

Ada scanned the figures lined up on either side of the entrance. "What, *all* of them?"

He gave a laugh. "It'll keep me busy for a couple of days, but better than letting them all get smashed."

"With Claudia around, it's probably not a bad idea." She waited a moment then took a deep breath. The moment of truth. "So how was your trip?"

"About what I expected. Displays, inventory, ordering stock. Mostly business."

Her spine went rigid. *Mostly* business? "Where did you stay?"

Having filled the barrow, Josh stepped around it to take up

the handles. "A bed and breakfast."

"Sounds…intimate."

He aimed the barrow for the archway and paused. "Lauren had her room, I had mine. Like I said – business."

Ada exhaled as she watched him walk off. In that one simple statement he'd addressed all her fears. What more of a declaration did she need? Clearly he had no feelings for Lauren. She'd been wrong to doubt him even for a second.

CHAPTER 62

Josh was three steps from the office door when a stocky figure hurtled out and crashed into him, knocking him back. He put out a hand to steady them both. "Hey, buddy, what's up?"

Crying audibly, Simon pulled away and hurried past him through the shop and out the door. Josh watched him go, debated briefly whether to follow, then blew out a sigh and entered the office.

Lauren stood with her back to him, staring out the window. He waited, wondering if she knew he was there or whether it might just be better to leave.

He'd decided on the latter and was turning away when he heard her whisper.

"You know what the worst thing was about today? It wasn't the mess or the lost inventory. It wasn't knowing that somewhere out there there's a person who hates me enough to do such a thing. It isn't even the sickening experience of feeling unsafe in my own home. It was having to tell Simon..."

When her words trailed off he moved a step closer. "Ada said you asked her to take over the job of locking up at night. I gather you just told him?"

"I told him."

Lauren shut her eyes. She could still hear Simon's anguished words: *No! I didn't forget! I locked the door. I locked them all. I know I did!"*

"He denied he forgot?"

"Yes. But what other explanation is there for the no-forced entry?"

"I've been thinking about that. Is there any way Claudia could've stolen a key before she left here?"

She turned at last, her eyes red-rimmed. "Olsen asked me that as well. I told him it's possible, but highly unlikely."

"Why unlikely? How many copies of the keys do you have?"

"Three. Mel has a set in case of emergency and I have two – one's a spare I keep at the house, the other I use to get in every morning and leave in the top drawer." She pointed to her desk. "They're all accounted for."

"Is your drawer kept locked?"

"No, but there's almost always someone in here."

"*Almost* always. And no-one would think twice of an employee wandering in here in any case."

"Unless it was Claudia. I never did trust her."

"Even so, conceivably she could've gotten away with it. She could've snuck in here, taken the key, had it copied when she went out for lunch, and returned it later before it was missed."

"The question is, why? Why would she have been planning a break-in *before* I fired her. If her vandalism is purely payback for what she considers my unfair treatment..."

"Maybe it isn't. Maybe she's got some other grievance against you."

"Great." She slumped. "I hadn't even considered that."

For a moment she looked so defeated, so utterly spent, he

nearly reached out. She looked up at last. "I'll let Olsen know your theory. You could be right. Was there anything else?"

His imagination or did she look hopeful? The decision he'd made pressed at his lips, but after all she'd been through today he couldn't bring himself to speak it. Tomorrow would be soon enough. If he could keep his distance till then.

"I just wanted to make sure you're okay."

"Well, I've certainly been better." She forced a smile. "But, yes, thank you, I'll be all right."

Ada turned away from the office and raced up the hallway to the shop. The conversation on which she'd just eavesdropped filled her with such joyful energy she was back at her station behind the counter by the time Josh emerged from the corridor.

Head down, clearly unaware of her presence, he marched for the door.

"Josh?" she said, stopping him dead.

She rushed out from behind the counter and stood in his path, wringing her hands. Two weeks ago, even two days, she'd never have had the courage for this. But knowing he'd just walked away from Lauren, seeing the proof with her own eyes that there was nothing between them, gave her the strength to take this step in the direction she now knew they were headed.

Gazing up into his stunning blue eyes, eyes endearingly surprised and confused, she blurted her words. "There's a craft fair in Hadley Common this weekend. I wonder if you'd like to go to it with me?"

He blinked for a moment, uncomprehending, then shook his head. "Sorry, I can't. I've got something else on this weekend. Another time maybe."

CHAPTER 63

Lauren savored the satisfying slap of her running shoes against the asphalt. At a steady but not-too-taxing clip, she moved from one pool of streetlight to the next.

She'd have much preferred to run on the beach. But with all that was happening, and especially after the day she'd had, she hadn't dared leave the house after dark unless to a public well-lit area. The familiar streets of her neighborhood seemed the safest option.

Running at night wasn't her first choice in any case. But she needed to get out and clear her head. To rid herself of the stress of recent events and thoughts of one encounter in particular. Yet no matter how far or fast she had run, the latter had followed her on every turn.

That afternoon, as Josh had stood before her in her office, she'd been sure there was something he'd wanted to say. As she had at the bed and breakfast two nights ago – was it only two nights? It seemed so much longer – she'd sensed something more had been about to happen. And then, just like that, with no provocation she could see, he'd simply said his goodbye and left.

She'd almost gone after him, run up the hall, dragged him

back and insisted he tell her what was wrong. Because something was clearly on his mind. She could almost see the gears turning, the pros and cons of whatever it was being carefully weighed every time he looked in her eyes. Or at least she thought she could.

Could she be that wrong about a man? She wasn't an expert by any stretch but she could generally tell when one was interested. Josh was as unreadable as a blank page. One minute he seemed poised to reach out to her, the next he couldn't get away fast enough.

Had she done or said something to put him off? Given him some signal to keep his distance that she wasn't aware of? Looking back over the time she'd known him there seemed a long string of missed connections, unexplained reactions. Either there was something eating at him or she hadn't a clue how to read him.

As she rounded the last bend heading home, a mile of straight road stretched before her. With cranberry bogs on either side and moonlight dancing across its surface, it beckoned her on, a trafficless runway from which to take off. She'd settled into a soothing rhythm, and as the endorphins at last kicked in, she felt her mind clearing.

This was the feeling, the reason she ran. For this sense of space and freedom. She'd worried her encounter with Theodore Phelps might rob her of it again. But so far, on this, her first run since that incident happened, she'd felt not the slightest twinge of cramp. Perhaps she was over that trauma at last.

Or new ones had temporarily overshadowed it.

The lane leading up to the drive to her house had just come in sight when she heard a car approaching behind her. As it got nearer, she found herself tracking the sound of its engine, listening for any sudden acceleration. It passed without any untoward sign.

She watched the tail lights fading before her, growing distant. Slowly her peace and composure returned.

Until the lights swung an arc across the road and headlights started coming back at her.

She slowed to a stop. Frozen like the proverbial deer, she squinted into the strengthening beam. Someone lost? Missed their turn? Looking for an unfamiliar address? She wasn't waiting around to find out.

The lane she'd passed a short way back seemed her best bet. With houses close on either side she'd have help if she needed it. To the sound of the engine growing louder behind her – her imagination, or was it accelerating? – she ducked up the lane.

Two houses along, she stopped and turned in time to see the car drive sedately past. She stood for a moment catching her breath then looked ahead again. The lane came out on another road that would lead her home; might as well keep going this way.

At the end she paused to look both ways. The street was deserted. Houses aglow in their spacious yards, cars parked at the edge of their lawns. Her safe, comfortable, familiar neighborhood.

She'd just turned in the direction of home when light splashed her silhouette on the road before her. The rev of an engine. She spun back and winced at the blinding headlights hurtling toward her. With no time even to leap from its path, she braced for an impact that never came.

The car screeched to a stop beside her. "You fucking bitch. Where do you get off telling the cops I trashed your shop?"

Lauren stood gasping, as stunned by her near-miss as the girl's sudden appearance. "Claudia?"

"They were at my house for over an hour. My parents were freaked."

Anger ignited like a match in haystack. "And you're blaming *me* for that?"

"I didn't do it! And if you don't stop telling them I did—"

"What about the statue and bird bath out by my fountain." Lauren stepped closer. "You telling me you didn't break those either?"

"I don't know what you're talking about. I never touched—"

"Like you never slashed those bags of fertilizer or graffitied my sign?"

The girl's look changed, growing almost prideful. "All right maybe that was me. But you'll never prove it."

"The police haven't finished investigating yet. Maybe they will. Maybe they'll prove you did the other things too. The fact you've been stalking me for two weeks certainly gives them a reason to try."

"Stalking you? What—?"

"I'm sure they'll be very interested to know you're harassing me now as well. Verbal abuse, threats, nearly running me down in the street."

The girl leaned out, made a show of looking around them, then smiled up at her. "I don't see any witnesses, do you?" Gunning the engine, she roared away.

CHAPTER 64

Too shaken to run, Lauren walked the rest of the way home. The entire way she debated who she'd call first when she got there – the police, Mel, or the only person she really wanted to.

By the top of her driveway she'd made her decision. But rounding the house she was stunned to find the man himself standing in the light outside her back door.

"Looking for me?" She stepped into the open.

Josh turned around. "Didn't think anyone was home."

Just the sight of him lifted her spirits. The fact he'd actually come to her house… "I went for a run. Just getting back." She was drawing breath to tell him what happened but something in his expression stopped her. "What's wrong?"

"Nothing. Nothing to do with the shop that is. It's just I've been thinking."

I've been thinking. Never the best words to start a conversation, especially with a guy.

She pulled out her key. "Come in, we'll talk about it."

"No, I won't stay. I just wanted…" He took a breath and tried again, this time managing to meet her gaze. "About my offer to buy into the business."

A trap door opened in the pit of her stomach. "You're having second thoughts."

"We agreed nothing was finalized, right? It was all in the preliminary discussion stage."

She gave him a moment to writhe on his hook. "I gather there's been some change of plan."

"Another option's opened up for me. I won't go into details other than to say it's something I've wanted for a long time."

Something you couldn't have gotten with me. She forced out her words. "Well, that's terrific." *For one of us anyway.*

"After what happened today at work I was going to leave it till tomorrow to tell you. Then I got home and thought more about it and...I know the timing's pretty lousy but..."

She stifled a laugh.

"I decided it would be worse to wait."

"I agree. I'm glad you told me."

"Are you upset?"

"Upset, no. Disappointed, sure. But, hey, that's business."

He studied her face. "There's something else."

It was like seeing the headlights rushing toward her all over again.

"I thought you should know I intend to give notice at the end of the summer."

This time there was a definite impact.

"I'll stick around till you close for the season but then I'm moving on."

"I see."

They stared at each other.

"Okay. Well." She nodded. "Thank you for letting me know all that. You're right it would've been worse to leave it. Always better to keep things out in the open, I say."

"You are upset."

"Look, forget it, it's just one of those things. Like you said, we never finalized anything. Nothing you can do."

He stood for a moment then turned to his car, opened the door and picked something up off his front seat.

She stared at the box he held out to her. Her father's baseball. "No, that's yours. You bought it remember."

"I want you to have it."

She gritted her teeth to hold in the words, the ones she truly wanted to speak. "You hang onto it. When I get the money, I'll buy it back."

CHAPTER 65

Lauren came into the nursery kitchen and spotted Josh from across the room. She hadn't meant to seek him out but as always her gaze gravitated to him.

For a second she thought about walking out again, reluctant to face him this early in the day – they hadn't even opened yet – and after their difficult exchange last night. But Mel was standing at the counter beside him and it was Mel she'd come to the kitchen to see.

The hell with it. She wasn't about to start trying to avoid him. If they were going to finish out the season together she'd just better deal with what had happened.

She started toward them. "Guess who I ran into last night?"

When the pair turned around she nearly stopped again, this time in reaction to Mel's appearance. The woman's normally glowing complexion was ghostly pale making the circles beneath her eyes even darker. Morning sickness or the burden of what she felt responsible for?

"Who?" Mel prompted.

Lauren recovered. "I went for a jog and ran into Claudia."

They stared, incredulous, as she told them about the car

that had nearly run her down and the conversation she'd had with the driver.

"When did all this happen?" Josh said when she'd finished.

"About eight o'clock."

He regarded her over the rim of his coffee mug. Clearly he'd worked out it had happened before they'd had their talk and was wondering why she hadn't mentioned it. Did he feel bad that he hadn't supported her? Or grateful he'd been spared that onerous task?

"Was she driving the Datsun?" he said.

"No, some kind of silvery wagon. I didn't see the make."

"Doesn't mean it wasn't her we saw in that parking lot on the trip."

"Or the other times that car's been tailing me."

"Hang on a minute," Mel interrupted. "Someone's been following you and this is the first I'm hearing about it?"

"I wasn't sure." She threw up a hands. "Hell, I'm still not sure."

"So did you believe what Claudia told you?" Mel said. "That she didn't trash the shop?"

"I don't know. She readily confessed to the fertilizer bags and graffitying the sign yet denied the break-in or damaging the statues. Why would she admit to some things and not others?"

"I'll tell you why." Josh drained the last of his coffee. "Because breaking and entering's a far more serious charge than vandalism. She caused a hell of a lot more damage in the shop." He rinsed his mug and set it in the strainer. "I'll go open up."

Lauren turned to Mel the instant he'd left. "Are you all right? You don't look well."

"Someone's stalking you, you nearly get run down in the street, and you're asking me if *I'm* all right?"

"I told the police and they're looking into it. I'm more concerned about you at the moment. Honestly, Mel, you're very pale."

"It's nothing. That remedy I was taking for morning sickness doesn't seem to be working any more. Either that or I picked up some virus." She waved a hand. "In any case it's not that bad, I'll be all right."

"No, forget it. If you're not feeling well I want you to go home. Take the day off."

"But there's still so much to do after yesterday."

"Never mind that. Ada's coming in after lunch so she'll help me. You need to rest. In fact take tomorrow off as well." When the woman looked away, Lauren took her arm. "Hey, what is it?"

"Things aren't good at home right now. Peter and I..." She shook her head. "We had a really big fight last night. He accused me of not being careful enough to prevent...you know, the baby."

"I thought he was okay with the pregnancy." Lauren slid an arm around her.

"So did I. Like an idiot I didn't realize how much more stress he was feeling about the job thing. You know he actually got a second call from the Portland people telling him he didn't make it. As if the first call wasn't enough! And now... Well, getting arrested won't exactly improve his chances of landing another one, will it?" She gave a weak smile. "So if it's all the same, I'd rather stick around here today. If you can stand the sight of me."

Lauren held her close for a moment then stepped back. "Whatever you want. But light jobs only. And you come in here and rest whenever you need to."

Outside, Lauren went looking for Simon. He'd arrived and gone straight to work without stopping in to greet everyone as he normally did. That was a bad enough sign on its own, but seeing him standing alone in the yard, despondently performing his chore of watering, made her heart ache. This was turning into his worst summer ever. First the ducklings and now losing his precious locking-up job.

"Simon, can I talk to you a minute."

Instead of his usual eager smile he simply shut off the hose and dropped it. He wandered lethargically over to join her and plunked down on the bench beside her. She couldn't bear to see him this way.

"Simon, there's something important I have to ask you. It's about a special job I need someone to do and I want to know if you would consider it."

As she'd hoped, that got his attention. "How special is it?"

"Very special. Without someone to do this job the nursery could be in serious trouble."

His eyes got bigger. "As special as locking the doors at night?"

"Every bit. Possibly even a little more. Want to hear what it is?"

He nodded.

"Well, you know that Mel's going to have a baby."

A smile twitched at the corner of his mouth. "She's going to get fat and we'll be able to feel the baby kicking right through her stomach."

"That's right. What you might not know is that when a woman is going to have a baby it's not good for her to do certain things."

"Like what?"

"Well, like picking up anything heavy for one. Another is reaching, stretching up high, like to put something up on a shelf. And she especially shouldn't do both together."

Simon frowned in intense concentration.

"That means that for the rest of the summer Mel won't be able to help me deliver any orders for hanging baskets – the ones we do for cafes and restaurants. They're too heavy for her to lift and she can't go up a ladder to hang them. So, I'll need someone else to help me with that."

She waited as he connected the dots. Then the explosion. "I could do it!"

"Oh, Simon, that would be such a help. Thank you. The job is officially yours. I'll let you know as soon as the next order comes in."

She left him grinning from ear to ear. Nothing lifted her spirits more than Simon's smile.

CHAPTER 66

Lauren heard the shout through the office window – an outburst not of anger but pain. She dropped her lunch, shot to her feet behind her desk, and ran from the room.

She reached the shop just as Simon burst in from the yard. "Josh got hurt! Josh got hurt!" She calmed him and followed him back outside.

Beyond the archway several customers stood in a cluster. In their midst she found Josh sprawled on the gravel clutching his knee, the wheelbarrow in pieces beside him.

"What happened?" she said, kneeling down.

"Must've overloaded the barrow." Gritting his teeth, he nodded at the statues he'd been preparing to move, now lying smashed just inches away. "Damn thing collapsed and fell against my leg."

"You think it's broken?"

"No." He struggled to unclench his jaw. "Just over-extended. I'll be okay."

Lauren frowned. Over-extended? The cry she'd heard suggested a far worse injury than that. Still, the limb had no odd angles she could see, no bones sticking out.

She pushed to her feet, thanked the customers for their

help and dispersed the group. When she turned back, Josh was holding out his hand. She and Simon took an arm each and pulled him up. He stood on one leg, balanced between them, touched his other foot to the ground, and let out a curse.

Lauren pulled her phone from her pocket.

"What are you doing?"

"Calling an ambulance. I think we'd better get you checked out."

"Don't be ridiculous. I'm fine." With Simon's help he struggled to take a step toward the archway. If not for the solid figure supporting him, he'd have collapsed in a heap.

She arched her brows. "Yeah, I can see that."

The grey-shingled saltbox stood on a lot just a stone's throw from a sheltered cove. Lauren pulled her car up before it, shut off the engine and got out. From the back seat she retrieved the crutches Josh had been given at the emergency room, carried them around to the passenger door and handed them to him as he struggled out, his knee firmly bandaged.

He fumbled in his pocket and handed her his keys. She walked ahead of him up the path and had his front door open by the time he reached it. He hobbled past her through the entryway and disappeared deeper into the house.

Lauren waited. Was he coming back? She closed the door and crossed to the doorway through which he had vanished to find him standing in a darkened living room. She felt beside her, found a light switch and flicked it on. Even this didn't draw his attention.

"Are you going to tell me what's going on?"

As though her words had roused him from sleep, he lifted his head. He opened the cupboard he was standing before, grabbed a bottle and glass from a shelf and started pouring himself a drink. "Nothing's going on. Everything's fine."

"Right." She shrugged. "Don't know where I got that impression. Could be because we just spent the entire afternoon at the hospital and you couldn't share a single thought. Or maybe it was the battle I went through simply to get you there in the first place, your refusing to let me call an ambulance."

"It's a cruciate ligament, not cardiac arrest."

"Bad enough to land you on crutches for a week. What were you planning to do, hop everywhere? If I hadn't driven you—"

"Lauren, look..." He swallowed the last of the scotch he had poured. "I thank you for driving me to the hospital, I thank you for bringing me home again, and I thank you for your concern. But really, I can manage from here."

Despite the talk she'd given herself – to have no expectations of this man, to keep things purely business between them – she couldn't deflect the sting of his words.

She watched as he poured another drink. "That's your idea of managing, is it?"

His gaze flicked toward her, a wordless warning.

"You know, whatever your problem is, you really need to work it out."

"You mean, the way you've worked out yours?"

A hint of challenge had invaded his tone. At last a crack in the stone veneer? "What's that supposed to mean?"

"Nothing. Forget it."

"Oh, no you don't. You don't get to make a comment like that and then back off. What did you mean?"

"How are the nightmares going, Lauren?" He turned to face her. "Had any more since we're back from our trip?"

She stared at him, speechless. What did her nightmares have to do with his refusing to get in an ambulance? And what was with his sudden intensity?

"They're not getting any better, are they?" he goaded. "And still you cling to your insane delusion that helping the survivors will absolve your guilt."

The words set her back like a splash of cold water. A moment ago she'd been the aggressor. Now, suddenly, the tables had turned. "Josh, what—"

"Answer me – has it helped or hasn't it? Everything you've done. Paying for Roger Phelps's funeral. Hiring Ada. Has any of it made the slightest difference to how you feel about what happened?"

"I...I told you it's not about absolving guilt, it's about repaying a debt of gratitude."

"Gratitude." He laughed.

She took a step toward him. "I don't see what's so hard to understand. A good man, encumbered with a serious debility, gives his life for a total stranger, and you don't feel that warrants some kind of payback?"

"He's dead, Lauren. You can't pay him back."

"Which is why I'm helping his only daughter, the woman who took care of him all those years. The person who gave her life for him the same way he gave his for me."

He shook his head and turned to the window.

Lauren waited then eased up behind him. "Josh, please, tell me, what is it?"

He was silent so long she was certain she'd lost him. Then, in a whisper, "I grew up here on the cape, you know. Spent all my summers at the beach as a kid. You know how long it's been since I've been there?"

"To the beach?"

"Fifteen years. The same length of time since I've been in a hospital."

Lauren frowned. How could anyone live on a cape and not visit the beach occasionally? Hell, he lived less than a block away from one.

"Josh, what does that have to do...?"

"I used to go with a friend of mine. We did pretty much everything together from the day we met in kindergarten, but the beach was our favorite place in the world. Fishing, swimming, riding the waves – the ocean was home.

"One day we rode to Windy Point, swam out passed the breaker wall and got caught in the undertow. A man fishing off the rocks saw us and swam out to help." His voice dropped further. "The tide was too strong. He could only save one of us."

She felt the chill of his words seeping through her. The same nightmare she had experienced. But for someone so young...

He turned to face her. "So by your logic I should have spent the rest of my life trying to make it up to his parents."

She looked at him, aghast. "No, of course not. You were a child. No-one would expect—"

"I was fifteen. Old enough to know I was a much stronger swimmer than Mitchell. That I never should've dared him—" He clamped his jaw.

She took his glass and set it aside. "Listen to me—"

"So here I am watching you all these weeks, going through the same hell I went through. Jesus, Lauren, you think I didn't see Mitchell's face everywhere I looked for months afterwards? You think I still can't hear his cries?"

"Josh, please..."

"Those 'old friends' I went to see on our buying trip? It

was them, his parents. A couple who'd once treated me practically like another son. I saw them all right. From a distance. I was too much of a coward to go in and face them."

Lauren held her breath, afraid to break the tenuous thread.

He lifted his hand, brushed his fingertips down of her cheek. "All those times I wanted to comfort you, wanted to take it all away. And at the same time another part of me was screaming to get as far away from you as possible."

"Josh, listen." She took both his hands and held them tightly. "What would you say to a fifteen year old boy – now, today – who had done what you had?"

He grew very still. "You did it. You killed him."

She stifled a gasp, gutted at the thought of the pain he'd been carrying all these years. Yet despite what he'd said, she felt the faintest glimmer of hope. They'd finally gotten things out in the open. To move forward together however they'd have to get past the final barrier standing between them.

She touched his face. "If you believe that, how have you lived with it all these years?"

"By staying shut down. By not allowing myself to feel." His eyes lit with bleak understanding. "In all likelihood the *real* reason my fiance left me."

She unfurled his fist and pressed his open palm to her throat. "And what if you *could* feel again? What then?"

His gaze dropped from her eyes to her lips.

And then he was kissing them.

CHAPTER 67

Ada steered her car through the darkened streets of Josh's neighborhood. She hadn't stopped thinking about him all afternoon, worrying whether he was all right. She hadn't meant for him to be hurt so badly. When she arrived at work and Simon had told her what happened she'd wanted to run straight to him and explain. But of course she couldn't go to the hospital with Lauren there with him.

The hours of waiting had been absolute torture. She'd only wanted to give him a warning, to let him know how much he'd hurt her by saying 'no' to her yesterday. She knew he cared, he'd made that clear. Why did he have to keep playing these games?

All right, maybe he'd wanted to keep their love a secret at first. Maybe he'd suspected Lauren had feelings for him and hadn't wanted to upset her. After all, she was his boss. But that had all been sorted out now. Wasn't it time they let people know how they felt for each other? Instead he'd rejected her invitation, offering only the lamest excuse, making her feel...

She clutched the steering wheel, twisting the rubber against her palms. No-one made her feel like she didn't matter, like she wasn't important. *No-one!*

She took a deep breath and blew it out. There it was again, that awful fire. Her anger just got the better of her sometimes. That's why she had to go and talk to him. To explain it to him, to make him understand.

For once she'd do more than sit in her car and watch him through the windows, like she'd done all those other times late at night. She loved to watch him when he wasn't aware – reading in his chair, listening to music, watching TV.

But not this time. This time she'd go up and knock on his door. She had to talk to him. Once she'd explained to him why she'd done it, he'd see it as proof of how much she loved him.

Turning the corner onto his street, she slowed at the sight of the car parked in front of his house. What was Lauren still doing here? They must have been delayed a long time at the hospital. Yes, that was it. She'd heard those emergency rooms were just awful.

At the thought of Josh in a place like that, she felt the slightest twinge of guilt. She really was going to have to make this up to him. She'd park here at the end of the street and wait until she saw Lauren leave. Surely the woman wouldn't be long; she'd only come to drop Josh off home.

Ada sat drumming her fingers on the steering wheel. She smiled faintly, enjoying the thought of looking after Josh in his recovery. If he had his leg in a cast and couldn't move around, she could wait on him, cook for him, bring him his meals. Maybe even bathe him. She blushed at the thought. Yes, if there was one thing she knew how to do it was take care of someone.

She checked her watch. What was taking so long? Maybe Lauren had helped him inside. Maybe he'd offered her a cup of coffee. Just to be nice.

She climbed from the car, slammed the door and started up the street to his house. She was sure they weren't doing anything. But maybe she'd just sneak a look to make sure.

CHAPTER 68

Lauren slid silently out of bed and gathered her clothes from the chair where she'd left them the night before. She dressed by the pale rays of morning sunlight seeping through Josh's bedroom window, and with a last longing look at the man in the bed, turned for the door.

"Where do you think you're sneaking off to?" Josh winced as he rolled over onto his back.

"Oh, be careful, watch that leg." She settled on the edge of the bed beside him. "How's it feeling this morning?"

"I'll live." He pulled her down into a lingering kiss. When they drew apart, he looked over at the clock on the nightstand. "Why so early?"

"I was going to go for a run on your beach, if that's all right."

"Knock yourself out. Just don't go anywhere near the lighthouse, it's falling apart. Although, you know..." He brushed a finger across her lips. "You could probably get all the exercise you needed without ever leaving this room."

"Is that right?" She smiled with her eyes. "You just want me to stick around and make you breakfast."

"As long as you're the main course."

She laughed as he pulled her over on top of him.

Afterwards, as she lay in his arms, Josh's expression grew suddenly serious. "I want you to know I never meant to play games with you. The offer I made to buy into the business… At the time I thought I could make it work. But then…"

"It's okay. I understand."

He kissed the finger she'd placed to his lips, then drew her hand away. "I don't think you do. What I'm saying is… What I'm *asking* is… Is there any chance I can withdraw my withdrawal?"

"About a partnership?" She calmed her excitement. "What happened to the other option that came up?"

"Sorry, I lied. I was just finding it increasingly difficult to keep things strictly business between us."

As if she didn't know what that was like. "What changed your mind?"

He laughed. "I'd say that battle's been well and truly lost, wouldn't you. Nothing to do now but forge ahead and hope for the best." His smile faded. "Time I faced a few demons of my own."

"We can help each other."

"I'm counting on it. So is that a yes?"

"How about we discuss it tonight over dinner? I'll come back after work and cook it for you."

"I don't know if I can wait that long."

He started to lean in for another kiss but Lauren withdrew. "Later, cowboy. Otherwise I'll never get to work." She climbed off the bed and straightened beside him. "Are you going to be okay on your own?"

"I think I can handle a few days sitting around with my feet up."

"What do you want for dinner?" she said from the

doorway. "You like Italian?"

"Anything you make is fine with me." His expression turned fearful. "As long as it's not that cake you made the first week you hired me."

She picked up the pillow at her feet and threw it.

Outside Lauren climbed in her car. Too late for a run. She had to head home and have her shower in time to open up the nursery.

Despite the dramas that had been happening at work she felt on a high. She'd feared last night would be a one-night thing, but from the way Josh was talking he seemed to want more than a business partnership.

It all made sense now. His reluctance, his distance, his anger over her befriending Ada. Each time she'd faced some remnant of her experience with Phelps he'd been forced to re-live his own painful memories. She hoped his disclosure over what had happened to him as a teen had broken down the barrier between them.

As she started her car, she noticed the chain stretched across the foot of the drive leading into the grounds next door. Beyond a straggling privet hedge she could just make out the top of a greenhouse. The For Sale sign out front had a 'sold' sticker pasted across it.

A second rusted sign hung on the chain: Lighthouse Gardens. The name rang a bell but she couldn't think why. Had this been the site of Josh's old business? If so, he might've mentioned it at some stage.

She stared out at the deteriorating site. So sad to see something once cherished go to ruin. Sadder still that it wasn't by choice. Perhaps, after all he had lost, Josh could find a fulfilling new partnership in her business. And with her.

CHAPTER 69

Ada stalked toward the office door. The pain in her head had gotten so bad she could hardly see.

Last night, after peering through Josh's front window, the blackness had consumed her like never before. Given the chance, she'd have smashed every window of Lauren's car, climbed in and torn the insides to shreds with her bare hands. But an elderly couple had come along walking their dog and she'd been forced to leave without the satisfaction.

This morning, however, she'd felt oddly grateful. The delay had given her a chance to think. She didn't have to rush her retaliation, she could take her time, plan it through, savor it more. In fact the relief born of that realization had led her to another, more unusual decision. She might not need to retaliate at all. *If* the two of them begged her forgiveness.

She knew about men and their baser instincts. Josh's lapse was purely the result of human weakness. He loved only her, of that she was sure. But presented with the combination of opportunity and temptation, he'd simply succumbed. As any man would.

As for Lauren, they'd just have to see. If she was honest

and confessed what she'd done – luring Josh to stray – Ada might feel inclined to forgive her. Yes, despite the enormous wrong they had done her, she was willing to give them every chance. Provided they did their best to atone.

A foot from the office she stopped and calmed herself, removing from her expression and posture any hint of the rage she was battling. When certain she had composed herself, she tapped on the frame and stepped through the door.

Seated at her desk, Lauren looked up. "Good morning, Ada. You're in early today."

For an instant her fury nearly broke free. Instead of the shamefaced shock she'd expected, the woman greeted her with an open smile. If anything, Lauren appeared more lovely, more glowingly happy than Ada had ever seen her.

"I came to find out how Josh is doing," she said through her teeth. "How's his leg?"

"Didn't Mel tell you? I called her after we left the hospital."

"I must've already gone home."

"Yes, it probably was a bit late by then. Well, the good news is, he didn't break it. Just a bit of damage to his knee. The doctor says it will heal on its own without needing surgery."

Ada stared back. That was it? No faltering confession? No groveling bid for forgiveness? She was just going to pretend it never happened? "Thank goodness. I'm so relieved. Is he in much pain?"

"Unfortunately, yes, but the doctor's given him something for it. He's having the rest of this week off. He'll see the doctor again on Monday and find out then if he can come back to work."

"I hope he won't be away too long. I'll miss him."

"Yes, so will I."

The words, the smile, were simply too much. Her control in tatters, Ada quickly backed toward the door. "Well, I better get to work. If you talk to Josh, give him my best."

"I certainly will."

Ada rushed out. How could the woman feel not the slightest measure of remorse? After the magnitude of her crime—

Halfway up the hall realization struck. Josh and Lauren didn't realize she knew. That was the only explanation for it. And how could they? They didn't know she'd been outside his house last night watching them together, that she'd actually seen…

Her fingernails bit into her palms. Yes, that was it. Clearly they thought they'd gotten away with it. Poor dumb Ada would never find out.

Well, let the two of them go on thinking that.

It wasn't till later that afternoon that Lauren noticed the broken statues and toppled wheelbarrow still lying at the edge of the parking lot where Josh had his accident. Little wonder the mess had been overlooked, seeing as it would normally have fallen to Josh himself to clean it up. With Simon busy and Mel still feeling under the weather, Lauren got to work on the job herself.

She retrieved the pull cart from the barn, loaded the broken pieces of statues and carted them to the dumpster out back. All that remained upon her return was the broken wheelbarrow.

She squatted beside it to determine what would be the best way to move it. One of the legs had broken off – no doubt what had caused the accident – but the wheel itself was still attached so the easiest way…

Frowning, she picked up the detached leg. Fully intact. It hadn't snapped off, it had fallen off. Would someone as fastidious with tools as Josh have let the bolts become that loose?

She spotted the offending hardware nearby and picked it up. The edges were scored with multiple groves to the point they'd been partially stripped away. Someone had either tightened or loosened the bolt only recently. Could that someone have been Claudia?

She straightened at the sound of approaching footsteps to see Ada rushing toward her from the archway. "Come quick. It's Mel."

Ada watched the ambulance speed down the driveway, with Lauren in her car right behind it. She'd promised the woman she would close up the nursery in her absence. And of course she would. What were friends for?

But first she had an errand to see to.

In the kitchen she opened the cupboard above the counter and took down the bottle containing Mel's morning sickness pills – the herbal, over-the-counter remedy Mel had been taking for the last two weeks. Or thought she'd been taking.

Ada tipped the capsules out into a dish. With a smile she replaced them with the ones from her pocket and returned the bottle to its shelf.

"I locked up the potting shed and the barn."

She whirled to find Simon standing behind her. Damn the retard, he'd scared her to death.

Exhaling loudly, she closed the cupboard and pocketed the pills from the dish. He'd think nothing of seeing her here – they all kept various belongings in the cupboard. "Thank you,

Simon. I'll tell Lauren what a good job you did."

He fidgeted with the keys in his hand. "Is Mel going to be all right?"

"Yes, of course."

"But...she was bleeding."

"That sometimes happens with women who are expecting babies. It's nothing to worry about, she'll be fine."

He gazed around the room, clearly at a loss. "It feels funny going home so early."

An idea sprang to her mind with his words. She hadn't planned it, but with everyone gone... "Actually, we don't have to go right away."

"We don't?"

"Lauren said to lock up, she didn't say we had to leave."

Simon stood gawping. Did she have to explain everything to him? "Lauren only wanted us to close because there aren't enough of us to serve customers. I'm sure she wouldn't mind if we stayed a while."

He gave an enormous shrug. "What would we do?"

Yes, what exactly. Her mind kicked over. The barn? Hard to make it look like an accident when Simon normally didn't go in there. The greenhouse? All that lovely glass but... "I know. I've been meaning to tell you – I think I saw a new batch of ducklings down at the pond. We should go look at them."

His eyes widened. "Oh, can we, please?"

"Let's do it right now." She put out her hand to him. "Just you and me."

They turned for the door and stopped at the sight of the figure standing there.

"Simon?" Ezra stepped into the room. "I thought you said you'd be out front. I've been waiting there for you."

"Oh." Simon looked back at Ada. "I forgot. I already called my Dad to come get me." She forced a smile. "That's all right, Simon, we'll do it another time."

CHAPTER 70

Pacing outside the emergency entrance, Lauren tapped a number into her phone. Josh picked up after only two rings. "I'm afraid you're on your own for dinner. I'm at the hospital again."

"Why, what happened? Are you all right?"

"I'm fine. It's Mel. She…started bleeding at work today."

A heartbeat of silence. "Jesus, the baby? Is she okay?"

"I don't know yet. They wouldn't let me ride in the ambulance so I drove in my car. By the time I got here they'd taken her in and I haven't spoken to a doctor yet."

"Well did anything happen? Did she fall? Overdo it somehow?"

"No, nothing. She's been taking it really easy in fact. She hasn't felt well for a couple of days but we figured it was just morning sickness." She blew out a breath. "Now it looks like it could be something more serious."

"Now, you don't know that. She could be fine. My sister spotted when she was pregnant and gave birth to healthy little girl."

Lauren closed her eyes against the image of the bloody paper towels strewn across the nursery's bathroom floor. This was more than a little spotting.

"You want me to come and wait with you?" Josh said.

"How would you get here? You're not exactly fit to drive and your car's at the nursery in any case."

"I'll take a cab."

"No, it's okay. You need to keep that leg elevated. Besides Peter'll be here in a couple of hours. I'll call you as soon as I know anything."

Lauren rose from the hospital bench when she spotted the doctor coming up the hall.

"Miss Donnelly?"

"Yes."

"You came in with Mrs. Haines? You're her employer, is that correct?"

"Yes. Mel's also my best friend. Please, how is she?"

"She's going to be fine."

Lauren slumped, fighting back tears, then instantly straightened. "And the baby?"

"Why don't we sit down?"

Chilled by the words, she lowered herself to the bench. "She lost it, didn't she?"

"I'm afraid so. I'm very sorry."

She bowed her head. "Oh, God, poor Mel."

The doctor surveyed the empty corridor. "I take it her husband hasn't arrived yet."

"He's out of town for a job interview. I called him and he's on his way back but he probably won't get here much before ten."

"I see. I wonder, would you mind answering a few questions for me?"

"Yes, of course."

He took her through all the ones Josh had asked – any falls, recent illness, any bleeding prior to this – till he got to a couple she hadn't considered.

"Is Mel on any medication you know of?"

"Just vitamins. And an herbal remedy for morning sickness."

The man looked up.

"She said it was approved by her doctor."

He nodded, making a note of the fact. "I understand you run a nursery. Has Mel come in contact with any poisons lately? Have you done any spraying in the last week or so?"

"No, nothing. As soon as we found out she was pregnant we've been very careful about all that." She paled at the thought. "You think something at work might've caused this?"

His smile was caring. "We may never be sure. Your friend bled more than I would've expected and we had to transfuse her, which is one reason I'm asking these questions. In all likelihood the miscarriage had nothing to do with work; it was simply something wrong with the fetus."

"But she'll be all right?"

"I expect her to make a full recovery. The bleeding has stopped and at this stage I don't see any reason why she can't fall pregnant again."

"Can I see her?"

"She's asleep right now and probably will be for the rest of the night. But you're welcome to go in and sit with her."

Lauren stared down at the figure in the bed. In the light from the corridor, Mel's face glowed ghostly pale. The woman hadn't stirred a muscle since Lauren had taken up her vigil an hour ago.

She, on the other hand, had grown ever more restless by

the moment. One word the doctor had spoken earlier kept popping up in her thoughts.

Poison.

When she'd called Josh to give him the news of Mel's miscarriage, she'd felt little more than a vague disquiet beneath her grief. But the longer she sat here mulling it over, the clearer that impression had become till it pressed on her mind with all the power of full-blown suspicion.

Unable to contain herself any longer, she rose from her chair, stepped into the hall, and phoned a number she'd recently acquired. "Detective Olsen? It's Lauren Donnelly. You came to my nursery the other morning to investigate a break-in."

"Miss Donnelly, yes, what can I do for you?"

"I have some information to give you. I'm not sure if it's related to the break-in but I thought you should know."

"Hang on a minute, I'll just grab a pen."

Shuffling sounds. She visualized him sitting at a cluttered desk, burrowing through mounds of unfinished paperwork, fast food wrappers, empty coffee cups.

Then he was back. "Go ahead."

"One of my workers had an accident yesterday." She gave him the details of Josh's mishap and the condition of the bolt she'd found that morning.

"You're suggesting the wheelbarrow was deliberately tampered with?"

She blew out a sigh. It did sound a stretch to hear him say it. "Look, it isn't just what happened yesterday. I'm at the hospital this very moment because another of my workers, Mel Haynes, who was three months pregnant had a miscarriage at work today."

A slight pause. "I'm sorry to hear that."

"The doctor asked me if she'd been in contact with any poisons."

"Had she?"

"No, not at work she hasn't. At least nothing relating to her job."

"There'd be plenty around at a nursery though. Insecticides, herbicides…"

"Detective, we're not exactly inexperienced in handling those things. I assure you we've been very careful."

"So what you're saying is, if Mel *had* been in contact with poison, it wasn't an accident."

She let the words tumble around in her head. Was that really what she was saying, what she would have this man believe?

She steeled herself. "Yes."

"Did the doctor note anything about her condition that would lead him to think that?"

"Not that he told me. But he might not have checked. From the way he spoke her miscarriage could be just one of those things."

In the silence she felt him gauging his words. "Perhaps it was. Woman have miscarriages all the time. My wife had one when we first started trying for a family."

"Yes, maybe that is all it was. But doesn't it strike you as a little odd… My place gets broken into, stock is vandalized, two of my workers have serious accidents within a day of each other, and an ex-employee nearly runs me down in the street. You don't think there could be a connection there?"

The silence was even longer this time. "You closed the nursery after Mel was taken to the hospital?"

"Yes. One of my workers did."

"All right, keep it that way. Don't open tomorrow. And

don't you or anyone else go in there. I'll come by in the morning and see what I can find."

"Detective, would it be all right if I did some watering? I have stock in the yard and unless I keep it—"

"How about I meet you there at seven? It shouldn't take more than an hour or two to look around, see if we need to follow this further."

She slumped with relief. "Thank you so much. Seven o'clock would be fine."

CHAPTER 71

Lauren paced in front of the archway. It had been after midnight when Peter finally arrived at the hospital to relieve her keeping watch at Mel's bedside, yet she'd been up since five reviewing her suspicions. She had to admit that by the morning light they didn't look nearly as certain as yesterday. In fact she could see so many holes in her theory, she wondered why Olsen had agreed to meet with her at all.

Despite her desire to be with Josh, she'd opted to spend the night at home so she could be sure of meeting the detective on time. Bad enough if she'd dragged him here on a wild goose chase, she couldn't risk keeping the poor man waiting.

Spotting his car coming up the drive, she walked over to stand near the wheelbarrow. She watched him pull up, climb from his car – not the squad car, he must be off duty – and come toward her. They greeted each other.

"I just walked through the grounds to open up," she assured him. "I haven't gone inside at all."

"Good. So this is the wheelbarrow involved in the accident?"

"Yes. And here's the bolt I found beside it the following morning. Yesterday morning."

He examined the bolt, then squatted to have a look at the barrow. "Where do you store it at the end of the day?"

"In the barn usually. But..." She shifted. "If it's being used for an on-going project it might simply be left under cover."

"In there, you mean." He nodded through the archway, then pushed to his feet. "And was that where it was the night before the accident?"

"Yes."

"So basically anyone who came through those gates could've tampered with it."

She sighed. Hole number one in her theory. "Yes. But, if it was deliberate, why would anyone but Claudia want to?"

"Why would *she* want to? What does she have against Mr. Stedman? You're the one who fired her."

"Maybe Josh wasn't the target. Maybe she figured I'd be using it."

"Then what would her motive have been for poisoning your friend? Mrs. Haynes."

Argument numbers two and three. Her theory was starting to look like Swiss cheese. "Maybe that was meant for me as well. Or else..." The thought was almost too disturbing to consider. "Maybe she thought she could hurt me most by hurting the people I care about."

He stared at her a moment, that hang-dog expression giving nothing away, then started for the archway. "Let's go inside."

Lauren unlocked the shop door, flicked on the lights and disarmed the security.

Olsen stood gazing about the room. "Your workers have lockers?"

"Lockers, no. Everyone leaves their things in the kitchen." She guided him through and gestured to the row of hooks on the wall. "Coats go here, handbags in the drawer down there or in my office."

"What about other personal items? Things they leave here

every day."

"Well, everyone has a bit of cupboard space."

He opened the door she'd indicated and stood perusing the row of coffee mugs. "Which is Mel's?"

She pointed to one.

He picked it up with a pen through its handle and slipped it into a plastic bag. Whatever he might think of them personally, he was certainly taking her concerns seriously.

Spotting something further back on the shelf, he donned latex gloves, reached in and came out with a bottle of pills. "These hers too?"

"Yes. Something she was taking for morning sickness. An herbal remedy."

"That what she told you? There's nothing on the label."

"Yes, I think she kept the main bottle at home and brought these to work in a spare one."

He opened the lid and shook some capsules onto one gloved palm. "She buy these or make them up herself?"

"I'm pretty sure she bought them."

"How long she been taking them?" He sniffed them, then tipped them back in the bottle.

"As far as I know just a couple of weeks." Lauren didn't like the look of his frown. "Detective, I know Mel would never have taken anything without making sure it was safe."

He slipped the bottle in another bag. "Her husband's been out of work a while."

The change in topic threw her a second. "That's right. How did you—?"

"The statement she gave us after the break-in. She said the reason she forgot to lock up was because her husband had been arrested." He closed the cupboard and moved to the next one. "Got drunk apparently after failing to get the job he was going for. Sounds like the guy's in pretty rough shape. Like maybe they both are."

"They're feeling the strain a bit, I'm sure."

He popped the lid on the electric kettle, sniffed its contents, closed it again. "Having a baby's an expensive business."

Lauren frowned. "I'm afraid I don't—"

"Last night after we spoke on the phone I got to wondering what other kinds of poisons you'd have around a nursery. You said you'd been careful with spraying so I thought, what about the plants themselves? So I Googled it." He straightened from peering into the fridge. "Did you know there are a number of herbs that can bring on miscarriage?"

"Well yes, but you would have to ingest them. Which is what I've been saying – someone could've..." Her words trailed off at a disturbing thought.

"Or maybe someone didn't."

For a moment the world felt strangely off kilter. "You're not suggesting—?"

"You'd be amazed how many websites there are on do-it-yourself herbal abortion."

"No. No way." She took a step back.

"It's cheap, easy, and no-one has to know. Unless you overdose, of course, which causes hemorrhaging. Wasn't that what the doctor said happened to your friend?"

"No, you're wrong. Mel would never... She wanted this baby."

For once the man's hang-dog expression seemed wholly appropriate. He held up the bottle. "I'll get these tested just to be sure."

CHAPTER 72

Lauren slid the sprig of dried thyme into the wreath's wire frame. She'd worked in solitude all afternoon, filling orders and trying to conquer her growing unease. Despite her attempts, she'd been unable to lose herself in the creative outlet she'd always loved. She couldn't put aside the disturbing question Olsen had raised.

A part of her simply couldn't believe that Mel would terminate her own pregnancy. Yet only two days ago Mel had told her of the fight she and Peter had had, that he'd accused her of not being careful enough to prevent the pregnancy. Clearly there were some issues there. Was Olsen right in his suspicions?

One way to find out the truth, of course, would be to simply call Mel and ask her. But she just couldn't bring herself to do it. She didn't want to force Mel into making such an admission before she was physically or emotionally ready. And if Olsen was wrong, Mel might never forgive her for asking.

In completing his inspection of the grounds, the detective had found nothing else suspicious. When he'd left the nursery just after lunch, he'd promised to get in touch as soon as he received the results of the tests on Mel's capsules. She would just have to wait until then.

As she slid the last sprig of thyme in place her cell phone rang and she walked to the end of the table to get it. Josh had called her several times, checking to make sure she was all right. She hadn't even admitted her fears to him. She simply couldn't bring herself…

But this wasn't Josh.

"Hello, Ada."

"I'm calling to see how you are?"

Why was everyone concerned about her? She wasn't the one who'd just lost a baby. "I'm fine, thank you."

"Are you at the hospital?"

"No, I'm at work. Just filling some orders. Trying to keep up."

"I didn't know you'd be working today. Why didn't you tell me, I could've helped you. You want me to come in and give you a hand?"

"No, it's all right, I won't be much longer. Thanks for the offer though."

"Well, if you need anything, please call me."

"Thank you, Ada. You're a good friend."

After hanging up, Lauren placed the finished wreath in the fridge, debated whether to quit for the day, and decided against it. If she was going to stay on top of the orders she had to do at least one more.

She shuffled through the loose sheets of paper, discarding the ones that would take several hours, and paused at one for a funeral wreath. Still too big.

She was just about to set it aside when the name caught her eye. Garevick. Simon's last name. Not a particularly common one. What were the odds?

She scanned down the page, read the requested inscription for the card and felt her heart stop.

Rest in peace, Simon Garevick.

Ada closed her phone and sat back on her blanket in the sand. She didn't know if she was relieved or disappointed. Clearly Lauren hadn't seen the order yet. If she had, Ada might now have to rush the next stage of her plan and in a way that would be much more exciting. Still, better to be thorough and take her time to avoid mistakes.

She gazed out over the deserted beach to the dark clouds sweeping across the sky. The wind had picked up in the last few minutes, trying to tear the towel out from under her and ruffling the shirt of the man building sandcastles at her feet.

He stopped and looked up. "It's gonna rain. I should call Dad to come and get me."

Ada smiled. "Not yet, Simon. There's something really special I want to show you just up the beach beyond those dunes."

She pushed to her feet, picked up the towel and held out her hand. "Come with me."

"Ezra, it's Lauren. Is Simon there?" Lauren fought to keep her voice steady. She'd already called the number on the order but the person who answered denied ever placing it.

"Lauren, how are you? Simon told me about Mel going to the hospital. Is she all right?"

Keeping a stranglehold on her nerves, she gave him the details as fast as she could, then repeated her request.

"No, I'm sorry, Simon's not here. He said you gave everyone the day off so he went the beach. I dropped him there just after lunch. I hope he got that right and you weren't expecting him—"

"What beach did you take him to?"

"North Shore cove."

"Have you heard from him since you dropped him off?"

"No. Why? We arranged that I'd pick him up from the ice cream parlor at five o'clock. Though I might head down there a little early, it looks like rain. Is anything wrong?"

Lauren debated. In the state she was in and with all that had happened, there was every chance she was overreacting. A misunderstanding. Someone thinking one thing while writing another could explain how Simon's name got on the order. She'd done it herself on the odd occasion.

"No, it's just... I tried to call him but he didn't answer."

Ezra huffed. "And you're surprised? He probably set his phone down somewhere and forgot about it."

"Yes, I thought that might've been it. If you could get him to call me as soon as you see him I'd really appreciate it."

"Yes, of course."

She forced a laugh. "You know the strangest thing happened today. We got an order for a wreath for someone named Simon Garevick."

"Is that right? What a coincidence."

"It isn't exactly a common name, is it. I wondered if it might've been a relative of yours."

"No, there's no other Simons in our family. He's one of a kind."

CHAPTER 73

It was 4:30 by the time Lauren reached North Shore cove but it seemed much later. Thick clouds had gathered to block out the sun and thunder grumbled in the distance.

She pulled up into the seaside parking lot and scanned the beach in both directions. Not a soul in sight. A chill wind whipped her hair in her face when she rolled down the window. No-one along the shoreline either.

She sat debating. Maybe she was totally losing it. Maybe she'd worked herself up to a state where she couldn't think rationally anymore. But despite Ezra's promise, she found she just couldn't sit and wait for Simon to call her back. She had to find him, had to assure herself he was all right.

Rest in peace, Simon Garevick. The words drove a spike of fear through her heart just thinking about them!

She pulled from the parking lot and drove along the shops that lined the foreshore. Ezra had said he was meeting Simon at the ice cream parlor at five o'clock. With this unexpected change in the weather maybe Simon had gone there early. She drove past the parlor but couldn't see him waiting out front. Leaving her car in a loading zone, she dashed inside but he wasn't there either.

Back in her car, she chose a direction and drove along the shore road, hoping to spot him down on the beach. Beyond the shelter of the little cove, the waves were bigger, churned by the force of the approaching storm. Simon, with his fear of big surf, would never have come this way voluntarily. And he couldn't have walked this far in any case. She turned and went back.

Her fear was edging toward outright panic by the time she reached the parlor again. Maybe Ezra had got there and picked Simon up before she'd even arrived the first time. But seeing the man's car standing out front shattered her only remaining hope.

Emerging from the parlor, Ezra spotted her, waved, and headed over. She buzzed her passenger window down.

"Lauren! What are you doing here?" The wind all but tore the words from his lips.

There was no point pretending. "I'm looking for Simon."

"I told you I'd get him to call you later." He pulled up his collar. "What's so important you had to come out in weather like this?"

She leaned and opened her passenger door. "Please, get in."

Ten minutes later she was on her own, once again driving the shore road, this time in the opposite direction. Ezra, unconvinced by her modified version of events – or perhaps just reluctant to share her concerns – had opted to stay and wait at the parlor, certain Simon would soon show up. That left her with the options of abandoning her search or extending it to the eastern side of the cove. She'd chosen the latter.

Less than a mile further however, the road veered away from the shore and her view of the beach was blocked by dunes. She parked in a small roadside turnoff, left her car and proceeded on foot.

The dunes were lose hummocks of sand, tufted with grass that slashed her legs and hands like blades. Blinded by the grit that scoured their crests, she maneuvered the troughs to the water's edge, then floundered to the top of a larger one and peered out along the darkening shore.

"Simon!" She called his name again and again. But between the wind and pounding surf she knew she'd have to be standing on top of him before he would hear her.

She stumbled down the dune's far side. The stretch of beach she'd glimpsed from its crest had held not another living soul. But a stone's throw further, a ridge of sand jutted toward the water in a wall that obscured the area beyond.

Even as she fought to the summit she heard a sound that chilled her through. The faintest cry, carried on staccato gusts wind.

Simon! Or had it just been a gull?

At the top, she stood braced against the gale, a narrow crescent of rocky beach curving before her. In the premature twilight she could make out no shadow the size of a person. But neither was there a bird in sight.

She squinted against the driving sand. The last wave to have pummeled the beach was draining back to a fresh line of breakers building off shore. And there in the briefly denuded strip, a small dark shape the size of a basketball. A rock surely. But darker than the others scattered around it.

In her charge down the slope, she stumbled and pitched headlong, tumbled to the bottom. Stunned, grazed, mouth full of sand, she pushed to her feet.

In that guarded hollow the sound came again.

Not a screech, but a cry.

Not bird, but human.

CHAPTER 74

Ezra tossed his phone on the dashboard. Useless. Simon had either lost his again or somehow switched it off by mistake.

Or was there another explanation?

He gripped the steering wheel and peered through the misty rain-lashed windscreen, hoping to spot his son's lumbering form hurrying up the sidewalk to meet him. Lauren's words rang in his head but he pushed them away. This girl, this Claudia who'd caused them so much trouble at work… Why would she come after Simon? What had he ever done to her? Surely Lauren was mistaken.

Unless she hadn't told him everything.

He twisted the wheel. What had she said? There'd been some damage done to stock. A worker was injured, then Mel's miscarriage, and now… An order for a wreath with Simon's name on it. What did that prove? It might not mean anything.

He pulled his handkerchief from his pocket and cleared a patch on the misty glass. Not a soul in sight. Where was the boy! It wouldn't be the first time he'd lost his phone but it wasn't like him to be late to meet him.

He opened his door, climbed from the car and ran into the ice cream parlor. Pulling the photo of Simon from his wallet, he handed it to the man behind the counter. "This is my disabled son. He was supposed to meet me here at five o'clock but he hasn't turned up. If he comes in would you please tell him to wait here for me. I'm going to look for him."

The sobs got louder as Lauren hurtled down the beach, sprinting toward the shape she'd mistaken for a rock. Only as she skidded to a stop beside him could she make out Simon's face in the gloom, his body buried beneath the sand.

"Simon, it's Lauren! It's all right, I'm here, I'll get you out."

She dug at the sand around his neck. Did he even comprehend she was there? He just kept wailing incoherently.

She heard more than saw the next wave coming and braced for the impact. It slammed her side and bowled her over. The ebbing swept her back again just as Simon's head reappeared. The sound of his choking ripped at her heart.

"Listen to me. You have to hold your breath when the next wave comes. I'll tell you when." But instructions were useless. The second he got enough air in his lungs he was sobbing again.

She went back to digging, trying to throw the sand further away. Most of what she'd already freed had been washed back in. The swell was enormous – storm surge on top of the in-coming tide. How would she ever—

"Simon, get ready. The next wave's coming." But her words only fuelled his hysteria.

"No! *No!*"

She grabbed his face in both her hands. "Listen to me! Close your—"

He was still screaming when the wave crashed over them.

CHAPTER 75

Ezra drove slowly along the shore road. In the growing darkness he wouldn't see anyone on the beach. It didn't matter. What he was looking for now was Lauren's car. Lauren had had the best chance of finding Simon. If he was anywhere safe, he would be with her.

He spotted her car parked in a turn-off and pulled in behind it. He grabbed the flashlight from his glove compartment, climbed out, and rushed to look inside it.

Wind snatched his hat and whipped it away.

The car was empty. He shone his flashlight beam at the ground – to see footprints leading down to the beach.

Lauren wallowed on hands and knees, fighting her way through the waist-deep water. The wave took forever to wash away. This time when Simon's head reappeared his silence was more terrifying than his screams.

"Simon? *Simon!*"

A feeble cough. His head lolled forward, foam flowing from his nose and mouth.

She clawed at the sand, buried shell fragments ripping her flesh. A gesture horribly reminiscent of her actions on ice two months earlier. *No. Dear god, please, not again!*

She'd uncovered his shoulder and the length of one arm when she sensed the next wave about to descend. She sprawled face down, took a huge gulp of air, and clamped her mouth over his. Holding his nose, she slowly exhaled as the wall of surging water swept over them. If not for her arm now wedged beneath him she'd be swept away.

Beneath the deluge, her terror built. Her lungs screamed. Fighting her body's demand for air, she refused to let go, refused the deliverance inches away. *No, you can't have him!*

When at last she straightened, gasping for breath, it was to see the next wave already forming. They were coming faster, lingering longer, receding less before building again. Another few minutes, two at most, and Simon's head would be fully submerged.

In the knowledge this would be her last chance, she ripped at the sand, scraping the layer from above his legs. With his freed arm draped around her shoulders, she heaved upwards as the next wave engulfed them. The force of its eddies, combined with the pull she continued to exert, did what all her digging couldn't, swirling away the remaining sand and floating his body to the surface.

They collapsed in a heap. She struggled to her feet and slipped her hands beneath his arms. Rain and salt spray lashed her face as she dragged him beyond the reach of the waves.

On her knees beside him she called his name, cried out when he didn't respond. She clamped his nose, arched his neck, forced her breath into dying lungs. When the first salty splutter burst from his lips, she laughed and rocked him in her arms.

A flash of lightning. She braced for the follow-up crash of thunder then looked around when it didn't come.

From the crest of the dune, hysterical beams criss-crossed the sand. One swept past her then wheeled back, fixed on her face. Squinting, she raised a hand to wave.

"I see them! Down here!"

Ezra's voice had never sounded so sweet.

CHAPTER 76

Lauren stared down at the ER floor, the same jagged speck in the linoleum she'd noticed on her last two recent visits. Through a muddling sense of deja vu, she felt someone settle on the bench beside her.

"Tell me more about this order for the funeral wreath." Olsen slipped a cup of vending machine coffee into her hand. "When did you find it?"

"Around four o'clock."

"Was there anything to say when it had been received? Who wrote it down?"

"No. I don't think it came in in the usual way."

"How do you mean?"

She took a sip of the bitter drink, hoping it would help to clear her thoughts. "Orders are placed either by phone or in person and it's usually me or Mel who records them. I know *I* didn't take this one because I'd certainly remember. And if Mel had, I'm sure she would've mentioned it to me."

"You didn't recognize the handwriting?"

"No, it was scribbled. Could've been anyone's."

"I don't suppose Mel's still here at the hospital so we could ask her."

"I checked. She went home this afternoon."

Olsen nodded. "Well assuming for the moment she didn't take the order, what about your other employees?"

"Apart from Simon, there's just Josh and Ada, and I'm sure they would've said something as well."

"So whoever attacked Simon on the beach would've had to fill out the order form and slip it in with the others himself without anyone noticing."

She turned to look at him. "*Him*self? You can't possibly think this was anyone but Claudia."

"How could she have gotten into the office without someone seeing her?"

"I don't know, but she managed it somehow. I've been to this hospital three times in as many days. First Josh, then Mel, now..." Her voice choked off.

"We still don't know if any of these incidents are related; or if any but Simon's and the break-in were deliberate."

She frowned. Why was he being so obtuse about this? "Did you talk to Claudia after you left the nursery today?"

"I went to her house but her parents said she'd gone away, visiting her grand folks in New York."

"When did she leave?"

"Yesterday."

"And you believe them?"

He shrugged. "I believe *they* believe that's where she is."

"Well, have you checked?"

"The mother claims Claudia called her when she arrived in New York, but they haven't spoken since. I've had someone trying to reach them there but so far no luck. The grandparents don't have cell phones apparently and Claudia isn't answering hers."

"So there's a chance she didn't go away after all. Maybe she's been right here the whole time. Hell, she could've called her parents from just up the road."

"Look, Lauren..." He swiveled to face her. "You could sell

me on this girl smashing a pot or tearing up a few bags of fertilizer. I could even believe she damaged those statues, dented your car, and maybe even trashed your office. But as for the rest—"

"You can't possibly think this is all a coincidence."

"You admitted yourself, anyone could've got to that wheelbarrow. And even if Mel didn't cause her own miscarriage, there are any number of reasonable expla—"

"You think Simon buried himself in the sand? You have a reasonable explanation for that!" Lauren looked around at the nurses and patients who'd turned to stare at her.

"Of course not," he soothed. "Someone obviously did that to him. And when we catch them, the charge will be attempted murder. But as for that person being Claudia—"

"She never liked him, not from the first day she started with us. She resented that he had more authority than she did, and hated him telling her what to do."

"Fair enough. But did Simon like her?"

Lauren blinked at him. "In the beginning maybe, but by the time she left, he was downright afraid of her. And after what she's done since—"

"Then how did she manage to bury him in the sand?"

The words were a door slammed in her face.

Olsen rested his elbows on his knees. "Think about it. How did Claudia – someone Simon fears and distrusts – coax him to that secluded beach? She's not a big girl. She couldn't have dragged him or forced him there, he'd have to go willingly."

"Well, maybe she tricked him...maybe..." She felt desperation welling inside her and clamped down hard on it.

Olsen eased back. "Look, just because I haven't spoken to Claudia again doesn't mean I haven't been checking into this since I left you."

"Checking into it how?"

"I interviewed one of your other workers." Olsen stared down into his coffee. "Did you know that before he came to work for you Josh Stedman owned his own nursery?"

"I did. He had it on his resume. It was part of the reason we hired him." Lauren felt a twinge of disquiet. Why was he refusing to meet her gaze? "We talked about it actually. His business went under about two years ago."

"He tell you what happened? Why it failed?"

She thought back to the conversation she and Josh had had in her office. "He said it'd been in trouble for a while but the ultimate blow was when a rival business underbid him for a crucial contract."

Olsen turned to her at last, his wordless stare drawing her toward her own conclusion. A contract bid… Two years ago…

Oh my God. "The Gallway contract. We won that bid, the biggest on the Cape. I remember it because it got us out of the hole we were in."

"And the business you beat in the final round?"

"Lighthouse Gardens. I knew I'd heard that name before." She closed her eyes. "Why did Josh never say anything? Why did he…" Her eyes flew open. "You think he still holds a grudge against me and that *he's* the one…"

"Gives him as much of a motive as Claudia. Maybe more."

"I don't believe it." She shot to her feet. "No, you're wrong. It couldn't be."

Pacing before him, she thought back over the list of offenses. Josh *could* have graffitied the sign and damaged the stock, but as for the rest… "He couldn't have broken into my shop. He was with me on a buying trip at the time."

"I thought you got back the night of the break-in."

"Well, yes, we did."

"You spend the night with him?"

She swallowed. "No."

"Then how do you know what he did after he dropped you off?"

She stared a moment then dropped back onto the bench beside him. "This is insane. You're telling me Josh staged his own accident?"

"To turn suspicion away from himself?" Olsen shrugged. "It's possible. Or else it was a legitimate accident. He also had every opportunity to plant the order for the funeral wreath."

Lauren shook her head. "Josh took Simon to a baseball game. He's always been good to him. They tell jokes, they're friends, they—" But even as she said the words she knew they proved nothing. All she had was her own gut feeling. "If you believe Josh is responsible, why haven't you arrested him?"

"Same reason we haven't arrested Claudia. No evidence. Yet." Olsen drained the last of his coffee, then patted her arm. "Leave it with me."

Tossing the cup in the bin beside him, he pushed to his feet. "You okay to drive yourself home? One of my men left your car out back."

"I'm not leaving."

"Might as well, there's nothing you can do here. They've sedated your friend and he'll sleep till morning. We might be able to question him then, but the doc thinks he may be too traumatized to remember much."

Olsen's words were the final defeat. "Thank you. I'll get home on my own."

CHAPTER 77

Ted eased his Datsun to a stop on the darkened track and watched Lauren's car continue up the driveway to her house.

He'd been careful tailing her home from the hospital, staying well back and only turning onto her private lane after her car had disappeared around the first bend. She'd grown so watchful these last few weeks, nearly catching him on several occasions, he'd had to make sure she hadn't spotted him.

And yet a part of him wished she had.

That same part was urging him even now to continue up to the house, knock on her door, and ask to speak with her. To finally unburden himself of his fears and tell her what he'd come to believe. For she wasn't the only one he'd been watching. He'd been keeping tabs on Ada as well. And while his niece's actions had seemed odd at times there'd been nothing to really confirm his suspicions.

Until today.

Today she'd met that boy at the beach – Simon, the disabled one from work. From his vantage point atop the bluff, Ted had seen them walk up the shore together and disappear around the dunes.

A half hour later, Ada had returned to her car alone and

driven off. Ted had assumed the boy was picked up – if he'd only walked down the beach to check! – and now that same boy lay in the hospital. Wasn't that enough to go to the police with?

But of course he couldn't. Not yet. He had to at least give Ada the chance to turn herself in. He owed his brother's daughter that much.

In the house on the other side of the pond the lights came on. Lauren was home and hopefully safe. Time to do what he knew he must.

Lauren locked her door and walked through the foyer into the kitchen. In the silence of the empty house, the phone's ring hit her ears like a scream, spurring her heart to an instant gallop.

She took a few breaths, reached out for it, then stopped, debating. At this late hour there were only a handful of people it could be, one of whom she wasn't ready to talk to yet – the same one she wanted to talk to most. She drew back her hand.

The phone kept ringing. What if it was Ezra calling with word about Simon's condition? She picked it up. "Hello?"

"Don't hang up. Just let me explain."

She clutched the receiver and closed her eyes. The voice she'd both dreaded and needed to hear.

"Lauren, are you there?"

Her mouth opened but no sound emerged.

"All right, don't answer; I'll do the talking. The cops just left here. Olsen told me what happened to Simon. Thank God you got to him in time. I just hope... Look, are you all right? Just tell me that."

What could she say when she didn't know the answer herself?

A frustrated sigh. "Olsen grilled me pretty good on my

whereabouts this afternoon so I gather I've become a suspect. I told him I've been home here since last night but of course I can't prove it.

"But damn it, I don't care about any of that. I know they'll work out it wasn't me. What worries me is… Olsen was here earlier as well. Among other things, he questioned me about my old business. I know he told you, and I know how it sounds, but you have to believe—"

"I remember after Roger Phelps's funeral." Lauren hadn't realized her intention to speak till she heard her own words. "You got in my car. I didn't understand why you were angry. It all makes sense now."

"All right, I admit I did hold a grudge in the beginning but it didn't last. Once I got to know you everything changed."

"When, Josh? When did it change? Before or after you paid for the franchise? Before or after you offered to buy into the business?" When she'd first learned Josh had lost his nursery because of her she'd felt simply awful. But at the thought he might've been plotting against her…

"Lauren, please—"

"Was that your plan? To keep feeding in more and more money until you owned the whole thing, until you'd bought me out entirely?"

"What? No!"

"Then why keep it secret?"

"I thought about telling you. I almost did a couple of times. But after things started to change between us I didn't see the point?"

"Didn't see the point?"

"It was all in the past; I wanted to forget it. Dredging it up again, hashing it over would only have made you feel bad."

There was suddenly nothing more she could say. She

couldn't even think straight let alone make any sense out of this.

"All right, I should have told you. But the fact I didn't, doesn't change the fact I'm over it now. Lauren, please, the things that have been happening at the nursery… You have to know it wasn't me. I would never hurt Simon. I would never hurt you. For god's sake, I love you. Can't you see that?"

She couldn't answer. She wanted to believe, perhaps she even did. But just at that moment she was too exhausted, too confused to have any idea what she thought or felt.

"I know you've been through a lot today, but please come over. My door's unlocked, we can talk about this. I'm sure we can work things out if we just—"

Silently she laid the phone in its cradle.

CHAPTER 78

Ted pulled into Ada's driveway, doused his headlights and shut off the engine. The house was dark. It was after ten so hopefully she was inside asleep. He climbed from his car, only to find himself glued to the spot.

Just go home you silly old goat. It's not your concern, let the police handle it.

Shaking his head he forced himself forward along the path. It was long past time he stopped listening to that voice. If he'd acted on his suspicions sooner maybe that poor boy wouldn't have been hurt.

On the porch he gave a light knock on the door. Why had he waited so long to do this? The possibility – however remote he'd thought it at first – that Ada had abused and tormented Roger, should have moved him to confront her straight away.

But the voice had been even stronger then, dispassionate and coolly logical, insisting he uncover more facts before taking action.

Yet, looking back now, he had to wonder – was it really just about lack of proof? Or had that voice been a cover for something else, knowledge of a much different kind? The deep-down conviction that, if Ada *had* been abusing Roger, it was nothing the bastard hadn't deserved.

Ted closed his eyes as images came flooding back. All the times Roger had bullied and tormented him when they were boys. The nastier tricks he'd played on him as they got older.

He shook off the thoughts. This wasn't just about Roger any more. It was about other people. Innocent people. It was about a woman who's childhood of abuse had pushed her to become an abuser herself.

Ted reached out and pounded on the door. Yes, it was time. He had to do something, before someone else got hurt. Or worse. If he couldn't convince Ada to turn herself in, he'd have no choice but to do it himself.

Wind swept past him, rattling a shutter and the trees overhead. He stepped back and peered along the front of the house. No lights had come on, despite all his noise. Where could she be at this time of night? The possibilities only disturbed him further.

He drew in a deep breath and blew it out. She'd forced his hand. He had to go to the police himself.

But with what? Hunches and feelings? The voice had been right about that at least – without something more, they'd laugh in his face.

He reached in his pocket and pulled out the note Roger had given him. It certainly wasn't proof of much – he'd hardly found it convincing himself. But what if...

His gaze moved back to the darkened house. If Roger had managed to keep from Ada not just the note but the fact he could write it, what more might he have kept secret from her? Letters? A diary? Outpourings of despair scratched into closet or basement walls? Places where she'd kept him confined? Could any of those things still be inside?

He stepped from the porch and picked up a rock at the

edge of the flower bed. Feeling beneath it, he found the spare key, returned to the door, and let himself in.

Standing in the entryway in the dark, he called up the hall, "Ada? You here?"

He didn't know what he'd do if she answered. How would he explain his presence here? By the look of it she wasn't home, but if she suddenly returned and found him snooping around her house…

As he closed the front door, the solution came to him. He'd say he'd been worried about her and when she hadn't answered his knock, he'd come in to see if she was all right. That sounded reasonable enough. In which case, better to be open about it than to sneak around like a geriatric thief. He flicked on the light.

Straight ahead of him was the kitchen, to his right, the living room. Unlikely any testaments of Roger's ordeal would linger in either place. His best hope of finding evidence, damning or otherwise, would be the man's bedroom. He turned and started up the hall.

At its end, he peered into Ada's room. The bed was empty and neatly made. Again the question – where could she be?

He stepped to the closed door across the hall. A chill washed over him when he touched the knob – like laying his hand on the latch of a tomb. He braced himself and eased it open.

Light from the hallway flooded past him, splashing his shadow on the opposite wall. Along with that of a large hanging noose.

He sucked in his breath, then slowly exhaled. A leather strap dangled from the metal arm above the headboard. Roger's frame. The one he'd used to help him get in and out of bed.

Ted clamped a fist to his chest. Despite the relief it was nothing more sinister, his pulse was racing. Roger had died nearly three months ago. Why hadn't Ada gotten rid of this stuff?

He forced himself forward, slid his hands beneath the mattress and worked his way down the side of the bed. When he reached the bottom, he pulled the frame away from the wall, and did the same on the other side. Nothing.

He pushed the bed back into place and checked the nightstand, then the tall boy. The drawers were all empty. In cleaning them out, Ada would have found any secret notes or journals surely. *If* there had been any.

His shadow crept across the floor before him, then slithered up the closet door. He opened it and stared in surprise at the row of neatly-pressed shirts and trousers. Why had she emptied all the drawers and not taken the clothes from the closet?

He reached up and felt along the top shelf. No photo albums, no documents folder, no shoeboxes full of memorabilia – none of the things that cluttered his own closet at home. Either Roger had never had any, or Ada had taken it all away. So why leave the clothes?

His gaze dropped to the hanging garments. For whatever reason she'd left them here, they could be concealing something further back in the closet. Something Ada didn't even know about. Something Roger had hidden there hoping she would never find.

Ted whisked the hangers to either side. Darkness filled the space beyond. With his last hope gone, he slumped in defeat. Then yelped when someone rushed out from the shadows. He leapt back as the figure arched past him and crashed to the floor.

He stared at the man now lying at his feet, then eased closer. It *was* a man, at least it appeared to be. Dressed in a familiar red flannel shirt and cotton pants. But the thud it had made when it hit the floor boards sounded more hollow than flesh and bone.

He nudged it with his toe. The figure rocked slightly.

Confusion quickly followed relief. A mannequin? In Roger's closet? What the—?

Even more disquieting, why was it dressed in Roger's clothes? Had Ada been telling the truth about her feelings for her father? If she'd acquired a dummy and dressed it in his clothes because she couldn't come to terms with his death, it painted her more pathetic than dangerous. Had he been wrong about her all this time?

He rolled the dummy over with his foot. And clamped a hand across his mouth to smother his cry.

A single sightless eye gazed up at him, the other obliterated by the screwdriver still protruding from the socket. The 'skin' of the face was blistered and pitted as though having been splashed with corrosive. Silently pleading release from its torment, the figure extended a broken arm with a hand bearing slash marks and two missing fingers.

Ted stumbled away from the closet. He staggered backwards across the room, then wheeled for the hallway. Only to find someone blocking his path.

"What are you doing here?" Ada reached out and turned on the light. Her gaze dropped to the dummy at his feet.

"My god, child, what have you done? All those years...this was how...?" He swallowed his gore. "Ada, please, you must listen to me. It has to stop. You're sick, you need help."

"What are you talking about?" She spoke the words

without inflection, her face devoid of all expression.

"I know what you did to him. He told me, Ada. He wrote me a note."

At last a reaction, her eyes growing wide. "He—"

"Yes, he could write. He kept it from you. In the note he begged me. I didn't want to believe at first, but now..." He put out his hand. "I was too late then, I don't want to be too late again. I know it's you who's been causing all the trouble at the nursery."

"You don't know anything."

"I don't have proof about that worker's accident or the woman's miscarriage but all the same I know it was you. Because I saw you today. I saw you walk up the beach with that boy, and when you came back he wasn't with you, and now he's in the hospital."

Her face darkened. "You've been following me?"

"Since the funeral." Ted took her arm. "Please, you have to turn yourself in. Even if I don't tell the police what I know, it's only a matter of time before they work it out for themselves."

A rictus smile tightened her lips. She tipped her head. "Time is all I need, Uncle Ted."

CHAPTER 79

Josh jerked upright in his chair. Still half asleep, he started to swing his leg to the floor and stifled a cry. Gritting his teeth, he eased the leg back down on the coffee table and did his best to breathe through the pain.

When his knee had stopped screaming he gazed about him. For a moment he didn't know what had woken him. Then he heard movement in the kitchen.

"Lauren?"

He'd left the light on above the stove, the door unlocked, in the hope she would come. Hearing the soft tread of her footsteps, his heart beat faster.

At last a silhouette appeared in the doorway. Something unclenched inside his chest. He reached out and turned on the end table lamp.

The moment drew out in a tenuous thread, chill realization seeping through him. Perhaps it had been there all along, hiding in the shadows of his subconscious, refusing to step out into the light. Perhaps with everything else on his mind, a voice as subtle as intuition couldn't be heard above louder, more demanding concerns. But in that instant he knew without doubt, the cogs aligning with perfect precision.

"Ada."

"You're surprised to see me. I understand. We said we wouldn't come together until this was over, but I'm afraid I just had to see you."

His thoughts tumbled over themselves. *We* said? Come together? Until this was over?

She crossed the room, the lamp light rising toward her face. "I won't stay. I just came to let you know I'm all right and that it's almost over. I'm going to have to move things along a little faster than we planned but it's become necessary. I've learned... Well, you'll just have to trust me."

She stopped, standing over him. "You do trust me, don't you, Josh?"

Not concern or confusion delayed his reply, but the sudden fury burning inside him. This monster could well have destroyed three lives and she wasn't done yet? "Of course," he gritted.

She cocked her head and frowned at his leg. "You poor thing. What did she do to you?" She dropped to kneel beside his chair. "Don't worry, my darling, when this is over I'll take good care of you. If there's one thing I know how to do, it's look after the ones I love."

Her smile set insects acrawl on his flesh. He braced as she lifted her hand to his knee, clenched his jaw as she began to massage it, drawing fresh screams from his damaged ligaments. Like confronting a rabid dog, something told him not to react.

A grunt slipped through his teeth nonetheless. Her smile broadened. Nausea churned in the pit of his stomach at the thought she'd taken his pain for passion.

Beneath it all, the anger goaded him – grab her now, knock her unconscious – but a blade of awareness knifed through his thoughts. In his current condition he could do neither.

She pushed to her feet. "I'll come back for you when it's done." Sausage fingers trailed down his cheek. "That's what you want, isn't it, my love?"

Despite the caress, he caught the steely chill in the words. Such an alien feeling. Knowing that, in his present state, a woman was stronger. A dangerous, seriously unstable woman.

He prayed his expression would pass for a smile. "Of course it is. I've been waiting for you."

"Have you?" Her hand stilled. "You know, I heard what you said to her that time in her office – that she never should have hired me."

Panic flickered at the edge of his mind. "Ada, that wasn't—"

"It's all right, I know you didn't mean it. You were only trying to make her feel bad because of what she did to you, right?"

He tensed as she started round the back of his chair.

"She's done terrible things to both of us. Different of course, but equally bad. Like how she tried to steal you away from me." She bent to his ear. "How difficult that must've been for you."

He swallowed and held himself deadly still.

"You'd think I wouldn't understand, but I do. Even I can see she's beautiful. In the most superficial way of course. That kind of beauty can never make up for the ugliness inside a person. But you know that, don't you? That's how you were able to be strong."

Her face moved into view before him, her breath a corruptness on his lips. "I *could* stay, you know. Just for a while. There's time."

She leaned in closer, hovered a moment, then drew back. "But, no, you're right. We've waited this long, we can wait a bit longer. Better to have it all sorted out before we can begin our lives together."

She stepped back, dropping her arms to her sides. Only then did he see what she'd been hiding behind her back.

"Ada, wait—"

"Don't worry, my darling. You'll be as safe as if you were in my arms."

CHAPTER 80

Lauren lay staring up at the ceiling. Despite her exhaustion she couldn't sleep. Her frenzied thoughts kept darting from one source of anguish to the next – Josh, Claudia, Simon, Mel. For the moment they had settled on Josh.

She couldn't stop thinking of all the things she hadn't told him, all the things she should have said. Like how sorry she was for what had happened two years ago. More than his business had been lost, she knew. From the way he'd spoken, the one time he'd opened up to her about it, his fiance had left him as well. Purely a result of losing his livelihood? Or would it have happened in any case?

She sighed at the painful truth of the matter. Submitting bids to potential customers was part of the business. And of course you did your best to win, to beat out all the competition. She'd never stopped to think what it would be like to actually know the other person, to see what her victory had cost them. And yet if she had it to do over again…

At the time, she'd been desperate to get her parents' business back on its feet. To at least make a start rebuilding it to what she had known in her childhood. In the years she'd been away her father's preoccupation with her mother's illness had resulted in its steady decline. The Gallway deal had meant the difference between survival or bankruptcy.

Unfortunately, the stakes had been exactly the same for Josh.

She pushed up to sit on the edge of the bed, rubbed her eyes, then headed to the bathroom. At the sink she poured herself a glass of water and turned to gaze out the window as she drank. Maybe she wasn't cut out for this business. Maybe she'd never been. Maybe…

A twinkle of light down by the nursery caught her eye. Looking toward it, she saw only the black outlines of the various buildings. Just a firefly.

She was turning away to head back to bed when she saw it again. Frowning, she moved closer to the window.

For a moment, nothing. Then she spied it – a flashlight beam moving through the woods of the neighboring allotment. A parcel of land with no dwelling on it.

The light flickered through the trees, moving toward the nursery's lower driveway. When it reached the boundary it turned and started up along the fence line toward the barn.

Lauren raced back into the bedroom. She reached to turn on the bedside light then thought better of it. No sense alerting whoever it was that she was awake and possibly watching. Let them think they hadn't been seen.

She groped across the bedside table, then slumped when she remembered she'd lost her cell at the beach that day, digging Simon out of the sand. She'd have to call Olsen from the phone downstairs.

She pulled off her nightgown and quickly dressed.

Three ferocious wellsprings of pain. Leg. Head. Shoulder. Like children vying for his attention they tugged and prodded, jabbed and screamed until they'd roused him from his daze.

He opened his eyes. Darkness as thick as when they'd been shut. A blindfold? No, his face felt clear.

Flat on his back, arms at his sides, Josh curled his fingers and felt the wooden boards beneath them. Table or floor? Groaning, he forced himself up on one elbow.

Down near his feet, barely discernible, a single horizontal thread of light seeped from beneath a closed door. With the sight, came the memory of what had happened – Ada, damn her! She'd clubbed him with something, the baseball bat that stood in the hall – and fresh on its heels, knowledge of what she planned to do next.

I just came to tell you it's almost over...have to move things along a bit faster. I'll come back for you when it's done...the only thing still standing between us...

His stomach clenched. There was only one person she could've been talking about.

He fought to his feet, groped for the door, found the knob but it wouldn't turn. On the fourth try throwing his good shoulder against it he heard the sweet sound of splintering wood. One last heave and the door flew open. With a shout of pain, he crashed to the floor.

He pushed up again, found the nearest wall, followed it until he got his bearings. The bitch had locked him in his hall closet. Which meant the living room was to his left.

Clutching the door frame, he pulled himself up, and turned on the light. His cell phone wasn't on the coffee table. Nor on the floor, nor any of the chairs. She must've taken it.

He turned and hobbled into the kitchen, used the counter for support to reach the wall phone. He snatched the receiver from the hook.

And heard not the slightest sputter of dial tone.

CHAPTER 81

"Olsen here."

The voice on the end of the phone sounded thick, rusty with sleep. "Detective, it's Lauren Donnelly. I'm sorry to call you at this hour but there's someone prowling around my house."

"What, inside?" All hint of grogginess was gone in an instant.

"Down by the nursery. I saw a light from my upstairs window. It's moving through the woods next door, coming up my driveway."

"Can you still see it?"

"Hang on." At the kitchen window she craned her neck, trying to glimpse past the intervening shrubbery. "Yes, it's still there. Looks like it's moving through the parking lot now."

"I'm sending a car. Be there in five minutes. Lock all your doors and stay inside."

"I will. Thank you."

As soon as she set down the phone it hit her – how was the patrol car going to get in? Olsen didn't know about the private driveway behind her house, he'd send them to the nursery gate which was currently locked.

Unless she went down to the road and opened it.

She tried him again but the line was busy. She could sit and keep trying or…

Five minutes, he'd said. No time to waste. She wouldn't

have to go near the buildings; she could cut down through the lower field.

She grabbed her keys and ran from the house.

Turning his car from the narrow lane, Josh started up the private drive leading to the back of Lauren's house. In the darkness he could see that her lights weren't on. Either she was safely asleep inside or... With a silent prayer he wasn't too late, he sped around the side to the kitchen and skidded to a stop.

He hauled himself from the driver's seat, grabbed his crutches out of the back, then limped up the path and pounded on the door. "Lauren! It's Josh! Open up!"

He listened as his shouts died away, then stood back and looked up at the windows. No lights had come on. Surely he'd made enough noise to wake her.

He tried the door and found it locked.

He was turning to search for another way in when a glint through the trees drew his gaze. Down at the nursery, someone was moving around near the barn. Lauren or an intruder? Or both?

Lauren pushed through a break in the trees and emerged back onto the upper driveway. She'd cut through the field to open the gate and returned the same way, encountering no-one. The police would be arriving any second. She'd wait for them here.

From her vantage point above the shop she searched for the light she'd seen earlier. When it suddenly appeared much closer than expected she nearly turned and ran for the house. But the sight of the intruder *inside* the barn made her stop short. What could they possibly be doing in there? Setting up another pitchfork ambush?

Despite her fears, she edged a bit closer. The glow now filling the barn's front window seemed too bright for a flashlight beam.

It was also flickering.

Outrage ignited. Olsen thought her tormentor was Josh, but in her heart she knew it wasn't. This was Claudia, damn her! And one half-pint teenage brat was *not* going to burn down her beautiful barn!

She started forward, had passed the shop before she heard the crunch of gravel behind her. She whirled to find a figure hobbling toward her on crutches. "Josh!"

"Lauren, thank God, I came to warn you. I know who's been—"

"There's someone in the barn! I think they're trying to set it on fire."

Clutching each other, they turned as one. From their closer aspect, the figure that moved past the barn's front window was plainly visible.

"Oh my god, it can't be." She turned back to Josh. "You knew it was Ada?"

He opened his mouth but the sound she next heard was not his voice. It came from the barn, a great rush of air, not quite an explosion – ravenous flame greedily encountering a highly combustible source of fuel.

In seconds the yard was awash in light, the darkness driven back to the edge of the woods by the strength of the flames. And above their rapidly growing roar, two other sounds.

Approaching sirens.

And a woman's screams.

CHAPTER 82

Lauren sat numbly in the nursery kitchen, Josh at her side, Olsen in the chair before them. "She's dead?" she whispered, still struggling to process the horror. "You're absolutely certain?"

"The fire crew can see her body, they just can't reach it yet," Olsen said. "As soon as things cool off in there and they're sure the place won't collapse, they'll go in and get her. Then you folks can get on with your lives."

Get on with our lives. Would that ever be possible again?

She closed her eyes against the memory of the Ada's screams, of her own futile efforts to help her, the feel of Josh's arms tight around her, holding her back from entering the building. Despite all the woman had done, no-one deserved to die that way.

She looked up at Olsen. "I never even thought to tell you what happened with Ada's father. She never, for one moment, gave the slightest indication she held a grudge. In fact…it was just the opposite."

"There's no way you could've known," Josh said. "Nothing about her was what it seemed."

"He's right." Olsen rubbed his bloodshot eyes. "She

334

must've been planning this from the start. She pretended to forgive you, then insinuated herself into your life with the ultimate aim of seeking revenge."

"So how much of all that's happened was Claudia and how much was Ada?"

"I think we can safely assume at this point that Ada was behind the attack on Simon. She had access to the office to plant the order for the funeral wreath and no-one would question her going in there."

"Plus Simon trusted her; he'd have gone with her willingly on the beach." Lauren cringed at the awful thought. Dear, sweet, innocent Simon. "But why? What did he ever do to her?"

Olsen seemed reluctant to answer. "I'd say simply being someone you cared about made him a target. I guess she figured robbing you of your loved ones settled the score for you robbing her of her father."

"Mel's miscarriage." Lauren winced. "Ada had free access to the kitchen. She could easily have tampered with the pills Mel was taking."

The Detective nodded. "If it turns out the miscarriage was due to poisoning then, yes, I'd say that was Ada as well. The same with the bolt on the wheelbarrow. As for the break-in..." He shrugged. "Maybe Claudia was telling the truth on that one."

"My God. To think I trusted her." Lauren felt Josh's arm close around her.

Olsen rose. "Look, why don't you two go get some rest?"

Lauren shook her head. "There's no way I can sleep here tonight. The sounds, the smoke...knowing that Ada..." She glanced toward the barn. "That she's still in there..."

Josh looked to Olsen. "What if I take her back to my

place? Are your people done there?"

"They are, and they've reconnected your phone. The fire crew'll be here till morning at least. Probably won't be able to retrieve the body much before then." Olsen thought it over then nodded. "You might as well go. I'll call you when it's good to come back."

An hour later, propped in his bed, Josh watched Lauren step from the bathroom, shed her towel and slither under the covers with him. As she nestled against his side, he breathed in the glorious scent of her skin. All but the faintest whiff of smoke had been washed away by her lengthy shower.

"I can't blame Ada for wanting to hurt me," she said as she settled her head on his shoulder. "In her mind, at least, she had a good reason. But I'll never forgive her for what she did to Mel and Simon. Or you."

Josh kissed the top of her head, then reached over and shut off the light. As he lay gently stroking her shoulder he found himself frowning at the ceiling. Something had been nagging at the back of his mind since leaving the nursery. "I'm not sure Olsen got it all right though."

"Why, what do you think he was wrong about?" Lauren's voice was already fading.

"Well, for one thing, Ada's motive. I don't think she came after you or the others as payback for her father's death."

"What other reason could she have had?"

"I'm not sure. Something she said to me when she was here. Or didn't say. She talked about her and me going away together, the plans we'd made, about you trying to steal me away from her. But never once did she mention her father." He shook his head. "It just doesn't seem like..."

His words trailed off at the sound of her breathing – deep

and steady. Gazing down, he smiled at the sight of her curled against him, eyes closed. At the thought of how close he'd come to losing her, he drew her tighter into his arms.

And smiled at the grunt he got in return.

CHAPTER 83

She opened her eyes. Josh's bedroom. Bird song and late morning sunlight filled the room. The other side of the bed was empty but if the wafts of coffee were any indication, she knew where he was.

Lauren got up, slipped on her clothes and padded down the hall to the kitchen. Josh was seated at the table, his leg propped on a neighboring chair, sipping coffee and reading the paper.

He looked up when she entered the room. "Sleeping Beauty."

"Don't know about the Beauty part but I certainly slept. The first decent sleep in months it feels like."

"Good. You needed it."

She wandered over, slid her arms around his neck and stood with her cheek to the top of his head. For the moment this was all she needed. To feel his solid strength supporting her. "What time is it? You had breakfast yet?"

"Eleven thirty. And, no, I haven't. Only been up a short while myself." He was silent a moment. "I called Ezra."

She straightened abruptly and sat down beside him. "And?"

"The doctors are confident Simon will make a full recovery. They're keeping him sedated for now but they'll start counseling as soon as he's ready."

Lauren took a deep breath and let it out slowly. "God, poor Simon."

Josh leaned toward her. "Have I ever told you how amazing you are? You saved his life, you know. Never forget that."

She managed a smile. Yes, she had. Did that mean her debt was finally paid?

He squeezed her hand. "How about I fix us both some brunch?"

"Sounds great. Do I have time for a run first?"

"At the rate I move around the kitchen these days, you could run the Boston marathon."

She pushed to her feet. "Don't think I'll need quite that long. Twenty minutes tops. Just enough to clear my head." She leaned down and pressed a kiss to his lips.

"I'll have it ready by the time you get back," he said.

The ocean air smelled wonderfully fresh. Lauren drew it deep in her lungs, ridding them of the last hint of smoke from the night before. Setting her sights on the spit of rock at the end of the beach, she took off at an easy jog.

A hundred yards on, she notched up the pace. The exertion was having its desired effect, clearing her thoughts. Between here and the spit she would focus on nothing but physical sensations – the warmth of the midday sun on her shoulders, the gentle sounds of the waves on the rocks, the heat slowly building in her muscles. Time enough to think when she got back.

Halfway along the curved stretch of shore, the craggy

outline of the old lighthouse loomed just ahead. Set on the point of a huge shelf of granite, the matron of the sea held silent court over a landslide of boulders tumbled at her feet. Even in its decline it was lovely.

A sound like a bird drifted on the wind. Lauren gazed up, searched the sky, but couldn't see it. It came again, closer this time, inexplicably piercing her calm with a shard of dread. Not so much like a bird after all. More like…

She stumbled to a halt. It sounded like Simon's cries for help at the cove two days ago. A sound so fresh it still rang in her ears. She spun around in search of the source.

The shoreline was empty.

CHAPTER 84

Josh set two plates on the kitchen table, then hobbled over to answer the phone. "Olsen here. Can I speak to Ms. Donnelly?"

Startled by the sharpness of the man's request, he took a second before responding. "Sorry, Detective, she's gone for a run. She only just left, but she won't be long. Would you like me to get her to—?"

"Where is she exactly?"

"On the beach just up the road from my house." He heard Olsen give his address to someone. By the traffic noises in the background he judged they were in a car. "Anything I can help you with?"

"Last night at the nursery, before the fire... Did *you* see Ada inside the barn?"

"Yeah. We both did. Through the front window."

"You're sure about that?"

Josh was becoming increasingly unsettled. Where the hell was he going with this? "I am, and Lauren hasn't expressed any doubts. Why, what's wrong?"

"We recovered the body early this morning. It was too badly burnt for positive ID but one thing's certain – it isn't

Ada."

"What? But…if the body's burnt, how do you know—"

"Because it's a man."

The revelation knocked him back. "I don't understand. You're saying there were *two* of them? She had an accomplice?"

"We found a car. A blue late model Datsun sedan left in the woods adjacent to the nursery. Isn't that the car that's been following Lauren?"

"Sure sounds like the one."

"It's registered to a Theodore Phelps. Ada's Uncle."

Josh leaned heavily against the counter, as much to take weight off his throbbing knee as to process his shock. "Well, that makes sense I guess. He'd have as much of a motive as Ada – Lauren caused his brother's death."

Silence stretched at the other end. "We just came from searching both their homes. In Ted's we found nothing. At Ada's there was evidence of a struggle in one of the bedrooms – blood on the floor."

Josh felt his patience rapidly waning. "Detective, forgive me, but I wish to hell you'd get to the point."

"We don't think Theodore was helping Ada. We think she killed him and planted his body at the scene of the fire."

His mouth went dry. "What the hell for?"

"To stage her own death."

CHAPTER 85

Lauren bowed her head and shut her eyes. Was this how it was going to be? Another lingering after-effect? Like seeing Roger Phelps's face in every pool and rainwater barrel, she was now going to hear Simon's screams every time she came to the beach? It wasn't fair. She hadn't caused Simon's death, she'd saved him. He was alive and safe, recovering in a hospital bed. Why would…

Slowly she lifted her head and frowned. Damn it, unless she was totally losing it, this wasn't her imagination. She could definitely hear someone calling for help.

She turned in a circle and finally got a fix on the sound. Not out but *up*. She gazed toward the sky and sucked in her breath.

Someone was hanging from the lighthouse railing!

At the end of his street, at the end of the path leading down to the shore, Josh stood staring along the beach. Fear and helplessness churned in his gut. His crutches would be useless on sand, he could go no further. How was he going to reach Lauren and warn her?

Olsen was on his way, he'd said. Until the police had Ada

in custody they were putting Lauren under police protection. He'd told Josh to wait for him at the house. But Josh had found that order impossible to obey.

If Ada had staged her own death in the hope of buying herself some time, she wasn't going to sit around wasting it. She'd make her move the first chance she got. And this was the first time Lauren had been out of his sight since the fire.

He shaded his eyes and squinted against the glare of the sun. The beach was curved yet fully exposed. If Lauren was coming back this way – a safe bet seeing that spits of land blocked access by foot at either end – he ought to be able to see her by now. Unless for some reason she'd changed her mind and opted to run on the road instead.

He was turning to check the street behind him when the breeze lifted a sound to his ears. A bird? A child? Someone calling out? He swore when it flitted off again. Even worse than hearing it, was having it dissolve before he could identify it.

He clamped his jaw. It had come from the beach, that much was certain, yet there was still no sign of Lauren anywhere. The only place she could be on the shore and *not* be visible was behind the light house.

Or inside it.

He dropped his crutches and set out hobbling across the sand.

CHAPTER 86

Lauren raced up the lighthouse stairs, feet pounding the iron steps. The graffitied wall blurred at her shoulder. To cries from above, she stormed up the spiral past a series of glassless windows.

A single landing broke the ascent. She raced around it, dodging litter and piles of mortar crumbled from the walls, and continued her race on the other side.

Breathless, she burst through the door at the top. After the gloom of the tower's interior, the sun was blinding. She squinted, frantic, at last spotting the hands on the railing, clutching the lowest rung of the balustrade.

The rails above were clearly rusted. No way they would support her weight. She threw herself forward onto her stomach, her only hope to pull the victim through the gap beneath.

At the edge, she reached down over the side. "I've got you! I'm here!"

But something was wrong. The arms she latched onto were stiff and hard, not living tissue; the hair on the head just inches from her face, as dry and dead as that of a corpse.

A spasm of shock jerked her hands. In an instant too quick

to reclaim her grip, she saw his fingers slip from the rung.

She clawed the air, a useless gesture, as though she might yet draw him back. Watched as he tumbled end over end, limbs outflung, clothing whipped. Cried out in a strangled wail when he hit the jagged rocks below.

Horror turned to disbelief as body parts flew in all directions. An age seemed to pass before reality broke through her shock.

Plastic, not flesh.

A lifeless dummy.

Not a person but a storefront mannequin!

Then whose were the cries she had heard on the beach?

The sense of danger came too late. With her body already half over the side, the shove from behind was all it took to finish the job.

CHAPTER 87

Josh paused to catch his breath. Why was limping so much harder than walking? He was only halfway to the lighthouse and already debating if he should turn back.

Was this really his best course of action? The sound he'd heard a few moments ago could've been seagulls; a flock had been going over at the time. He hadn't heard anything since. Nothing to suggest there was someone at the lighthouse, let alone someone in trouble.

He turned and looked back along the shore. Still no-one in sight. For all he knew, Lauren *had* gone for her run on the streets. So while he was here on this fool's errand, she might already have returned to the house – which, in his haste, he'd forgotten to lock.

Indecision twisted his gut. Ada was definitely coming after Lauren. She could've been watching the house all night, waiting for her chance to move in and sabotage something inside. And he'd just given her the perfect opportunity.

With a groan he turned and started back. He got three limping steps toward the road before stopping. In the brief lull between in-coming waves there had been a sound. Different this time. But no mistaking it. Or its source.

*

Lauren clung to the lowest rail. She'd managed to grab it as she'd gone over. Now as she fought to maintain her grip, she looked up to see her assailant's face peering down from the platform above.

For a moment the words seemed to stick in her throat. "My god. But you're..."

"Dead?" Ada smiled. "No, not quite. Not as much as poor Uncle Ted. I really did like him, once upon a time. Until he turned into a Nosey Parker."

The woman looked out to scan the horizon. "I've never seen the view from up here. Lovely, isn't it?" She looked back down. "I can understand you might not be able to appreciate it at the moment so you'll just have to trust me. Though they say it isn't too safe anymore." She grabbed the railing and gave it a shake.

Lauren gasped as her only support rocked in its moorings. She stretched with her foot, feeling for any projection below, but the wall was recessed beyond her reach.

Ada nudged some loose bits of concrete over the side. "Looks like they're right. Still, neither of us are going to be here that long so we don't need to worry."

"Ada, please, you have to believe me. I never meant to hurt your father. If there was any way I could take back what happened—"

The woman laughed. "Oh, I just love it. Even now you haven't a clue." Her look darkened. "You're pathetic, you know that. All those things you did for me – paying for the funeral, giving me a job, turning a blind eye whenever I broke something, even when I did it on purpose... At first I thought it was because you cared, because you wanted to be my friend. But that wasn't it at all, was it?"

Ada scanned the area around her. Spotting something off to the side she vanished from view.

Lauren heard the ring of an iron bar dragged over concrete. When she looked up again, Ada had returned; clutched in her hands, a section of railing long since rusted away from its stays.

"You were just feeling guilty, that's all. You never cared." The woman hefted the pipe to her shoulder. "Just a sniveling baby trying to sooth her own conscience."

Lauren screamed as the pipe arched down. It slammed the upper rail of the balustrade bending it nearly down to the lower, bare inches from her fingers.

As Ada prepared for a second swing, her words tumbled out. "Ada, that's not true. I did care, I did want to be your friend. I still do."

"Liar!" The bar crashed down. The top rail collapsed. In the instant before it could shatter her hands, Lauren slid her grip aside.

Panting more from excitement than strain, Ada squatted down beside her. "You want to know what makes it all so funny?" Her voice was a whisper, a vocal caress. "All your struggles for absolution? Your bids to atone? They were totally pointless."

Ada brought her face to rail, beaming with pride. "You never killed my father. I did."

CHAPTER 88

A stone's throw from the foot of the lighthouse, Josh heard another scream and looked up. His heart nearly stopped. Lauren was hanging from the railing above while Ada took swipes at her hands with a pipe. Cursing his leg, he hobbled the final yards to the building and made for the door.

In his scramble, he failed to allow for lack of flex in his bandaged knee. His toe caught the step and he sprawled across the concrete interior.

He stifled his cry of anger and pain. He'd landed on his injured knee. Could he even stand on it now?

He dragged himself to the base of the stairs. Using its banister to haul himself up, gritting his teeth, he started up the spiral staircase.

You didn't kill my father. I did.

Lauren couldn't process the words. Her arms were screaming, her fingers numb, the edge of the concrete jabbed at her throat. "Ada...please..."

"You never wondered why the ice was weak in just that spot? When every other stream and pond on the cape was frozen solid?"

Despite her terror, the words sank in. Yes, she had wondered. Of course she had. How many times—

"I went out in the night and chopped up the ice. It didn't work the first few times, the ice kept freezing again by morning. Took me a while to get the timing just right. Plus I found a little rock salt helped."

She cocked her head. "See, I knew that's where he crossed every day." Her look turned savage. "He was always trying to run away, telling people lies about me. I figured, if he wanted to escape so bad, I ought to help him."

She pushed to her feet, "You nearly ruined everything, you know," and lifted the bar to her shoulder once more.

Lauren looked down. A sea of jagged rocks sprawled below her, waiting to split her body apart. "Help. Somebody help me. Please!"

Ada smiled. "I remember those words. The same ones you yelled at the stream that day, when you fell through the ice." At Lauren's incredulous look, she laughed. "That's right, I heard you. I watched the whole thing from my kitchen window. Dad saving you. You saving Dad. Or trying to. Better than reality TV any day."

Her smile died. "And this is where it finally ends."

Lauren screamed. Not at the sight of the pipe arching upwards, but the unexpected feel of something sliding around her waist.

The something – an arm! – gripped her tightly, drawing her body toward the lighthouse wall. Someone was down there! On the landing below, reaching out through the open window! They must've seen—

Even knowing what they were trying to do, she couldn't force herself to let go. Whoever it was might not have the strength to pull her to safety. They both could fall. The railing was her only salvation. Her failing grip her only hope.

Fighting her rescuer to the last, she watched Ada swing the pipe toward her hands. Not till the final split second before impact did she her give up her hold.

And then she was falling.

CHAPTER 89

Flushed with exertion, Ada dropped the pipe and pushed off from where she had slumped against the lighthouse wall. She'd done it. The bitch was finally gone.

Savoring the moment, she walked slowly to the edge to look down. And there it was. Lauren's body laying broken and smashed on the rocks below.

For an instant something welled inside her. Lauren. Who had once been a friend. Who'd given her work when no-one else would. Who'd forgiven her mistakes, befriended her to Mel and whose arms she'd more than once felt around her.

With a sneer she pushed the memories aside. Of course that had all been a lie.

Lauren's scream echoed around them as she tumbled through the window. She opened her eyes to see the man laying sprawled beside her. "Josh! Oh my god. How did—"

"No time." He pushed himself to a sitting position. "We have to get out of here. And you've got to help me."

Lauren draped his arm around her shoulder, helped him to his feet. Together they started down the stairs.

*

Ada looked down for one last glimpse of her ultimate triumph. Her smile spread, then suddenly faltered.

Something was wrong. A pale patch she'd thought to be a strip of sand was actually an arm, lying some distance off from the torso. Looking closer, she saw a leg still further away. Even on rocks, a person didn't break apart like this. How—

Realization ripped through her mind. The mannequin! Then where was Lauren?

She circled the platform. Perhaps the body had landed nearby and, before she'd looked down, a wave had swept it off the rocks.

She stalked around the entire circuit, her fury building with every step, then stopped at a sudden glimpse of movement – two figures emerging from the lighthouse door and moving out along the beach.

Josh and Lauren.

Rage shattered the last of her reason. She slammed her fists down on the railing. A structure weakened by years of neglect and her own handiwork with the pipe.

She felt it snap like twig beneath her.

CHAPTER 90

The scream stopped them dead.

Clinging to Josh, Lauren spun around in time to see a body plummeting toward the rocks. She gasped and turned her face to his chest.

They stood together for a frozen moment, then Josh let himself slump to the sand. "Sorry, I'm done. Knee's given out for real this time."

"Stay here then. I'll be right back."

He snagged her arm. "Leave her. The cops are on the way, let them deal with it."

"If she landed in water she could still be alive."

"So what?"

She looked in his eyes, seeing both the pain and residual fear. Fear he'd arrive too late to save her?

She cupped his cheek. "I have to see. I'll be right back." She turned and sprinted around the lighthouse.

She found the body in a tidal pool, floating face up. As she scrambled over the rocks to reach it, she lost all hope the woman had survived. Her eyes were open and staring skyward – a sight that brought Lauren's hand to her mouth. It was the image of Roger in his final moments. Only Ada wasn't clawing the surface.

The last of her strength suddenly ebbed and she dropped down to sit at the edge of the pool. The aftermath of her ordeal crashed over her like a wave, leaving her with the ambiguous truth: where she and another had faced certain death, once again she alone had survived.

She gazed at Ada's upturned face. Maybe someday she'd understand. Why this woman had so despised her. Why she'd done what she had to Mel and Simon. Hateful, inexplicable things. Things she might never bring herself to forgive.

Still, it didn't mean she couldn't feel pity.

Lauren reached out, grabbed for the cuff of Ada's sleeve. The hand jerked free and clutched her arm. Eyes that had, a moment ago, stared sightlessly up at the sky, fixed on her with fierce intent.

Off balance, Lauren tried to pull free but felt herself tipping toward the water. The pool wasn't deep but if she fell headfirst on the rocks at the bottom…

With a cry of defiance, she wrenched her arm free and toppled back.

Righting herself, she sat peering down.

Inches below the water's surface, Ada's mouth opened in a silent scream. Slowly, as her father before her, her gaze grew dull.

CHAPTER 91

As much as she loved spring, autumn was Lauren's favorite season. Summer always gave up its reign with the most spectacular palette of color.

In the woods surrounding the nursery grounds, maple, oak, poplar and birch displayed every shade from primrose to claret. Holly and dogwood flaunted bright clusters of crimson fruit, and bittersweet paid for its parasitic ways by festooning its host in garlands of red and yellow berries.

It wasn't just nature that put on a show. The final harvest from the garden was gilded in the same brilliant hues: pumpkins – from the palm-sized Goblin to the monster Big Max; warted Hubbard, butternut, buttercup and acorn squash; gourds of every shape and description from Dinosaur Clubs to the lobed Turks Turban to the gnarled and twisting Crown of Thorns. And every cob of Indian corn had its own unique and dazzling rainbow.

Lauren stepped back to admire the bounty arranged on hay bales in front of the barn. It seemed the best place for this year's showcase, seeing as tonight was the building's official opening. A party was planned, lights had been strung, customers and friends alike invited.

With the second-hand siding she and Josh had gotten at an auction, the building hardly looked like a newcomer to the premises; more like the stout old friend she had known since childhood. Still, it was an occasion to celebrate, the restoration both a tribute to the future and symbolic triumph over past adversity.

It seemed she'd come to appreciate such things more in recent times than she used to.

At the sound of the tractor, she turned to find Josh coming up the drive. She waved to Simon seated in the trailer amid the mountain of corn stalks the pair had just cut.

Like all of them, Simon had his good days and bad. Counseling had helped, but in the end the best therapy had been coming back to work. Within a few weeks of his return, he'd been pretty much his old self again.

Across the yard, Mel stepped out the greenhouse door with the pull cart in tow, laden with assorted potted chrysanthemums. When she'd dragged it over, Lauren joined her in arranging them around the hay bale pyramid as the final touch to the seasonal display.

She set down her first two pots and straightened. "So how's Peter's new job working out?"

"Great. He loves it. He says all the months of waiting were worth it." Mel gave a wry look. "I'm not sure I share that sentiment entirely but I'm glad he's happy. Actually things are better all around between us."

"Good to hear it."

"Which reminds me." The woman leaned closer. "Just a bit of news between you and me: we're trying again."

Lauren's eyes widened when her meaning sank in. "You mean for a baby?"

"With Peter's new contract and things looking so much

better around here, we figured, why wait?"

"Oh Mel, that's wonderful! I'm so happy for you."

As she stepped back from giving the woman a hug, Josh pulled the trailer up beside them, then started reversing it toward the barn.

Lauren smiled at the wink he gave her. Today they'd be celebrating more than a barn warming. After festivities finished tonight he'd be 'officially' moving in with her, the boxes sitting in the back of his Sierra waiting to be unloaded into her house. Their business partnership had secured the nursery, their personal one would do much the same for the rest of her life.

When the trailer stopped, Simon jumped out and Josh climbed down from his seat on the tractor. She smiled as she watched them unloading the corn stalks while Mel began tying them into sheaves.

This was her family. The people she cared most about and for whom she would do almost anything. She wasn't responsible for all their happiness or all their sorrows. Yet they'd suffered dearly because of her and her debts to them she would freely repay.

2014 Daphne du Maurier Award Finalist

RUN TO ME

A woman on the edge. A boy on the run.
A race to save each other…

It's been two years since Shyler O'Neil's beloved son
Jesse was killed, but his final moments are as vivid to her
now as they were that dreadful day. Suffering from post-
traumatic stress, and convinced she did not do enough
to protect him, she retreats to an isolated cabin in the
woods of northern Maine.

Meanwhile, Zack Ballinger – a ten-year-old boy who
has never known a mother's love – finds himself in the
wrong place at the wrong time. He's seen too much and
is now running for his life.

Fleeing into the woods, Zack soon finds himself at Shyler's
cabin. He'll take whatever help she can give – even though,
for some reason, she keeps calling his Jesse…

With the pursuers hot on their heels 'mother' and 'son'
go on the run. Protecting Zack may well be Shyler's one
chance at redemption.

Or *she* is the child's greatest threat…

What readers have to say about Run To Me…

'The author makes good use of her rustic setting and clearly understands the value of sympathetic characters and the thrill of narrow escapes.'
Publishers Weekly

'Hester keeps the reader guessing right until the end. A terrific first novel from an author we'll no doubt see more of.'
Sophia Whitfield, Culture Street

'…a fantastic on-the-edge-of-your-seat novel…gripping and heartfelt at the same time…'
Nicole Frith, Ballarat Courier

'A clever thriller with a perfect mix of action and emotion.'
Ivy Fleming, Illawarra Mercury

'Thank you for giving us a thriller with some real heroes.'
Donna212 - 5 stars, Random House reviews

PROLOGUE

"Jesse, come down from there, you might fall."

"I'm throwing sticks in the water, Mommy. See how fast they float away."

Shyler came up behind her son where he stood on the railing's lowest bar. Sliding her arm around his waist, her cheek pressed to his, she peered over the side of the bridge.

"The water's moving really fast, isn't it? Must be all that rain we had. Now come on, sweetheart, we better get going. Your baseball training went late today; it's starting to get dark."

"All the sticks went under the bridge." He held up the last one. "I want to see where this one comes out."

"All right, one more, then we have to leave. Daddy'll be home soon."

With a five-year-old's flair he threw the stick, watched it hit the water, then jumped down to race to the other side.

"Look both ways before you cross." Though he quickly obeyed, though they'd not seen a car since the edge of town, she couldn't help double-checking to be sure.

That's when she saw the three men step out.

They emerged from the bushes at the end of the bridge as though they'd come up from the banks below. But with no poles or reels they couldn't have been fishing.

She moved to where Jesse was scanning the water.

"There it is, Mom!"

"I see it, honey." But in truth she was looking the other way, keeping watch from the corner of her eye.

The men had spread out across the road. Even before she could see their faces she knew the one in the middle was leader, just from the way the others watched him, held back behind him as they started toward her. Their sudden appearance could be totally innocent, random chance.

Still, why had they spread out across the road?

Jesse climbed down and took her hand. "Timmy brought a rabbit to school today. A live one."

"Did he? I bet that was nice." She turned him to head back the way they'd come. Maybe they'd walk home the other way today, just to be—

Two more men had stepped out behind them.

"It had real soft fur, and big floppy ears. Can I get a rabbit, Mom?"

"We'll see." Pulling him close, she looked from one group to the other. Clearly together, clearly an ambush. A mugging? Here? In their quiet little corner of New Hampshire?

"What is it, Mommy?"

She scanned the road in both directions. No cars, no people. The fields sweeping back to the woods either side held nothing but drying rows of corn. She knew there was a house just past the first turn. But trees lining the banks of the creek would screen them from view, muffle any cries for help. The bridge they had crossed nearly every day since Jesse started school had never felt so lonely and remote.

The men closed in, encircling them. Younger than she'd thought. Late teens perhaps. Taut and wiry, ragged as strays.

The one with his hands jammed in his pockets twitched like a puppet on invisible strings. Another with a snake tattoo on his neck, his eyes red-rimmed. The plaid flannel shirt on the gangly one made him a scarecrow, a jaunty beret an incongruous touch for the one incessantly scratching himself.

Stay calm. Don't provoke them.

She faced the fifth, the gang's leader. "What do you want?"

A scar tugged the side of his mouth like a fish hook. "Wallet," he said.

She fumbled in her purse, handed it over. The others pressed closer as Fish Hook looked through it.

"You gotta be kidding. Five lousy bucks, that's all you got?"

"That's all I brought with me."

An unseen hand jerked Puppet's strings. "Oh man, no way."

"That's bullshit, she's lying. She's gotta have more."

"Here, take my bag if you don't believe me." She held it out. The instant he snatched it, Puppet yanked Jesse away from her legs.

"No, please, let him go."

Scarecrow and Beret cut between them as Puppet lifted the boy to the railing. "Soon as you give us what we came for."

She strained to see past them – Jesse, his eyes now huge and frightened. "It's okay, baby, they'll be gone in a minute."

Scarecrow leered. "Yeah, baby, it's okay. Mama won't let her little boy fall."

She couldn't pry her gaze from Puppet. Those twitching hands, that nervous dance… "Please, let him down. There's rocks…the water… He can't swim."

They shoved her back.

Fish Hook was throwing things from her bag. "There's

nothing in here."

Bargain. Say anything. "There's an ATM in town. I've got lots of money in my account. You can have it all."

"Think we're stupid?" Puppet swung Jesse's legs over the edge.

"There's an iPod in my bag. A cell phone, credit cards."

"Not enough."

"I have nothing else!"

A jab from behind. "Empty your pockets."

"Car!" Snake said, before she could move.

"Don't see nothin."

"I hear it, man."

"Let's get outta here."

Fish Hook threw the bag down, jerked his head. The others ran after him.

All but Puppet.

"Hey, what am I supposed to…?" His look growing frantic as the car sounds got louder.

Raising her hands, a calming gesture, inching forward. "Please, be careful. Don't—"

He let go and ran.

She sprang to the rail, the moment imprinting itself like a scar. Silken hair sliding between her fingers.

The terrified scream she would never stop hearing.

'A cinematic, stay-up-all-night thriller – twisty, compelling, and relentlessly suspenseful. Diane Hester is a master of her craft.'

HANK PHILLIPPI RYAN – Anthony,
Agatha and Mary Higgins Clark award-winning author

HIT AND RUN

Raina Wilkins has little to live for.
Until she's forced on the run with a wanted killer
and a homeless teen with a deadly secret.

Driving alone on a dark autumn night Raina Wilkins hits a man who darts out from the Maine woods in front of her. The injured stranger jumps in her car and forces her to drive on at gunpoint but gets out soon after and disappears back into the forest.

Raina thinks never to see her again. But Alec DeMarco has left something behind in her car. Something others will kill to possess. When he returns to claim it, Raina is swept into a world of abduction, conspiracy and murder.
A world where even the police want her dead.

What readers have to say about Hit And Run…

'Gripping and intense, the fast-paced plot rocketed along keeping me on the edge of my seat.'
Goodreads reviewer, Brenda – 5 stars

'Loved it!!!! With plenty of action and suspense, and two awesome, fiesty female protagonists like Raina and Erin I thoroughly recommend this book…'
Shane 5 stars

'Surprised me with the ending; thought I had it all figured out. Boy was I wrong.'
Wanda C 5 stars

'I loved each and every character…plenty of suspense, action-packed and twists and turns! Highly recommended!'
Rita 5 stars

'Lots of twists, great characters, intriguing plot…a wonderful and thoroughly enjoyable read.'
Dianne – 5 stars

'What a page turner.'
Margaret – 5 stars

CHAPTER 1

The rock ledge trembled beneath her feet, quaking with the force of the tons of water surging over it. On the falls' far side saplings clung to the sheer cliff face, its tree-lined summit looming above her, silhouetted by a three-quarter moon.

In the presence of such a wonder of nature Raina felt small, insignificant. Salvation Falls. Boundary between chaos and calm. Gateway between the tranquil waters of Jessop's Lake and the churning rapids of Moosehead Run. Drawn by the hypnotic lure of its power, she stepped to the granite's edge and looked down.

Moonlight shimmered off the cascading flume, shattering into a thousand diamonds in the canyon plunge pool far below. Not the largest of Maine's many falls – its mouth a mere twenty-foot cleft in the rock, its drop a paltry two-and-a-half stories – but the boulders heaped about the pool's edge would ensure any misstep would be her last.

She inched closer. Loose pebbles rolled underfoot. A flurry of pine needles, nudged by her toe, fluttered soundlessly over the edge.

She closed her eyes. At once phantom laughter echoed around her, remnants of the childhood memories forever linked to this special place. The touch of Rick's hand. His shy smile. The way his hair dried to a tangle of curls whenever they emerged from a swim. Shared afternoons of guileless ease that held no hint of what was to come.

She opened her eyes and stared once again at the pool below. Wind off the lake pressed at her back, compounding the urge to lift her arms and lean toward the gulf until oblivion rose to take her.

What held her in place she couldn't say. Cowardice or a vestige of hope? Whatever the reason, it seemed she wasn't yet ready to embrace the release held forth in that final step.

With a last look at the beckoning drop-off she started back the way she'd come, negotiating the moonlit ledge with newfound caution. She followed the series of granite outcrops to the wooded track where she'd left her car, drove the quarter mile back to the road and turned for home.

Her detour to the falls had been spur of the moment. A mistake, she now realized, giving her a chance to contemplate the state of her life in far too remote and dangerous a setting. She should've gone straight home after the movie.

In the dark she groped along the console in search of a CD to jam in the player. She grabbed the first one her fingers lighted on and promptly dropped it.

Leaning aside to feel where it went, she never saw the shadowy figure that darted from the woods.

Until it bounced off the side of her car.

CHAPTER 2

On the dark wooded road she screeched to a halt and sat
clutching the wheel in a death grip. That sickening thud. That
jolt of something hitting her fender, something big. A deer?
Had to be. Oh god, what if she'd killed it? Worse, what if
she'd only injured it?

Raina looked in the rearview mirror and felt the air in her
lungs turn to ice. Bathed in the bloody glow of her brake
lights, the body lying in the road was human.

No! 'Oh my god! How could… Where did…'

Her heart battered against her ribs.

Seconds to grope for a rational thought, then she snatched
up her bag. With trembling hands she rifled through its
contents; fumbled, dropped, recovered her phone —

Light flooded the car's interior. She squinted as the
passenger door swung open. A rush of cold air. A figure folded
itself through the opening, collapsed on the seat.

And a stranger sat there staring back at her.

She caught but a snapshot of his face – wild dark eyes,
patrician nose, features twisted in a grimace of pain… Then
the door swung shut, plunging them into darkness again.

'Drive,' he said.

Shock and disbelief held her frozen. Tearing her gaze from the aberration, she checked the mirror. The body lying in the road was gone.

'Are you crazy? You shouldn't be walking around. Wait till the ambulance gets here before —'

'No ambulance.' The man looked back. 'Just drive, damn it.'

'What, to the hospital? I can't leave the scene of an accident. I have to report this, I have to call —'

Ripped from her hand, her phone went sailing out into the night. He turned from the window, the gun he clutched aimed at her face. 'I said "drive".'

A mile down the road her thoughts were in turmoil, her breath coming in short punches, the steering wheel greasy with sweat. A man with a gun. Sitting in her car. A man peering back over his shoulder.

'What's back there?'

'Nothing.'

'Then why won't you let me call an ambulance?' In the feeble glow of the dashboard lights she saw him wince, his jaw clench tight.

'This is insane. You're obviously hurt. You need help. You could be bleeding internally, go into shock. At least let me take you —'

'What part of "just drive" don't you understand?' The gun waved closer.

She swallowed. 'Fine. Drive where?'

No answer this time. He turned away. With a stifled groan he leaned toward the door.

Raina stole glances aside as she drove. He looked to be wearing a tweed jacket and pleated pants. Clearly not a hiker or fisherman. His jaw was clean-shaven, his dark hair longish but not unkempt. If they'd met on the street she might think him a teacher, a businessman maybe.

So where had he come from? She'd seen no car. No houses out here as far as she knew – this side of the lake was undeveloped. Not even cabins. Just a few boat shacks engulfed in acres of primal forest.

She peered at the tree trunks strobing past. What could be roaming these woods that would frighten him? Force a grown man of thirty, thirty-five, hale and hearty – until she'd slammed into him – to run out on the road without even looking. The gun, though hardly a hunter's weapon, would still protect him from scavenging bears, the odd coyote, a rutting moose. Unless…

Oh, god, those dilated pupils. Shock or delusion? Crack? Something harder? A drug-crazed madman had hijacked her car? An escaped lunatic? A wanted crim —

She yelped when something flopped in her lap. His hand. The gun still gripped lightly in his fingers. His body slumped against the seat.

She held her breath, fighting not to panic at the feel of the dead weight across her leg. If she startled him now, if he jolted awake, he might squeeze the trigger and accidently shoot her.

She leaned forward to glimpse his face. His eyes were closed. Out cold by the look. But no way to tell how deeply. If she moved would he wake? Then again, if her shriek hadn't roused him…

She straightened, twisting her grip on the steering wheel. This could be it. Her one and only chance to get him to the hospital.

Or pull the car over and get the hell out!

CHAPTER 3

Gravel crunched beneath the tires. Raina eased the car to a stop on the shoulder and cut the engine.

The man beside her still hadn't moved. Was he dead? No, in the silence she could hear him breathing.

Beyond the window darkness beckoned, the safety of the forest just a few feet away. A refuge she would never reach unless she could get his hand off her lap.

With the tips of her fingers she pinched a fold of his jacket sleeve, careful not to catch the flesh beneath, and slowly lifted his hand from her thigh. The gun slid to the floor with a clunk.

She froze, his cuff still gripped in her fingers.

Nothing. No movement, no fluttering eyelids, no change in breathing.

She lowered his arm across his lap.

When he didn't stir, she eased her handbag from the space between them, slid the keys from the ignition, and curled her fingers around the door handle.

The light! She reached up and switched it off.

Door open, she regarded the stranger one last time. Grab the gun? Throw it away and head for the hospital? Even without a weapon, if he woke and became enraged…

The man beside her let out a groan.

She launched to her feet and ran blindly into the forest.

Pain. A razor slashing his side, prying a tortured groan from his throat.

He reached for the source. Sticky wetness suffused his shirt. He raised the hand before his face but could make out only its basic outline in the mire of shadows filling the car.

As he stared, his fingers and the blood they were smeared with came into focus, awash in a strengthening glow of light. He straightened and turned in the seat.

Headlights were coming up the road behind him.

His heart leapt to a thready gallop, furnishing a burst of mental clarity. Beside him the driver's seat was empty, the woman gone – he leaned to grope along the steering column – and she'd taken the keys.

Another look back. His pursuers were still a half mile off but coming up fast. How far would he get on foot? Maybe if he could staunch the bleeding…

An open box sat on the car's rear seat. He pulled it toward him, felt inside and came up with a handful of woolen hats. Stuffing the handful into his shirt, he clamped it to his side with his elbow and opened the door.

He lifted his legs out, tried to stand. Blackness not of the night engulfed him. He dropped back, clenching his jaw till it passed.

He squinted at the light rapidly turning night into day. He had his answer – he'd never outrun them. The best he could hope for was to keep them from finding the thing they were after.

He pulled it from his pocket and shoved it beneath the seat.

*

The moon stippled sallow light through gaps in the forest canopy. Enough that Raina could make out the trunks of trees but not their lower clawing branches. Her face was stinging and raked with scratches before she'd gone a dozen yards. Still, she was safe. Even if the man revived, he'd never find her out here in the darkness.

A flicker of light through the trees caught her eye. Out on the road a car was approaching, coming from the same direction she had. It cleared the bend a short way back and began to lose speed.

Holding her breath, she watched it slow and veer off to pull up behind her own. Someone thinking she'd broken down, stopping to help?

The engine shut off. Car doors slammed. Footsteps on gravel.

She stood twisting the strap of her handbag. Go back? Call out to them? Reveal herself? They'd have a phone. She could get help.

No, she felt safe where she was for the moment. They'd look in her car, see the injured man and call 911. And when the ambulance and police arrived, *then* she'd come out and show herself.

And if the man with the gun woke up before that? Started shooting? Took these people hostage in place of her? And if they had a child in the car...?

'Damn!' She started back for the road.

Ahead through the trees, in the wash of headlights, something moved. A figure walking from her car to the one behind. The injured man or one of the others?

The person got in behind the wheel and slammed the door.

She quickened her pace.

The engine revved.

She ran for the road, stopped short of stepping out on the shoulder, and stood frowning as the car sped away. How could they just drive off like that? Hadn't they seen the injured man?

She turned to the darkened hulk of her car. No silhouette in the passenger's seat.

She eased closer, damned the crunch of her shoes on the gravel, and leaned down to peer through the driver's door.

Empty.

A bolt of fresh fear. She straightened and scanned the forest around her, straining to see into the impenetrable shadows. Was he there? Watching? Or had he run off? Considering the state he was in, how far could he get?

From across the road – the snap of a twig. Rustling, as something moved through the undergrowth. Something big.

She jumped in her car, locked the door, and sped for home.

ACKNOWLEDGEMENTS

Working so many hours alone can allow all manner of doubts to creep into an author's fertile imagination. That's why I feel truly blessed to have such a wonderful support network of family and writer friends who keep me centered and moving forward.

Firstly my critiquing partners, Alison Manthorpe, Mary Gudzenovs and Kathy Blacker. Thank you for your help, feedback, and encouragement through the months of putting this manuscript together. (Twenty years together and still going strong. You guys are the best!)

To the members of my local Eyre Writers for being such an active, supportive group – your passion inspires me!

And to my long-distance sage and morale booster, fellow author, Rowena Holloway, who on so many occasions has set me back on course again when I lost my way.

ABOUT THE AUTHOR

Born in New York, Diane Hester is a former violinist with the Rochester Philharmonic and the Adelaide Symphony. Her debut thriller, RUN TO ME, was short-listed in the 2014 Daphne du Maurier Awards. She now lives in Port Lincoln, South Australia with her husband Michael. Visit her at www.dianehester.com